Mustang Ridges isn't a town, a [illegible] old western movie. She's a feisty, single mom living in the small town of Lakeside, Texas where money does buy happiness and keeping up appearances is much more important than the truth.

OTHER BOOKS BY KATIE GRAYKOWSKI

The Marilyns
Place Your Betts
Getting Lucky

The Lonestars
Perfect Summer
Saving Grace
Changing Lanes

REST IN PIECES

By

Katie Graykowski

Formatting by Anessa Books

Dedication

For Paul...because you make me laugh.

ACKNOWLEDGMENTS

This book didn't write itself and no, I didn't wake up one morning and decide to write a mystery. This book has been in me for years, and thanks to some wonderful people, I was able to write it. Thank you to my Ruby Slippered Sisters who told me that it was okay to write a mystery. The biggest thank you in the world to Jane Myers Perrine my good friend, mentor, cheerleader, and ledge-talker-downer. Thanks to Austin RWA for giving me the confidence and skills to write. Thank you to Tracy Wolff and Emily McKay for believing in me even when I didn't believe in myself. Thanks to Salon Bellezza—Lindsay Kelly, you rock! To my stylist, Andrea Garcia, thanks for lending me your name—you are a talented, patient, and kind person. For Rachel Lane—I love your hair! For my mother and two brothers, family is the most important thing...sorry that I forget that sometimes. For my husband and daughter, thanks for making me laugh.

Thank you to my proofreaders, Rhonda, Sandra, Ella, Liz, Becky, Sherry, and Allison.

And thank you to my fans. Your emails keep me going.

CHAPTER 1

If the world was really going to end on Christmas Day, by God I was gonna meet Jesus with a full head of hair. My new hairstylist, Andrea, was gluing extensions to my existing hair that didn't add length so much as cure my hair anemia. Thin hair is a curse just like bad breath, or a funky second toe that's longer than the big toe—fortunately, I only suffer from hair anemia.

I flipped to the next page of the *National Enquirer*'s story on the Rapture and decided that the least the editor could have done was to plan the end of days for Black Friday. That way I wouldn't have to freeze my butt off camping outside Target, risking death by stampede to get a half-priced Xbox for Max's big Christmas present. Then again, these days it seemed Black Friday was as much a part of Thanksgiving as the turkey and cranberry sauce, which I always thought was more symbolic than tasty.

If I'd learned anything in the last forty-eight hours—besides that the world was going to end—it was that life is short. I still couldn't believe that Molly Miars, my son's kindergarten teacher—and my close friend—was dead. According to the Lakeside PD, she'd overdosed on heroin. The absurdity of this made me want to shake my head, but I'd been warned within an inch of my life not to move.

And since Andrea was currently wielding a burning-hot iron, I was prepared to do whatever she asked. She used the pick end of a long comb to separate a small chunk of my hair from its thin brown fellows. Then she wrapped the hair extension around the chunk of my hair, picked up the crimping iron, and clamped down, gluing new length to my hair.

Not that I could normally afford hair extensions, but Bee Creek Elementary had given me a pretty hefty gift certificate in recognition of all of my hard work as the

Parent Teacher Organization president. My good friend and PTO secretary, Haley Hansen, sat in the chair next to me. For all of her hard work, she'd gotten a twenty-five dollar gift card for Chili's.

Being president had its advantages.

Today we had an impromptu meeting—well, once our VP, Monica Garza, showed up. All she'd gotten was a coupon for a free Brazilian bikini wax.

Next year I was thinking of running on a platform of equality for all.

Usually the PTO met in the school cafeteria, but today we were having a special session at Salon Bellezza. Our highly un-esteemed treasurer, Lyle Grinchwalt—one of the Grinchwalts in Lee, Grinchwalt, and Grinchwalt, CPAs—was missing. Because he's a dick and probably gets his hair done at Supercuts, this meeting was minus the Grinch. I had it on good authority that he'd gotten a coupon for a bikini wax also, and I was dying to know if he'd used it.

I sipped on a glass of champagne. It was so dry that it sucked the spit out of my mouth, but it was free and it made me feel very fancy. Careful to move only my eyeballs, I glanced around. Somehow Salon Bellezza managed to be both opulent and cozy. Rich purple velvet settees were sprinkled between the beautician's chairs, and huge gilt-edged mirrors adorned the walls. It was part brothel, part boutique, and actually kind of homey, if you were Heidi Fleiss.

It was three forty-five on a Thursday, and I'd skipped out of work early.

"Don't move your head." Andrea picked up another clump of hair. Hitler couldn't have been this focused when he'd invaded France. I wanted to shoot my arm out in a Nazi salute, but I'd have to move my head.

I knew that Molly had been behind the hair salon gift certificate. Over enchiladas at Don Julio's, we'd often talked about my secret desire for an appointment at Salon

Bellezza. And it's not that the place is all that expensive, it's that I'm all that broke.

Molly and I were both have-nots living in a town chuck full of haves. Not long ago, our lovely little town of Lakeside, Texas, campaigned furiously to keep a Walmart out of our zip code, because the wealthy residents were convinced the large chain store would bring the wrong element into our community. I couldn't figure out why anyone believed that criminals would drive an hour out of Austin just to shop at our Walmart, but explaining that would have been futile and exhausting. In the end, the corporate giant chose a less hostile environment, and Molly and I were stuck paying top dollar for tampons and toilet paper. Well, I was. Hopefully Molly wouldn't need tampons and toilet paper in heaven.

"I'm here." Monica, my PTO VP and fellow have-not, breezed in tossing her black leather jacket on an end table and plopped down in the chair on the other side of Haley. With the toe of her black motorcycle boot, she rocked the beautician's chair back and forth. "Sorry I'm late, but traffic was a bitch. Highway 71 from South Austin was a parking lot."

"I now call this meeting of the Bee Creek Elementary Parent Teacher Organization to order."

My name is Mustang Ridges and no, I'm not a stripper. I'm the billing manager at Lakeside Regional Hospital, and if I could afford to change my name to something less stripper-like, I would. But sadly, until that time, I remain Mustang Ridges.

"Just a minute." Haley pulled her iPhone out of her Hermès. "Let me hit record so I can transcribe it later."

Meeting notes are part of the by-laws, but Haley took it to a new level. Usually, our meeting notes were verbatim. Which was both good and bad.

If Monica and I didn't love Haley, we'd have killed her years ago. As the wife of a prominent plastic surgeon, her dinner parties were gourmet catered, her clothes were haute couture, and her house was a mansion on Lake Travis. She was queen of the haves. But if I needed a kidney, she'd give me one of hers in a heartbeat, and then nurse me back to health by force-feeding me champagne and caviar.

I'd met Haley in college when she'd dated my cousin, Erik. When he'd been killed by a drunk driver just two days after his twenty-first birthday, Haley had mourned right along with my family. We'd been sisters ever since. Monica had come into our lives when her son Landon and my Max had become best friends in kindergarten.

We were an unlikely trio—two divorcées and a mega-rich socialite—but we complimented each other. At least that's what I told myself... really we weren't bringing Haley down so much as giving her life a more well-rounded experience. If it weren't for us, she never would have darkened the doors of Big Lots and found that she could buy Cheetos for a dollar a bag. She'd been so excited that I hadn't had the heart to tell her they were expired. I lived in fear that she'd figure that out one day and realize that Monica and I didn't have much to bring to the relationship.

"Are y'all going to the viewing?" Lindsey, Haley's stylist, brushed on a bluish color that would keep Haley's platinum blonde locks from turning back to whatever shade they were naturally. Since Haley never had roots, there was no telling.

I planned on being there early to say my good-byes in private. My little Max hadn't wanted to go to the service and I didn't have the heart to make my eight-year-old endure such a thing. It had been hard enough to sit him down and tell him that his good friend and most favorite former teacher was dead; I certainly didn't want his last memory of her to be in a casket. Seeing me cry had always upset him, so I'd arranged for him to stay at school in extended care until six.

Lindsay nodded. “I’m going to the viewing. My son, Tanner, had Miss Miars two years ago. I can’t imagine why a kindergarten teacher would overdose. She was always so cheerful. The kids loved her, and she was teacher of the year the last three years.” She continued to brush bluish cream onto Haley’s hair.

“She didn’t overdose.” Andrea picked up the crimping iron and attached another extension. “I did her hair. You can tell a lot about a person based on their hair.”

I glanced in the mirror at my ever-growing mass of brown locks. What did my hair say about me?

Andrea put down the crimping iron, separated another chunk of hair, and grabbed an extension. “She didn’t do drugs. My stepfather was her doctor, and he said she fainted at the sight of needles. Shooting herself full of heroin doesn’t make sense. If she used heroin like the police chief said she did, her hair color wouldn’t have taken. She always insisted on burnt orange number seventeen. God bless her, but it was a bad color for her. She wouldn’t listen to me when I told her blonde was her color. If she was a heroin addict, then I’m Marilyn Monroe.”

I completely agreed. Molly’s alleged heroin use just didn’t make sense. She didn’t drink alcohol or even the occasional beer, so it was hard for me to accept the idea of her overdosing on heroin. Molly and I went out to dinner almost every week and talked on the phone all the time. Surely I would have noticed if she was high, even just once. Maybe she was trying it for the first time and accidentally overdosed? That’s the direction my mind had taken when I first heard the news.

“If she didn’t OD, then what? She was murdered?” Monica picked up a *People* magazine and relaxed back in her seat. She loved T-shirts with funny sayings. Today’s read, “Buffy Staked Edward—End of Story.”

"That's a little out there. Don't you think?" I would have shaken my head, but it was under lockdown. "Murder, really?"

Besides, no one was ever murdered here. Lakeside is a retirement community, where business moguls and their trophy wives move to play golf and tennis and throw lavish charity balls just to prove to the world that money does buy happiness.

"The Lakeside Police Department said it was an overdose." I was still sticking with the tried-it-once-and-accidentally-overdosed theory, even though it didn't make sense. This was a woman who took pride in making Christmas ornaments out of kindergartners' handprints. I didn't want to believe that she was the type to do drugs, but heroin in her bloodstream was hard to ignore.

Still, murder? We didn't have murder in Lakeside, and I should know. My ex-husband, David, had been the chief of police until six months ago, when he decided that a permanent vacation on Grand Cayman with his bimbo girlfriend was ever so much more fun than being a husband, a father, and a cop. All I'd gotten in the divorce was an empty bank account and my sweet son, Max.

If I were smarter and if the stubborn streak that ran in my family had skipped a generation, I'd have moved away and left this town in the rearview mirror. But no one has ever accused me of being smart, and being stubborn was one of my best qualities. Besides, Lakeside is my home, and my son was born here. I may be a husbandless have-not, but I'm not a coward. Plus, if I couldn't join the haves, then I vowed to beat them at their own game by ruling my own little fiefdom—the Bee Creek Elementary PTO.

No, someone murdering Molly didn't make sense. "What would be the motive? An unsatisfactory report on some kindergartner's report card?"

Haley hunched her shoulders. "Everyone loved Miss Miars. Reese and Riley adored her. They cried at the end of last year when they graduated from kindergarten."

Because Haley was an overachiever, she'd had twin girls, Reese and Riley, who were also overachievers.

"It's odd." Monica crossed her legs and flipped through the magazine. "If there was any doubt about the overdose, the medical examiner would have ruled it a heart attack or something else to spare the family and so the life insurance would pay out. Insurance doesn't pay for an overdose or suicide." Not finding anything interesting, she tossed the magazine on the table next to her. "There must have been a lot of drugs in her system."

Monica was a claims examiner for a workers' compensation company. The woman could smell a con from a mile away.

I glanced at her. "Was there a life insurance policy?"

Who would the beneficiary be? Molly had an on-again, off-again relationship with our local eye doctor, but according to her, it was never anything serious. What about her family? In all the time we'd spent together, she'd mentioned her mother only once and the words weren't kind.

"I don't know. Let me see what I can find." Monica pulled out her phone and started typing. "My company is a subsidiary of Global Life, the largest life insurer in the United States." She typed some more and then looked up. "I don't see a policy with us, but I can check around tomorrow."

She turned her screen off and slid the phone back into her pocket. "If she did have a policy, I guess the beneficiary would be her mother."

Andrea paused long enough to prop her left fist on her hip. "Have you ever met Edna Miars?" She shook her head. "There really aren't words to describe her." She thought about it for a second. "Well, maybe soul-sucking vampire who leeches the joy out of everyone she meets."

It seemed she had lots of words to describe Edna.

"I've met her." Haley looked around like she was trying to collect words from thin air. "She was... um... she was the most unhappy person I've ever met."

No wonder Molly didn't talk about her mother. According to the world at large, she was a bitch.

"Tell us how you really feel." Monica leaned over so that she could look past Haley to me. "Remind me why we like her? She's like Snow White, but blonde and nicer." She glanced at Haley. "Do little pastel tweety-birds follow you around in the woods?"

Haley arched a Nike swoop eyebrow. "Sticks and stones."

"She makes a damn fine margarita." I winked at Haley. "And she's the only one who can afford bail money."

"Yes, I can see her appeal." Monica nodded.

"Once, Molly told me she'd sell her body if that's what it took to keep Edna at Lakeside Living." Andrea sectioned off another piece of hair.

"What's Lakeside Living?" I'd heard the name, but I couldn't place it.

"It's that new senior living community on the lake. I hear the one bedroom bungalows start at five hundred thousand." Haley gestured with her chardonnay glass. "And that's for the one with the view of the dumpster. If you want to see the lake, you're looking at a million plus."

"Trust me, Edna isn't living near a dumpster. She'd want the best of the best. Her tastes run past champagne straight to platinum." Andrea crimped the next extension in place. I think Andrea was starting to like me; she hadn't burned me in a whole fifteen minutes.

"How could a kindergarten teacher afford to pay for that?" Molly didn't have that kind of money. Once, when we worked the same booth at the school's fall carnival, she told me that she'd come from money. But after her father died, they'd had to scrape by.

"No clue." Andrea shrugged. "All I know is Molly would have done anything to keep the old woman from moving in with her."

Nothing made sense. Even though I was shocked and confused about the manner of Molly's death, I'd accepted the coroner's ruling and believed that it must have been a first-time overdose.

I had planned on going early to the viewing to say my good-byes and try to begin the healing process, but now something was gnawing at me... something I couldn't explain. I wanted to know just what exactly had happened to Molly Miars forty-eight hours ago. There had to be some evidence of her drug use, and I needed to see it for myself. Because if there was a chance she hadn't overdosed, I needed to know. The Lakeside Police Department had a long history of watching out for the rich and famous. The rest of us had to fend for ourselves. Molly had been part of the have-not club, and she was my friend. I'd never let a friend down, and I wasn't going to start now.

An hour later Monica, Haley, and I walked into viewing room number one at Lakeside Funeral and Final Rest.

"Watch the door. I want to look for needle marks." I walked down the center aisle that led right up to the pale pink casket surrounded by dozens upon dozens of large flower bouquets and funeral sprays. I smiled to myself. Molly was definitely well-liked in the community.

"I'm sorry, come again." Haley leaned forward like she hadn't heard me the first time.

"I'm going to check her body for needle marks." From the beginning, I hadn't been completely comfortable with the overdose idea, and now I wanted to prove to myself that I was right.

"Cool." Monica pulled the doors closed and stood in front of them. "Visitation starts in forty-five minutes and I'm sure the family will be here soon. I'll keep them busy."

"Here." Haley pulled a retractable police baton out of her purse and flicked it open. "Shove this through the door handles. It'll keep them closed."

Monica just stared at her for a moment and shook her head. "Where did you get that?"

"Amazon." Haley smiled and slid the baton through the door handle loops. "It was very highly rated."

"Sometimes I feel like I don't know you at all." Monica blew out a slow breath.

How could I not love these women? They were up for anything. Monica didn't ask any questions and Haley pulled out a tactical baton.

I turned back to the casket holding Molly's body. There was a weird orange light shining down on her face. Between that and the fluorescent lighting casting a green tint, she had the ethereal glow of an Oompa-Loompa. Maybe good lighting in a funeral home was a bad idea.

Molly was dressed in a fuchsia dress that clashed with her beautiful red hair and the pale pink satin lining the casket. And of course the dress was long sleeved, so I couldn't see any injection sites, track marks, or bruises.

"Don't most drug users inject in the arm?" I had no idea. That's what they did on TV. Swallowing down a serious gag reflex, I touched her wrist, intending to roll up her sleeve. When my fingers brushed her hand, I froze. It wasn't cold as I'd thought it would be, but it wasn't warm either. Not having any experience with dead bodies, I assumed they'd be cold.

"I'll Google it," Monica called over my left shoulder.

You could Google heroin injection sites? Who knew? I touched Molly's hand again and pulled my fingers away. Something oily smeared my fingertips. I rubbed my fingers together. It was thick, flesh-colored stage makeup.

"It says that they can inject anywhere there's a vein," Monica called from behind me. "Unless they inject in the same vein over and over, there won't be track marks. Also, you don't have to inject heroin. You can smoke it, too."

It occurred to me that I was learning more than I ever needed to know about heroin from an iPhone.

I touched Molly's hand again. It was hard and unyielding. Even dead flesh should be a little bit pliable, shouldn't it? With my index knuckle, I knocked on it. It sounded like a ripe watermelon. Molly's hand was hollow. Carefully, I picked it up. It was plastic, like a manikin, only with polished fingernails and even a ring.

The last time I'd seen Molly she'd had both of her hands.

"Um... do either of you know why Molly has a plastic hand?" I ran through every scenario I could think of and nope... I had nothing.

"What do you mean?" Monica called from the door. "Molly didn't have a plastic hand."

She walked over, leaned over the open casket, and touched the hand. "That's not right. How far up does it go?"

Monica worked the button at Molly's wrist until the cuff came loose. She rolled up the material as far as she could. The entire arm was plastic.

Haley's heels clip-clopped on the tile floor as she made her way to the casket.

Her eyes turned wild. "Oh God. Stop that! What are y'all doing?" She turned around as if to use her body to hide the open casket from nonexistent onlookers.

Monica took hold of the arm at the elbow and yanked. There was a pop and then a crack. The arm came loose at the shoulder and wobbled under the fabric.

Haley wrung her hands. "Oh God, you broke the body. That's so gross." She used her disapproving mommy voice. "It's so disrespectful."

"Why would she have a plastic arm?" How could overdosing result in her arm being replaced with a fake one? Was the rest of her plastic, too? Carefully, I knocked on her torso. It was hollow. I tried her other arm. Again, a hollow echo. "I think the whole body is plastic."

"Not that." Haley pointed to the head. "It looks real."

Monica thumped Molly on the cheek. "That's not plastic." She turned to me. "Check her legs."

I removed the large spray of pink roses from the lid and set it on the front row and then peered under the partially closed casket lid. It was dark. I felt around for a latch or some way to open the bottom portion of the casket. Not surprisingly, there wasn't a lock, because why would a dead person need a latch release on the inside of their casket? I grabbed the edge of the lid and pulled hard. It popped up as if it were spring loaded.

"We are going straight to hell." Haley glanced down and her eyes turned the size of Magic 8 Balls. "Mother shucker."

Monica threw her hands up. "I feel like such a failure. You spend so much time with me and you still can't cuss." She turned to me. "We need to step up the potty mouth around her."

"It's so hard with the kids around." I shrugged. "What can you do?"

Haley reached over, grabbed Monica by the chin, and tilted her head down.

"Holy. Shit." Monica had a PhD in cussing.

I looked down. Holy shit was right.

From the waist up, Molly Miars was plastic, but from the waist down, she was missing.

CHAPTER 2

The door rattled behind us. We turned around in unison and stared at it. Light knocking started up.

"Is there someone in there?" a deep male voice called from the other side of the door.

"Yes, give us a minute," I yelled.

"Haley, go and stall. Monica and I will..." I gestured toward the casket, "Close her up."

"We're saying a private farewell. Molly was a dear friend. Just give us a moment," Haley said in a loud, fake, teary voice as she walked to the door.

"Certainly, but the viewing starts in twenty minutes." The male voice was firm, but consoling.

I yanked on the bottom lid, but it didn't budge. I yanked harder. The casket rocked back and forth, but the lid didn't close.

I turned to Monica, who'd whipped Molly's dress up and was photographing her plastic parts.

"Do I want to know why you're doing that?" In an evening crammed full of weirdness, this shouldn't have shocked me, but hey, I guess I'm easily shock-able.

"So I can research where they came from." She pointed to a tiny patch of numbers. "I think those are serial numbers."

I leaned over. There was indeed a small tag with numbers on the bottom of the torso. It was good to know that fake plastic body parts came with a VIN.

"Hurry. We need to figure out how to close this thing." I walked around to the back and checked the hinges. They were locked in place. I felt around for a lever or a latch, but I couldn't find anything. Mentally, I went to my old standby for fixing most things—bang on it with a hammer, but damn it, I didn't have a hammer. "Either of you have a hammer?"

Haley unlooped her purse from under her arm, opened the front pocket, and pulled out a small black gun. "Use the butt of this. It's a Smith and Wesson nine millimeter."

Monica looked at me. "Yep, we don't know her at all."

Haley's arm reared back like she was going to toss it to me.

"Don't throw it. I assume that it's loaded. Throwing a loaded gun can't be good." Growing up in Texas and having married a cop, I'd been around guns my whole life, but I'd never handled one myself.

"The safety's on and there's no bullet in the chamber. It's fine." She tossed the gun to me. I caught it like a softball and used it to bang on the hinges. They finally gave way. The bottom lid clattered closed with a loud thud.

"What's going on in there?" The man on the other side of the door was back. "I insist that you open this door immediately."

"Just a few more minutes." Haley said. "Molly was so special to us."

The man started pounding, and the doors rattled against the baton.

"I can't hold him off much longer." Haley leaned against the doors, using her body weight to keep them closed.

I grabbed the floral spray of pink roses and slapped it on top of the closed lid.

Monica tucked the dress back into place and we stuffed the bottom under the closed lid.

"I'm having a little trouble with the arm. I can't pop it back into place." Monica had the arm up and was wiggling it. "There's a bolt or something sticking out."

She dropped the arm and there was a good two-inch gap between the upper arm and the shoulder. The fuchsia material sagged in the separation.

"Do something fast. I'm about to take out the police baton. I can't stall him much longer." Haley's body rattled with the doors as the pounding got louder.

"She's lying on her hair. Let's pull it out and cover her shoulders. She has... um... had long hair." I couldn't think of anything else. Molly's right shoulder was considerably lower than her left. It was noticeable.

"I'm not touching her head again. I already verified that it was her actual head. I'm not touching dead hair." Monica threw her hands up and stepped back. "You're on your own."

It looked like the buck stopped with the president of the PTO. "Fine."

Gently, I slid my hand underneath Molly's head and tugged out a good bit of her red hair. I smoothed it over her right shoulder, and then I grabbed more and smoothed it over her left. It wasn't bad, but clearly whoever had fixed her hair had used some serious hair gel to slick it back. Now that I had disturbed the slicked-back 'do, the hair flopped down over her face in a crusty tidal wave. We needed a headband or something to pull this off. I scanned the room for something that would work.

"Haley, throw me that scarf around your neck." It wasn't perfect, but we didn't have much choice.

"Why?" She kept throwing her body weight against the doors to keep them closed.

"I need it to make the hair look right." Short of weaving pink carnations in her hair, which was too flower girl at a royal wedding, I didn't have any other choice.

"But I like this scarf. It doesn't go with her outfit." She picked up the edge of her black and red scarf. "Will I get it back?"

Slowly, Monica turned around to stare at her. "Do you want it back after this?"

I cocked my head to the left and shot her a look. "We don't have much time."

After rolling her eyes, Haley untied the scarf one-handed. I ran over, grabbed it, and was back at the casket in a flash. Again punching down the old gag reflex, I looped the scarf behind Molly's ears and tied it. My fingers grazed something metal. I felt around. Apparently a metal rod was how the funeral home or whoever had secured the head to the plastic body. My hand slipped and my finger grazed the crease where the neck met the plastic. Revulsion sent a shiver down my spine. I pulled my hand away.

What could have happened to Molly that would result in a pole connecting her head to a fake body?

The addition of the scarf wasn't much better, but it would have to do. If you didn't look too closely, the mismatched shoulders weren't that noticeable. With any luck, Molly wouldn't have a mourner who was OCD.

Monica checked out my handywork. "Not bad."

She nodded to Haley. "Let them in."

I grabbed a handful of tissues from a nearby table and wiped my hands as I made my way down the center aisle. I checked my watch. "It's five thirty. We need to pick up the kids from extended care."

Max and Landon went to extended care. Haley had a live-in nanny named Anise who took care of the twins after school.

"I had Anise pick them up over an hour ago. All the kids are playing at my house. Daniel texted me on the way over saying that he had a late case at the hospital, so I had Anise order a couple of pizzas for the kids. She'll feed them and make sure their homework is done." Haley was so matter-of-fact.

Being a single mom and not used to the help, I could have cried with relief.

Both Monica and I put our arms around Haley and hugged her.

"Have we told you lately that we love you?" Monica whispered.

"You just love me for my nanny." Haley smiled.

"I'm not going to lie, she does bring something to the table." Monica dropped her arm.

Haley stepped back and the doors burst open.

"Is everything okay?" A large man in a gray suit and a skinny blue tie rushed in. According to his nametag, he was "Chester Dunhill—Chief Bereavement Coordinator."

Considering that the deceased was made of plastic and I'd just used a gun to bang the coffin into submission, everything was wonderful. "Yep, it's all good."

Which reminded me. I pulled the gun out of my back jeans pocket and handed it butt-first to Haley. "I forgot to give this back."

"Good heavens." Chester jumped back.

I just smiled sweetly and said, "I found it in one of the floral arrangements. It looks like Flowers.com is branching out with a Guns and Roses bouquet."

Chester managed to look both confused and consoling. Clearly the consoling look was so ingrained that he couldn't drop it even when it wasn't needed. I bet he was loads of fun at the office Christmas party.

"Ladies, why don't you take a seat up front? As good friends of the deceased, I'm sure you'd like to share a remembrance or two when the service starts." Chester nodded solemnly to the front row.

"No thank you. We've said our good-byes in private." I wasn't sticking around. I'd seen more—well, actually less—of Molly Miars than I had in years. While she was a friend, at this point the only good-bye I had to offer was to find out why her head had made it to her funeral but her body was MIA.

Monica put a hand on my shoulder. "It's what Molly would have wanted."

"Yes." Haley nodded. "Molly didn't like a lot of attention."

Five minutes later we stepped into the chilly night air. The parking lot was huge and filled to capacity. Molly sure had lots of people who felt they needed to pay their respects. I stuffed my arms into my jacket, shrugged it on, and buttoned the three front buttons.

Monica slipped one arm around me and the other around Haley.

"So we're thinking murder?" Her voice was barely a whisper.

"I don't know." I shook my head. "In my mind, I keep running through every reason I can think of that would end in a plastic body, but I can't think of a single scenario that fits. If all the police found was her head, we would have heard. This town is about as closed-mouthed as WikiLeaks. Nothing is private, especially a bodiless head."

"If all they found was the head, then how did they know she overdosed?" Ever the practical one, Monica loved a puzzle. "I guess they could check the fluid in her eyes or something. For that matter, I guess there was still blood. Too bad we didn't get a better look at her neck. Maybe we could have seen the cut marks."

Both Haley and I stopped walking and turned to look at her.

"Are you suggesting that someone chopped off her head?" Haley whispered under her breath. Even in the spotty light of the parking lot, it was clear that she was turning green.

"I'm not suggesting anything. I'm just saying that it would have been good to examine her neck. If we had, maybe we could have some sort of idea as to why her body is missing." Monica shrugged. "It's gross, but it would have been informative."

"I don't know much about the neck, but I do know that her head was secured to the plastic body with a metal rod." I dropped my gaze to the ground. "I felt it when I was tying the scarf. I didn't feel around the neck much, but from the split second of contact I had with it, I think the cut was clean. It didn't feel jagged."

Monica pulled out her phone, touched the notes icon, and typed, "Head removed cleanly. No jagged marks."

"What are you doing?" Haley looked around like the CIA was going to jump out of the bushes at any second and arrest us for talking about Molly Miars's body.

"Making notes." Monica shrugged. "You know, for the murder investigation."

"I don't know if we're talking murder here, but I think we can all agree that Molly's death is a little out of the ordinary." I looked from Haley to Monica and back again. "Right?"

"Absolutely." Haley nodded.

"You bet," Monica added.

"I think we owe it to Molly to find out more." I glanced up at the stars. "I don't think the police or anyone else cares. If they did, the head-missing-a-body news would be all over town. The new Lakeside police chief only investigates crimes committed against his wealthy supporters."

I knew this all too well. At work, my purse had been stolen right out of my desk and Chief Stanford hadn't cared a bit. I'd investigated on my own and found the culprit—a maintenance worker. After I made his life a living hell, he'd returned my things, along with an extra hundred bucks for my trouble. Being annoying had its advantages.

Because it didn't look like the Lakeside Police Department cared one way or the other about Molly, finding out what really happened was up to us. We cared. Hopefully, that was enough to find the truth.

"I'm in." Haley's shoulders went back. "She helped my girls, and I never thanked her."

"Hell, I'm in just because it's kinda cool." Monica zipped up her black leather jacket. "I love a puzzle."

"So we're in this together." I took a deep breath. "Wow, our PTO meetings just got a lot more interesting."

"Who cares about selling wrapping paper to raise money in a school district where money grows on trees? This is way more important." Haley nodded.

We stood together in the parking lot and stared at each other. What were we doing? Were we really going to do this?

"We need a cool name, like the PTO Death Club, or wait, PTODC might be better. If I write death club meeting on my calendar, my assistant will have a heart attack. I need this one to stick around. She seems to be able to count to ten and knows her alphabet." Monica yawned and then pointed to her car. "I'm over there."

"I'm two rows over." I turned to Haley. "We'll meet you at your house to pick up the boys."

Haley waved as she headed to her Land Rover.

It had been a strange day. Not only had we found our friend minus a body, but we were now officially investigating her death. Our lack of actual credibility aside, we—the PTO Death Club—were a force to be reckoned with. There were so many unanswered questions, not the least of which was, where was the body? I would grieve by finding out what happened. I needed to know, and I owed it to Molly. If I found that something else had happened, she deserved justice. But if I did find that she'd overdosed, I would find a way to deal with that.

Teaching kindergarten didn't rank at the top of the stressful job list, but then again, I didn't teach kindergarten. Molly had never seemed stressed. She loved her job. In fact, she'd just signed up to direct the school holiday play.

Where Molly was concerned, things weren't adding up. What did an overdose and a missing body have to do with one another? For that matter, why hadn't the Lakeside Police put two and two together and cried foul play?

That was fine. Molly had us now. The PTODC would figure out what happened—and no matter what it took, we were on Molly's side.

CHAPTER 3

At noon the next day, I pulled into the parking lot of the mighty Lakeside Police Department. It was a typical fall day in the Hill Country, a cloudless sixty degrees, but that did little to lighten my mood. I hadn't set foot in the Lakeside police station since the day before David left.

It hadn't been my finest hour, but in my defense, I'd just found out about his infidelity. My baseball bat and I took a little field trip over to the police station and bashed some heads—well, only one—David's. Nothing serious, but there was blood spilled, and his precious vintage Jaguar took the brunt of my rage. If it hadn't been for Officer Ben Jamison, who'd pulled me off "The Chief" and driven me home, I'd have ended up behind bars.

Today, I was hoping Officer Jamison was feeling charitable again. I balanced a box of a dozen cupcakes—red velvet, my favorite, because I didn't know Jamison's favorite—and two mocha lattes. Hey, if someone were trying to pump me for information, red velvet cupcakes and mocha lattes would definitely loosen my tongue.

Don't get the idea that I baked them. Six years ago I gave up cooking for Lent, and I haven't looked back. The fact that I'm Baptist is completely irrelevant.

With my butt, I pushed open one of the double chrome and glass doors, and walked up to the front desk, smiling broadly. "Esther. It's been too long."

Esther glanced up from her computer with a look that said it hadn't been long enough. Clearly, I'd underestimated her devotion to my ex-husband.

"I'm here to see Ben." My smile didn't waver. "Can you please tell him that I'm here?"

"He's out." Esther's two-pack-a-day voice put the gravel in gravelly. Her milky-brown, glaucoma-blue-eye-shadowed eyes scrunched up, and tattooed eyebrows bounced off her garish orange hairline. "On a call."

Ben's deep laugh boomed out of his office behind Esther.

My cheeks were starting to quiver under the strain of my smile, but I soldiered on. "That's funny. It sounds like he's right there."

I parked my cupcake box on her desk and looked down my nose at her.

Esther's prune-wrinkled face puckered up like she'd just sucked on a dill pickle. "Guess I was mistaken."

Liar, liar, pants on fire. No cupcakes for her.

"Ben!" I yelled. If I waited for Esther to pick up the phone and call him, I'd miss the Black Friday sales next month. Halloween was in three weeks; I was tempted to go as Esther. All I needed was a Freddy Krueger mask, lots of blue eye shadow, and an orange wig. Actually, it wasn't a bad idea.

Officer Ben Jamison stepped out of his office in all of his uniformed glory. His face lit up when he saw me. If Matthew McConaughey had a younger, cuter brother, Ben would be him. He even had the East Texas accent and the "aw shucks, ma'am" attitude.

He practically leapt over Esther to get to me. "Mustang, it's so good to see you."

As you might have guessed, there are no good nicknames for Mustang. Musty, Tangy, Mustangy, even the annoying Tang—they've all been tried and failed miserably.

"Ben, I brought cupcakes. Do you have a minute?" I threw Esther a snotty look and stepped around her desk.

"Sure." He took the cupcake box from me. Then, like we were long lost college roommates, he wrapped his arms around me in a hug. Holy hard pecs, Batman. Ben had been working out. The last time we met, he hadn't hugged me so much as tackled me. This time was much better.

With his hand at the small of my back, he ushered me into his office, set the cupcakes down on his messy desk, and gestured to the chair closest to him. He dropped his hand and stepped back just a bit. Instead of sitting in his desk chair, he leaned on the desk edge near me. He was so close that his knee bumped my thigh, and his crotch met me at eye level. It was hard not to look, it being two feet away and all.

Struggling a bit to move my eyes upward, I forced myself to focus on his face.

"What can I do for you?" Interest sparkled in his eyes, and I wondered if he'd caught me checking him out.

"I was hoping you could help me with something." Did I just jump in and ask for the Molly Miars file, or did I try to finesse it out of him?

"Cupcake?" I leaned over and opened the box. Finesse it was. I grabbed the biggest one. True, they were meant to ply Ben for information, but I was hungry. I was also the product of two older brothers who lived by the law that whoever got there first got the biggest cupcake.

I unwrapped the cupcake and took a huge bite. Tart cream cheese icing and bloodred-dyed dark chocolate cake swirled inside my mouth. My taste buds high-fived each other, and I took a moment to enjoy myself.

"Can't, I'm low carb." He patted his trim stomach. "Watching my weight."

That made me feel bad... sort of. I knew I should go low carb, but I have a loyalty problem. Carbs are my friends and have gotten me through some really tough times. I feel that I need to support them in this cruel, low-carb world we live in. It's the least I can do for my best buddy, red velvet.

I chewed the world's biggest bite and wondered if it would be rude to take the cupcakes and lattes with me when I left. I didn't want them to go to waste and he didn't want them.

After the eternity it took for me to chew and swallow, I got right to it. Finesse was overrated. "I want to talk to you about Molly Miars."

His smile drooped around the edges. "I don't understand."

"She was my friend." And I wondered why we'd only buried her head. "She didn't seem the type to... you know... overdose. Max adored her."

Was it too soon to ask to see her file?

"I don't know what I can tell you." He shrugged. "As I heard it, she was found at her house. She'd been dead for a couple of days."

"Who found her?" And did they find all of her?

"Chief Stanford got the call. Someone from the school called wanting us to do a welfare check because she hadn't shown up for work in two days and they hadn't heard from her."

Dennis Stanford had the body of a professional wrestler and the good sense God gave Cool Whip. I heard that last Christmas he'd reported his car stolen because he'd forgotten where he parked it. Two weeks later, he got a call from the Target store manager asking him to please come pick up his car. And that wasn't the first time. The man obviously had a memory problem. The only reason he'd been appointed to the chief's spot was because the good citizens of Lakeside could count on him to do as he was told.

Ben crossed his arms. "What's with all the questions?"

"She was my friend, and I can't quite reconcile the facts. She didn't do drugs, so the idea of her overdosing is, well..." I took a sip of my mocha latte. " ...hard to take."

His eyes softened. Pity wasn't my favorite emotion to inspire. The last time I'd seen him, he'd had the same look in his eyes.

"Any chance I can look at her file?" I smiled sweetly.

He looked around like he was afraid of being overheard and then leaned close to me. "Stay away from this case, Mustang. It's all wrong. Stanford threw procedure out the window. He handled everything himself and he isn't talking," he whispered close to her ear. "No one's talking about it."

In a small town, the only thing more dangerous than gossip was the lack of it. If Ben was right and something bad had happened to Molly and no one was talking about it... it must be really bad. Gossip was bread and butter in small towns—unless people were scared, and then their bread and butter stuck to the roof of their mouths.

"Was Molly... you know..." I tried to use my hands to gesture "whole," but I kept pantomiming a ball and didn't know why, so I linked my fingers and rested them in my lap. "You know, um... intact. Did they find all of her?"

His look went from concerned to skeptical—like he was humoring crazy Aunt Laverne who'd had one too many eggnogs and was now convinced that Tom Cruise had stolen her reading glasses.

"I'm pretty sure her body was in one piece." He nodded and smiled like yep, I was a nut job. "Oh... wait." He sat back. "There was something strange. I overheard the Chief say something about her dog." He thought about it for a minute. "Oh yeah, he said that the dog must have been loyal because he'd found it dead right by her side."

"He found Molly and her dog dead?" That was odd. Did her dog overdose, too? Or maybe he'd died first and she was so heartbroken that she pulled out the heroin she just happened to have lying around and injected it? Or was it a murder suicide—she killed the dog first and then herself?

"Was the heroin found near her body? For that matter, how do you know it was heroin?" Since I couldn't look for needle tracks on plastic arms, I was interested to find out how exactly they knew about the heroin.

"I don't know." He crossed his arms and looked like he was humoring me. "Look, we don't determine cause of death, the city coroner does. So regardless of what was found at the scene, we don't have anything to do with cause of death."

"Oh." I guessed that made sense.

"Is there anything else you can tell me about the case?" I hated to keep pressing, but I needed the info.

"Leave it alone. She died of an overdose." He shook his head. "There really wasn't much of a case. She was found dead and the toxicology came back positive for heroin. Open and shut."

Au contraire. This case was anything but open and shut. Nothing made sense. And the more questions I asked, the weirder things got.

"So, how's Max?" Ben tucked his thumbs into his belt on either side of his belt buckle as if to point out the stunning array of gadgets on his belt.

"He's good. Loves soccer and swimming." I sat forward, preparing to stand. Ben had always played with Max when the department had gotten together at my house for barbecues and parties.

"Maybe I could come by sometime, kick the ball around with him?" Ben smiled. Again with the pity.

"Sure." I tried to sound enthusiastic. Max needed a father figure around, but pity wasn't the basis for any kind of relationship. I analyzed his face and realized I saw more than pity in his eyes: there was guilt.

It hit me like a ton of bricks; he'd known about David's affair. Good Lord, who else knew? I sighed and shook my head. Everyone... except me. Wasn't the wife always the last to know?

I made a big show of checking my watch. "I really need to go. I only have fifteen minutes left on my lunch break."

Thank God Lakeside Hospital was only five minutes away.

"Sure, I understand." He rose. "It was good to see you."

I stood too. "You bet, and thanks for your help."

Not that he'd been all that much help—well, except for the dog. I nodded to myself, thinking. As a hospital employee, I had access to all kinds of medical information. Getting Molly's medical records was just a phone call away. I was starting to perk back up. If I were a villain in an old movie, I'd stroke my mustache in anticipation, but I don't have a mustache, and today I wasn't the villain, so I just grabbed the cupcakes, my mocha latte, and headed to the door.

"How about dinner tonight?" Ben called after me.

I turned back to him. "Look, you don't need to feel guilty. It doesn't matter about David and the bimbo. It's over and done. It's obvious that you knew, but I don't care."

And I kind of didn't. If I was being honest, I hadn't loved David in a very long time, but the embarrassment of being the victim of a cheating husband lived on forever. At least the whispering behind my back had stopped. Or I was pretty sure it had, but then I tend to ignore people, so it was hard to tell.

"So we're on for dinner?" Was it my imagination, or did his smile brighten a couple of degrees? "I'll pick up food after work and head over to your place."

"You know where I live?" Of course I'd had to sell my house and find something I could afford on my salary. Unfortunately, the only thing I'd been able to find that would keep Max at the same school was the guesthouse of Lakeside's most eccentric resident.

Astrid Petrie was in her sixties, worth hundreds of millions, and spoke to the dead. She was equal parts Austen's Lady Catherine de Bourgh and Hogwarts Divination Professor Trelawney. My rent was cheap, but I did have to attend the regularly scheduled Monday evening séance.

"Astrid's my aunt. She's, um..." Ben hunched his shoulders. "Well, let's just say she makes the family Thanksgiving way more fun than it should be."

I'd forgotten that Ben was a trust fund baby who worked because he wanted to and not because he needed the money. It wasn't his fault that he'd been born into a family full of oil billionaires.

"I can see that about her." I smiled and nodded. "Okay, dinner it is."

In two strides, he was at my side. "I'll walk you out."

With his hand at the small of my back, he led me through the front office, where I glared at Esther, and then we were out in the sunshine.

"I've thought about you a lot these last six months." He was so close that I could smell his aftershave, something exotic and woodsy. "I've almost called you so many times."

It was on the tip of my tongue to ask him why, but I just nodded. We reached my crappy Ford van—another tragedy of divorce, as I could no longer make the payments on my Ford Fusion. I went to open the door, but he opened it for me. My van didn't lock, which was fine because I didn't have anything anyone would want to steal.

"I'll see you tonight." I was about to slide behind the wheel when he pulled me into a tight hug.

"I can't wait." He finally let me go and stepped back. "See you soon."

I climbed into the driver's seat, closed the door, and waved good-bye.

I turned the screwdriver sticking out of the ignition keyhole and started Bessie, my brown 1997 Ford Aerostar.

It had come with a screwdriver instead of a key and for the five hundred bucks I'd paid for her, I hadn't asked any questions. It got me from point A to point B, and with no car payment, who was I to complain?

As I pulled out of the parking lot and onto Lakeside Drive, I glanced in the rearview mirror and saw Ben standing right where I'd left him, hands in his pockets, watching my car.

It had been a long time since a man had flirted with me. As men went, Ben was pretty to look at, but I had Max to consider. Ben turned around and I caught a glimpse of his backside. Nice. Okay, there were worse things than a handsome man bringing me dinner.

Damn, I forgot about the carbs. While he was hot, the carb-free thing could be a deal breaker.

What did I love more, sex or pasta?

That was a tough one.

CHAPTER 4

"I'm not taking no for an answer." Haley's voice was high-pitched and bossy. I rolled my eyes. I had Monica and Haley conferenced in on my way back to work. If only I could drive and FaceTime them, they would feel the full force of my eye roll.

"Both of you need to know how to handle yourselves. I'm taking you to the shooting range." Haley was in mom mode and when she got like this, there was no shutting her down.

I'd filled them in on what little I'd learned from Ben.

"How about this afternoon?" Monica yawned. "Sorry, I was up late last night researching Molly Miars. I found almost nothing. I think she's the only person in the world who doesn't have an online presence."

"I can't tonight. Ben's bringing dinner over." I yawned too. Yawning really is contagious, even over the phone.

"Somebody has a date," Monica sing-songed.

"Yeah, but he's low carb, so I don't see this going anywhere." Which pretty much summed up my dating life. I go on a lot of first dates, but second dates? Ehhh, my chances of winning the lottery seemed to be better.

I pulled into my parking space at Lakeside Regional Hospital with seven whole minutes to spare.

"Cougar alert. Ladies, we have a cougar alert." Monica sipped something. "He's hot. No denying that."

"He's only two years younger than me." The last time I'd dated someone younger than me, I'd felt like I was babysitting, only I wasn't getting paid.

Haley shuffled some papers. "What about tomorrow for the range? I'll call D and see if we can come around ten. It's Saturday though, so he may not be around."

"Ten works for me. I can have my mom take all the kids to the park. I'll even pack them a picnic lunch." Monica liked to cook.

We weren't exactly polar opposites, but we definitely weren't polar sames. I laughed at my own joke and there was a silence across the phone line. Look, if I didn't laugh at my own jokes, who would? Trouble was, I tended to laugh at jokes that I hadn't said out loud. It tended to confuse people.

"After I talk with D, I'll text you his address." Haley sounded like she was making a note to self.

"His address? I don't understand. I thought we were going to the gun range?" I opened my door, grabbed my purse, and headed out of the parking garage. While technically I was salaried and could take a longer lunch if I wanted, I liked to set a good example for the three whole employees I managed.

"He has an indoor gun range at his house. It's the only place to go shooting in Lakeside." Haley said. "And his butler is a gunsmith."

"Of course." Because everyone's butler was a gunsmith. Of all the crazy-extravagant things I'd seen in Lakeside, this didn't even rate in the top one hundred. Now, the full-on castle complete with moat-turned-lazy-river at the corner of Lakeside and Rough Hollow, that made the top one hundred. I've discovered that one man's moat was another man's lazy river. "Who's D?"

"Daman Rodriguez." Haley was so casual.

"Why does that name sound familiar?" I knew that name from somewhere. Maybe David had mentioned him.

"So you hang out with gangbangers now?" Monica was dead serious.

"What?" Gangbangers? The closest Lakeside had to gangbangers was the neighborhood watch—true, they wore matching red windbreakers, but that hardly qualified as gang colors.

"Just because he has tattoos doesn't mean he's in a gang." Haley's voice turned dreamy. "He's really pretty to look at."

"Damn, I didn't know you had a bad boy fetish." I heard the smile in Monica's voice. "Guns and bad boys—Hal, you are a complex woman."

Lakeside had a bad boy? Evidently I ran in the wrong circles.

I slid my electronic security badge through the scanner at the employee entrance. "Sorry ladies, I've got work to do."

"Tomorrow at ten. We expect details." Monica made some kissing noises.

"Bye." I hung up.

A bodiless head, a carb-less date, and now I find Haley is into bad boys. The *Enquirer* was right; the world really was going to end on Christmas.

Five minutes later I was seated at my desk and logging into our medical software program. I got up, closed the door to my office, and sat back down. I typed "Molly Miars" into the patient search window.

Fifteen records with different dates of service popped up. The first one was from seventeen years ago when Molly was ten and broke her arm. It seemed unlikely that she'd starting using heroin at the age of ten, so I scrolled down to more recent records.

Last year, she'd come into the emergency room for vomiting and diarrhea. A copy of her blood work had been sent to Dr. Lucy Enos, who was an OB-GYN. Why send the blood work to her OB-GYN? Lab results usually went to the primary care doctor. In the state of Texas, an OB-GYN could be a primary care doctor, but most women had a general practitioner as their primary because an OB-GYN didn't usually have time to treat the common cold. I glanced at the doctor's info again. Dr. Enos was in Austin. Why would Molly have driven all the way into Austin when we had an OB-GYN in Lakeside?

I moved to the next record. A couple of months ago, she'd been in for an ankle X-ray. A copy of the X-ray report had been sent to Austin City Orthopedics. Also curious, because Lakeside had an orthopedic doctor on staff at the hospital.

So Molly liked seeing doctors outside of her gossipy hometown. I nodded to myself. It wasn't a bad idea. I wish I'd thought of it.

I pulled up the X-ray report. The cause of injury at the top of the report stated that this was a gardening accident. That seemed odd—first, that she would tell the emergency room that she'd had something as stupid as a gardening accident, and second, that she'd make it up. Molly didn't garden. Many a time, she'd proudly proclaimed her inability to grow anything. She'd called herself a "black-thumb-smith."

I clicked print, and while all of her recent medical records spilled into the tray, I pulled up my web browser and searched for Dr. Enos's practice phone number. I needed to see all of Molly's medical records.

I found the number and picked up the phone. If there was anything I could count on, it was that most medical office employees were underpaid and overworked. I checked my watch. One forty-five.

I dialed.

"Enos Women's Health, can you hold please?" Perfect timing. Just back from lunch and in a hurry to answer the phones and check in tons of patients.

"Absolutely." As my mother always says, you catch more flies with honey than vinegar. It worked well with harassed front desk people.

After five minutes, she was back. "Thanks for holding, how may I help you?"

I pinched my nose together and said in my best nasally, haute voice. "This is Salina Atan at Lakeside Regional and I need Molly Miars's file. Can you send it over ASAP?"

I always used my most-hated coworker's name when ordering medical records that I really didn't need. Her email address is satan@LakesideHospital.org. Satan was the perfect name for her. She'd had an affair with my husband. Along with Giles Martin, the high school principal, and Stumpy Gregg, the World War II veteran who ran bingo night at the Knights of Columbus, and God only knows who else. Apparently, her tastes were eclectic.

"Sure. Why?" Clearly this receptionist wasn't as harassed as I'd hoped.

I pulled up Molly's medical record again and checked out the insurance information we had on file.

"United Healthcare is auditing us and her file is on the list." See what I did there? Listen, the only reason bullshit isn't my middle name is because I don't have a middle name.

"But she's dead." She may not be as busy as I'd like, but she wasn't the brightest crayon in the box.

"She has outstanding claims. They don't go away just because she's dead." I was so sweet and helpful that I almost strained something.

"Sure. What dates do you need? I have to enter a date range in the system or send the whole file." I could hear the phone ringing in the background.

"I can tell that you're busy, so just send the whole file and I'll take what I need." Ever the helpful one.

"Yeah, okay. I can fax directly from the program. What's your fax number?"

It's a little known fact that most medical offices still use fax machines as the primary form of information transfer. Don't know why.

"Thanks." I gave her my office fax number and hung up.

I called Austin City Orthopedics and did the same thing. I'm good.

Did Molly have a GP? I hadn't seen one in her file, and considering that she liked to find her medical professionals outside of Lakeside, there was no way to tell. Maybe one of the records I'd just requested would have more information.

I filled up the fax machine with paper and waited. It took all of five minutes before the records started spitting out.

Fifteen minutes later, I was the proud possessor of Molly Miars's medical files. I thumbed through them, found referrals for other physicians, and called their offices for her medical records. Close to a ream of paper later, I had everything medically known about Molly Miars.

Two and a half hours later, it felt like the world really was going to end. On the way home from work, I'd picked up Max and was now standing in front of my closet trying to decide if I should change into date clothes or jeans.

"Mom, whatcha doing?" Max plopped down on my bed.

"Having a personal crisis." Should I go boob shirt or just a regular shirt? How much of a date was this? Like 50 percent date and 50 percent Ben just wanted to see Max, or was it 90 percent date and 10 percent wanted to see Max? The level of date should dictate the level of boob shirt, but I didn't have a 50 percent boob shirt. For that matter, I didn't have a 90 percent boob shirt either.

"Does personal crisis hurt?" He finger-combed his unruly golden hair—a gift from his dad.

"You better believe it, buddy." I pulled out a black V-necked shirt and a loose V-necked green sweater. Both showed some cleavage, but not a lot. I held them up for Max. "Which one?"

"Which one what?" His blue eyes zeroed in on my face. "Why aren't you changing into sweatpants like usual?"

"Because Ben Jamison is coming over." And I don't always wear sweatpants around the house. Sometimes I wear yoga pants.

"Oh yeah." He shrugged. "Why is he coming over?"

It wasn't suspicion so much as boredom in his voice.

"He's bringing dinner." The black shirt and jeans seemed like a safe bet. Some cleavage, but not full-on boob shirt. "He's one of your dad's friends. He asked about you when I saw him today."

"You saw him today?" Now that was a full-out accusation. "Are you dating him, too?"

Max hadn't liked Chad, the last guy who'd taken me out. Luckily, I hadn't really liked Chad all that much either. He'd been a reporter who tried to romance the story of my ex-husband out of me. I was all for the free meal, but it turns out that free food wasn't worth the three hours I spent with Chad, even with the two baskets of dinner rolls I'd eaten by the time my steak arrived.

"He's just a friend of your dad's. Mainly he wants to see you. Don't you remember him? He's the guy who always played soccer with you when the guys came over." Max had always liked Ben.

He did that one-eyebrow-up thing, something I'd never been able to master. "Yeah, I remember him. You're not going to have sex with him, are you?"

Some might think it was too early, but Max and I started having the sex talk a couple of years ago when he'd asked where babies came from. I'd gotten way more in-depth than necessary, and now I realized that he was listening and apparently understanding a lot more closely than I'd thought.

What should I say to him? I never lied to Max.

"Not tonight. We're only having dinner." That was truthful.

His eyes narrowed. "Your hair is different. It's bigger or something."

"Thanks for noticing." I shook my head like a model in a shampoo commercial. "I got extensions. Do you like them?"

Max shrugged. "It's okay, I guess. Whatever. I hope this guy brings pizza."

"I wouldn't count on it." Ben would probably bring a side of beef and a pound of bacon. That was okay because I had a couple of frozen pizzas we could eat after he left. "How's the homework situation?"

"Finished in extended care. Except we have to do this stupid genealogy project. It's due in two weeks. I'm supposed to ask you and dad all these questions." He tried to sound like he didn't care, but I caught the sadness in his voice. "Have you heard from him?"

Max no longer cried for his father. It was a terrible thing to watch grief turn into resignation. I never bad-mouthed David in front of Max, but it took lots of restraint.

"Nope, sorry, buddy." I sat beside him. "Let me see those questions. We can always call Grandma and see if she knows the answers to them."

David's mom thought the sun rose and set in David's eyes, which of course meant she absolutely hated me. That was fine because the feeling was mutual. If I didn't love Max with every fiber of my being, I wouldn't have volunteered to call the old dragon.

"We'll figure this out together." I ruffled his hair. "So let's get serious now. What have you built on Minecraft today?"

"A new house with an underground bunker. Wanna see?" His eyes lit up. If my son was any indication, Minecraft brought more happiness to elementary school households than Santa, the Easter Bunny, and the Tooth Fairy combined.

"Absolutely. Let me just change and I'll be right out." I smoothed his hair down where I'd ruffled it.

"Wear the jeans and the red shirt. Emma's dad said you look hot in that shirt." He edged off the bed, walked out the door, and closed it behind him.

So kids these days discussed the hotness of their parents? Wow, things really had changed.

He was growing up way too fast. I shrugged out of my work clothes, slipped on the jeans and the red shirt Max had pointed to, and pulled on some fluffy socks. At least the socks were part of my normal after work wardrobe.

"Okay, Maximus Cuticus, I can't wait to see my new Minecraft house." I padded down the hall and headed toward the living room. Astrid's guesthouse had two tiny bedrooms, a small living room, and a surprisingly huge kitchen with what were probably state-of-the-art appliances, but they were completely lost on me. The year-round-heated pool, sauna, tennis court, and workout room were burdens I forced myself to live with every single day. We all have our crosses to bear.

My socks barely made any sound on the chocolate travertine floors.

As I walked into the living room, I pulled my now-thick hair up into a ponytail and secured it with an elastic band, then came up short. Ben and Max were head-to-head in front of our home laptop. One blond head melted into the other.

I shook my head. "Show me whatcha got."

"Hey." Ben turned around and smiled, his gaze starting at my head and slowly moving down. The look should have been lascivious but was just plain sexy. Smolder alert. My lady parts yawned awake, stood at attention, and said, "Yes please." Guess Max was right about the red shirt.

"Your hair is different. I meant to tell you earlier that it looks good... fuller or fluffier or something." He'd changed out of his uniform and into pressed khakis and a blue-green button down that matched his eyes. And he'd noticed my hair. David wouldn't have noticed my hair if I'd colored it purple and set it on fire.

"Thanks." I slid my hands into my back pockets and spied the enormous paper sack from It's All Good Barbecue sitting on the kitchen island. Probably I should offer to make a salad to go with dinner, but anyone who knows me knows that I hate salad and rarely have anything green—well, unless it's turned green—in my fridge.

"Max, please set the table." I glanced at Ben. "Wanna beer?"

"Okay Mom, just let me finish this." Max banged away on the keyboard building something on Minecraft.

"Wait... sorry. I forgot that you're low carb." I searched my brain for a low-carb beverage. "Want some water?"

"Beer's fine." Ben walked to the kitchen and started unloading the bag. "I didn't know what you like, so I got a little of everything."

I grabbed a bottle of Shiner from the fridge, opened it, and handed it to him. "I'll do that. Relax. You brought dinner, the least I can do is unpack it."

"That's the best offer I've had all day." He shrugged out of his jacket, hung it on the back of the chair, and then walked over to the front door and picked up a leather messenger bag. "I brought you a present."

"Cool. I need another messenger bag." I laughed. Again with appreciating my own jokes. At least I'd said that one out loud.

"Ha. Ha." He pulled out a manila file folder, brought it over, and handed it to me. "Here."

He glanced at Max off in Minecraft-land. "You need to keep it to yourself."

I unloaded the last large, paper-wrapped bundle, wiped my hands on a dish towel, and took the folder. Inside was a single photograph.

"That's the entire Molly Miars file." He was standing so close that I could see the gold flecks in his eyes.

Another serious smolder alert. I managed to pull my gaze away from his long enough to glance at the picture. It was a picture of Molly Miars's body, and her little dog too. My mind said the last part of that sentence in the voice of Dorothy's Wicked Witch of a neighbor.

"Thanks." I have to say that I expected a chalk outline. It was kind of disappointing that there wasn't one.

I glanced at Max to make sure he was still in Minecraft-land and looked down at the photo. It was in color; I don't know why I'd thought crime scene photos were black and white.

I studied the photo. Molly's body was on her left side at an odd angle, but her head was facing up with her eyes open. Her dog seemed to have been stabbed or something else that would cause an open wound because there was a trail of blood coming from somewhere out of the frame all the way to Molly. It was like he'd pulled himself over to her. Paolo, his name had been Paolo. Molly had called him her Pomeranian boyfriend.

"Can I keep this?" I needed to go over it with a magnifying glass, and the girls needed to see it. Maybe between all three of us, we could find a clue.

Ben shrugged. "I guess. It's a copy, the original's in evidence."

"You're the bestest." I gave him a quick hug. At least it started out as a quick hug, but Ben pulled me in tight against him. Sculpted abs and pecs crushed against me.

"Mommmm." Max sounded honestly scandalized.

Ben dropped his arms and stepped back.

Max's eyes were the size of cupcakes.

"What?" I put my hands on my hips. "Grown-ups hug and kiss and sometimes more than that."

"But you said you weren't going to have sex with him." Max cocked his head to the left.

I could feel my face light up like a red neon sign. Some women blush prettily, I turn lobster red. I avoided Ben's gaze.

"If you think that was sex, clearly I need to be more specific. We'll discuss it later." I slipped the picture back in the folder and finally turned to Ben. "I'll be right back. I need to put this away."

I needed to hide it somewhere that Max would never find it. When David was around and I wanted to hide something from him, my old standby was to put whatever it was in my tampon box. But this was larger than the tampon box. I walked into my bedroom and looked around. Under the mattress, just like they did it in the movies. After pulling up the corner and slipping the photo under it, I walked back into the kitchen.

Ben had unwrapped most of the food and set it on the kitchen table.

"Max, please set the table. This is the second time I've asked." I was using my mommy voice. I don't know where it came from, but it had showed up sometime after I'd given birth.

"Okay." He typed some more and then pushed away from the computer. He stood on his tiptoes to reach the cabinet, opened it, pulled three plates down, grabbed three forks and knives from the drawer in front of him, and went to the table. He set the plates down, a fork and a knife on either side, and then grabbed a handful of paper napkins from the basket in the middle of the table. He placed one under each knife.

"Good job, buddy." Ben nodded.

Max rolled his eyes up to meet Ben's. "Mom makes me do it a lot."

He made it sound like I beat him regularly, lock him in a closet, and only let him out to set the table.

"Moms can be like that. Mine made me make my bed every morning and take the trash out." Ben clapped a hand on Max's shoulder. "Moms can be tough."

I pulled two glasses out of the cabinet, filled them with ice from the door in the freezer, and then pressed the water button, filling them with water. I brought them to the table and set one in front of Max and the other in front of my plate. "Yep, we moms are a mean species. It's a wonder you lived through having one."

"I know." Ben grinned. "Does the ability to look at your child and know what they've done wrong come automatically or is there some practice involved?"

"Yep, it grows in the womb along with the baby. So do the eyes in the back of our heads, the ability to spot a lie a mile away, and hurling shoes to get your attention when you're too far away to feel the full weight of the mommy death glare. Motherhood is a package deal."

"Sounds like it." With his fork, Ben stabbed one of the three Fred-Flintstone-sized beef ribs and put it on his plate.

Max took one and they turned to look at me. Not that I wasn't a fan of giant-sized beef products, it's more that I was a chicken kind of girl.

I checked out all of the meat options. Chicken, turkey, and sausage, along with a mountain of brisket. That was a lot of dead animals. I picked up a white Styrofoam container and popped off the lid. "Cream corn... cool."

I poured a huge glob of corn onto my plate, along with some turkey. Using my knife, I cut off a hunk of chicken. I opened the remaining three Styrofoam containers to find squash casserole, potato salad, and coleslaw.

"I thought after dinner, we could kick the soccer ball around, if you'd like." Ben watched Max.

"Sure." Max's face lit up. "We've got a game tomorrow afternoon against the Strikers. They beat us last year."

"What position do you play?" Ben used a paper napkin to wipe his mouth and then took a sip of his beer.

"Midfielder," Max said around a huge bite of meat. I would have chided him for talking with his mouth full, but I've been known to do the same thing, so it seemed hypocritical.

"I don't know much about soccer, maybe you could teach me," Ben said.

"Sure." Max's tone was all importance.

"What time is your game?" I'd forgotten about it.

"I think it's at four. Why?" Max was gnawing on the rib bone. It seemed that Fred-Flintstone-sized meat brought out the caveman in my son.

"Haley's teaching me to shoot tomorrow morning. You're going to the park with Reese and Riley and Landon. Landon's grandmother's watching you. Y'all are picnicking."

"Cool." Max grinned. He had a crush on Riley.

"You're learning how to shoot a gun? Why?" Ben wiped his mouth again, sat back, and looked at me.

"Honestly, I'm not sure. My friend Haley seems to think I need to know how to handle a gun. She's taking us to someone's house. I can't remember his name, but he has a gun range in his house. His butler is a gunsmith."

I've always wanted a butler, but I've never understood what they do, besides opening the front door. Do they just wait around for someone to knock on the door? People rarely come to my door, so my butler would be pretty bored.

"Daman Rodriguez." Ben's eyes narrowed and five lines popped up on his forehead.

"Yes, I think that's right." I scooped up a forkful of creamed corn and popped it in my mouth. It was sweet and a little spicy with a hint of jalapeño.

"He's not a..." Ben looked like he was choosing his words carefully. "A very nice person. If you know what I mean." He shot me a look full of hidden meaning that I was supposed to get but didn't.

"Not nice" could mean a lot of things. Did Daman eat small children by the light of the full moon or tailgate the elderly? There were many, many levels of "not nice."

"I don't understand." I needed a qualifier.

He glanced at Max and then back at me. "Rodriguez is kind of shady."

"Okay." So did that mean he cheated on his taxes? Or was he a serial killer?

"I'm finished." Max scooted back from the table. "I'll go play in my room so y'all can finish dinner and talk about whatever it is that you don't want me to know."

I reached out and ruffled his hair. "You're such a smart kid."

Max shot me a grin. "I know."

Ben laughed. "Can't pull one over on you. Let me finish talking to your mom and then I'd like to kick the ball around with you. You can show me what a midfielder does."

"Awesome." Max high-fived Ben and then turned and walked down the hall to his bedroom.

Max seemed to genuinely like Ben.

"Great kid." Ben smiled at me.

"Yes, he is." I could go all false modesty, but Max is a great kid. "I don't know where he gets it."

"From you... he's you, only younger and male." Ben's eyes twinkled in the fluorescent light.

"Thanks." Could I make my eyes twinkle? I was going to have to work on that.

Ben glanced at the hallway to make sure Max was out of earshot. "Daman Rodriguez is the head of a Mexican drug cartel."

It took a full minute for my brain to process that little bit of news. "Drug cartel? In Lakeside?" I watched him very carefully for signs that he was either joking or hallucinating.

"Six months ago, he shows up out of nowhere, has money to burn, buys an unfinished house, and quadruples the size. I've run a background check on him. There is nothing prior to ten years ago. He didn't exist. Nothing." Ben crossed his legs at the knee—something I usually found effeminate in men, but there was nothing girly about Ben. He oozed so much alpha maleness that my ovaries tingled.

"So just because there's no record of him beyond ten years, he's a drug lord?" I had a hard time believing the drug cartel angle. What kind of drugs were we talking? Did he run the black market Viagra trade out of his house? Viagra was really the only drug that would be of any interest to the folks of Lakeside... except for Metamucil, and since that was legal, I couldn't see making a business out of it.

"He has a private airstrip and we think he's bringing in drugs from Mexico. There seem to be lots of planes coming and going from his land. We have him under surveillance, but we can't catch him at anything."

"The Lakeside PD has money for surveillance? Your budget must have grown quite a bit since David was in charge." First a drug kingpin and now surveillance? Maybe Ben had gotten mad cow disease from that low-carb lifestyle.

"Well, it's not so much surveillance as his neighbors spying on him. They have cameras aimed at his house. Never underestimate retirees. They have lots of free time." Ben took another sip of his beer.

Surveillance by nosy neighbor. Were they deputized first? In this neck of the woods, you couldn't throw a rock without hitting a retiree. I bet Ben had legions of seniors at the ready to spy on everyone.

"And with this highly sophisticated level of surveillance, what have you found out?" If they knew Daman was a drug lord, then why didn't they arrest him?

Ben avoided eye contact. "Nothing. He's squeaky clean."

I sat back and eyed him. "Nothing? Then how do you know he's a drug lord?"

"It's a hunch." He finally made eye contact. "How about I teach you how to use a gun? I'm off on Sunday. We could start then."

He sounded so hopeful.

"Sure." It seemed that everyone thought I needed to know how to use a firearm. Why didn't anyone want to teach me how to use nunchucks? Those were much cooler looking than handguns.

A slow, sexy grin ambled across his face. "It's a date. I'll pick you and Max up around two. Then we can have dinner after." Happiness radiated out of him.

"Wow, a second date." I smiled and shook my head. "I don't go on many of those. I'm the world's foremost authority on first dates."

"Really?" He laughed.

"You bet. You can ask me anything." I smiled so hard my cheeks hurt. He thought I was kidding. Well, the joke was on him.

He sat up and then leaned in close. "What do you think about this?"

His lips lightly brushed my closed ones while his hand cupped my cheek. Gently, his tongue parted my lips, darted inside my mouth, then looped slowly and deliciously around my own. Heat tingled through my body and my nipples went hard. Ben had some skills.

He pulled back, ran his thumb over my cheekbone one last time, and sat back.

"And?" He waited expectantly.

"What?" I had no idea what he was waiting for. I had to resist the urge to fan myself.

"What do you think about that?" The shit-eating grin on his face was way too confident.

I screwed up my face like I'd just bitten into a super-sour dill pickle. "It was okay. On a scale of one to ten, it was like a six." More like a six hundred, but since it had been a while since I'd had sex my scale could be a little off—or maybe completely broken.

"Liar." He pointed to the front of my shirt.

I looked down. My nipples were poking through the fabric. From now on, I was wearing a lightly padded bra. "Wow, it's cold in here."

"You're a terrible liar." He studied the front of my shirt and then looked away. "Nice."

"I'm a fantastic liar, thank you very much." And I was. Only the most accomplished of con artists could pull off a better lie than me.

"Keep telling yourself that if it helps you sleep at night." He winked. "That kiss was an eleven and you know it."

I shook my head. "Maybe a seven and only because there was tongue."

I tucked my index finger under his chin and pulled him into me. I kissed him hard, my tongue forcing its way into his mouth. I sucked lightly on his bottom lip and pulled back. "Now that was an eleven."

"Please, it was a five. Weak." But a dazed look had replaced his cocky smile.

"Who's the terrible liar now?" Score one for the divorcée who'd been jilted by a cheating bastard of a husband. My red shirt and I still had it. I glanced down. This might not qualify as a boob shirt, but it was definitely a nipple shirt.

"You're killing me with those." His gaze dropped to the front of my shirt.

"I don't know what you're talking about." I arched my back in a fake stretch.

"Now you're just being mean." Slowly his gaze made it all the way to my face. He dropped a light kiss on my nose and then stood and called in the direction of Max's bedroom, "Hey buddy, I'll meet you outside."

Talk about leaving me cold. "Now who's the mean one?"

The cocky grin was back. "You're even hotter in person than in my dreams."

"You dream about me?" I bit my lower lip. He was too cute for my own good.

"Yes, ma'am." He leaned down and whispered close to my ear. "I've had a crush on you for years."

CHAPTER 5

"Holy cow." Haley fanned herself with one hand and managed the steering wheel with the other as I relayed the facts of my date last night. We were in Haley's Range Rover, headed to Daman Rodriguez's house. "I can't believe he told you that he's had a crush on you for years. That's so sweet."

"You think everything is sweet." Monica stuck her head into the space between the driver's and passenger's seats. She'd failed to call shotgun before me and had lost out on the front seat. "He's hot... really hot. You should totally jump on that."

I bit my bottom lip in contemplation. "So does 'jump on that' take the place of 'tap that'? I can't be using the wrong phrase for sex. I'm a perfectionist."

A snort came from Monica's general direction.

I resented that snort. I could totally rock perfectionism once I got the hang of it. Trouble is, I'm a procrastinator, so perfectionism can wait until tomorrow.

"Speaking of hot." Haley turned onto an oak-lined street that I'd never seen before. We were in the heart of Lakeside, skirting Lake Travis. The properties here started in the tens of millions for a fixer-upper and went up from there. It was so far out of my price range that I never even ventured this close to the lake, partly for fear of being stopped by the local police because I drive a piece of crap. In this neck of the woods, driving a POS means you're here to mow someone's yard. There was nothing the patrol cops liked more than harassing the hired help.

I looked around. What I'd thought was a street was actually a driveway... to a really big mansion. Living in Lakeside, I'm used to the run-of-the-mill mansions. They usually have ten or so bedrooms, a six-car garage, and a couple of guesthouses. But this mega-mansion made all those look like one-room apartments in the projects.

At its middle the building had five stories of Texas white limestone that tapered down to a modest two stories on either side. Lots of arched columns and balconies lined the front and sides of the enormous house, giving it a distinctly Texas look. If Southfork and the Alamo got together and had a big, fat baby, this would be it.

We pulled up to the circle driveway and parked in front of a ten-tiered terra-cotta fountain that was larger than the swimming pool at the Lakeside Country Club. Not that I'd ever been swimming in the Lakeside Country Club's pool, but I did walk by it once when Bessie stopped running right in front of the club's gated entrance. Something about her gas tank being empty. Bessie needed feeding... Max always needed feeding... everyone was so needy.

"Who needs a house this big?" Monica looked as stunned as I'm sure I did. This was excessive in a town where excessive was the norm.

"He entertains a lot." Haley put the SUV in park and turned off the engine.

"Who? A mid-sized country? This is bigger than the Hilton Garden Inn by the mall. I don't know enough people to fill half this house, much less to invite to a party." Monica said. We were on the same page.

"The electric bill must be six figures a month." Mine was two hundred dollars last month and I was having a hard time accepting that. It was autumn-ish so I wasn't even running the air conditioner all that much. How could Max and I possibly have used up two hundred dollars in electricity last month? That was it, I was going to stop cooking all together. Clearly, warming stuff up in the microwave was using too much power.

"Daman hosts the winter cotillion here in his second ballroom." Haley smiled as she opened the driver's door and stepped onto the crushed granite driveway. "He always has it decorated like a Winter Wonderland."

"It's a shame he only lets you use the second ballroom instead of the first. You debutantes must feel like trailer trash. He probably decorates the first ballroom with diamonds." Monica rolled her eyes. Well, I didn't actually see her roll her eyes, but her tone strongly implied it. She jumped down onto the granite and closed her door.

I stepped out of the passenger's seat, and gravel crunched underneath my pale pink fake UGGs. I don't think the boots actually have a brand name, but they were only twenty bucks at Marshalls so I had to have them. Wind rattled off the lake and cut right through my sweater. Today it was chilly and in the low fifties. By Central Texas standards, we were about to freeze to death.

One of the enormous wrought-iron double front doors opened and an olive-skinned man with black hair stepped out. Deep dimples dented each cheek as he smiled at us. He bore a striking resemblance to Eddie Cibrian, only taller and more muscular. He waved, and diamond cuff links glittered in the sunlight. His dark gray trousers and pressed white button-down shirt seemed a tad formal for Saturday morning at home, but what did I know? Maybe all rich people dressed up while lounging on the sofa and watching Saturday morning cartoons. Maybe this was a Texas version of Downton Abbey. Why hadn't his butler answered the door? Besides the gunsmithing, it was really his only job. Man, he was lazy.

"Ladies, welcome to my home." His accented English was downright sexy.

I'd expected a Mexican drug lord to look like Danny Trejo or a Hispanic Don Corleone, anything but a Latin soap star. It was disappointing. I glanced at his shoes. Black cowboy boots. My first thought was that he could have at least worn some expensive, cheesy Italian loafers. My second thought was that I really needed to stop stereotyping people. Everyone had a hobby; mine was prejudging people. The fact that I was usually wrong about them didn't deter me one bit. I'm not a quitter.

"Damn," Monica said under her breath. "I call dibs."

After the shotgun-calling incident, she'd stepped up her game.

"Daman. Thank you for letting us take advantage of your hospitality on such short notice." Haley sauntered over to him.

I don't think I've ever sauntered... possibly sashayed but never sauntered. Monica and I just plain walked up to the front door.

Daman Rodriguez up close was even better looking. His black-coffee eyes were surrounded by so many eyelashes that it looked like he was wearing eyeliner. A tiny scar creased his brow, which was more charming than dangerous.

"Absolutely. I'm always happy to help out a friend." He leaned in and kissed her left cheek and then her right.

"Think it's too forward of me to ask him to be the father of my future children?" Monica whispered as she shot him a stunning smile.

"If you don't ask, the answer is always no." I winked at her.

"Good point." She nodded.

"These are my friends." Haley stepped back, giving us access to Daman. "This is Monica."

Monica stuck her chest out and cooed. "It's so good to finally meet you. I've heard so much about you."

"All good, I hope." His gaze darted to me. "And this must be Mustang."

Reluctantly, Monica stepped inside and out of the way.

"Nice to meet you." I smiled.

He turned up the wattage of his grin and all the estrogen in my body drunk-dialed my brain. I opened my mouth to ask how the drug lord business was treating him, but thought better of it. Ben didn't say it was supposed to be a secret, but I'm pretty sure it was implied. People should start stating the obvious instead of going around implying all sorts of things.

"I believe that you were married to our former police chief." Daman held out his hand for me to shake. I took it, but instead of the normal handshake he brought my hand to his lips and kissed the back. "Give him my best when you speak with him."

Slowly, he released my hand.

"I don't ever speak to him, but on the off chance that hell freezes over and I do, I'll give him the message." Was that TMI? Sometimes I have trouble with oversharing.

One corner of his mouth turned up, and damn if a third dimple didn't pop out on his chin. Handsome men should have a two-dimple limit.

He stepped aside so I could walk through the open door.

The interior of the house was breathtaking—literally, I sucked in a chlorinated, humid breath. The scent of roses fought with chlorine in a battle for dominance, but I had to give it to the chlorine. There must be an indoor pool somewhere close.

The front entryway boasted off-white, large travertine tiles set on the diagonal and a huge, round Mexican table holding a gigantic floral arrangement. I leaned over to make sure it was real. Yep, nothing fake here.

I looked up.

Beyond the table, two glass doors led to an atrium with tropical plants surrounding an indoor swimming pool complete with two waterfalls and three hot tubs. The source of the chlorine. The pool was larger than most five-star resorts could boast. Not that I'd been to any, but I had free cable thanks to Astrid's love of reality TV.

Two staircases with ornate wrought-iron rails—one on either side of the pool—spiraled up, joining the five floors. Each floor was open to the pool below so that the floors appeared to be little more than a series of balconies. Sunlight streamed in from the roof, which appeared to be all glass.

A waterslide started at the fifth floor and swirled and looped all the way down to the pool. I hoped he had an elevator because climbing all those stairs just for a few-seconds ride would suck.

"It sounds like you and your ex-husband aren't on the best of terms," Daman said.

I peeled my gaze away from the surroundings. "We aren't on any terms, good or bad."

New acquaintances always asked about my ex-husband. I never knew if it was to get the juiciest gossip or because they were making conversation or they didn't know what else to say.

His gaze lingered on my face. "If he were my husband, I'd feel the same."

Was I supposed to maintain eye contact, look away, or do something provocative? It's not that I was socially awkward, it's just that handsome men rarely lingered over any part of me. Usually, I attracted the wandering-eye types who live with their mothers and smell like Fritos... well, except for Ben. He was cute.

"If he were your husband, that would be a horrible waste of a very handsome man." Monica elbowed me to the side. She had mad elbowing skills. She'd spent four years as a Texas Roller Girl. Her name had been Monica the Masher. That always made me think of mashed potatoes.

"Would you ladies care for something to drink?" He looked past Monica and directly at me.

"A margarita would be wonderful." Monica flipped her hair back flirtatiously and it thwapped me in the face.

Somehow guns and liquor seemed like a bad idea.

"It's like eight-thirty in the morning," I said as I picked strands of Monica's hair out of my lip gloss. She really needed to work on the hair flipping thing, or at least make sure she was a good five feet away from the nearest bystander.

"How about coffee?" Daman put his hand in the small of my back and gestured to a silver tray holding a silver coffeepot, several china cups, croissants, bagels, and kolaches. Did the mega-rich have stashes of baked goods lying around on the off chance that hungry visitors would stop by?

Here was a lifestyle I could embrace: carbs and coffee, my two favorite things. My stomach rumbled loudly. Everyone turned to look at me.

"Sorry, no breakfast this morning." Or any morning. I just couldn't stomach the idea of eating until I'd been up for hours.

Daman picked up a plate and filled it with two croissants. "Here. You need to eat."

He handed the plate to me and then picked up the coffeepot. "How do you take your coffee?"

Oversolicitous much? In the last twenty-four hours, two hot guys seemed to be interested in me. It was nice... weird, but nice.

He was standing a little closer to me than was socially acceptable. In Texas, we like a good eighteen inches of personal space around us at all times. He'd cut that down to about half. He smelled fantastic—something citrusy and clean with something all man under it. I tried to suck in a discreet breath of air but ended up sounding like Darth Vader. Damn my nasal allergies.

"Thanks." Did I really have to eat all of this food? I totally could, plus I didn't want to offend a possible drug lord. In the movies, drug lords were mean and shot people for ending sentences with prepositions. I wasn't sure what a real-life drug lord would do if I didn't eat his croissants—chop off my head, draw and quarter me, force me to sing show tunes? They were equally bad.

I stuffed half the croissant in my mouth, which was impressive because Daman Rodriguez liked his croissants almost as big as he liked his houses. I chewed and chewed half of the world's largest croissant until I was finally able to swallow it. I shoved the other half in my mouth and chewed and chewed. It finally went down too. My eyes were watering and I was breathing heavily. I didn't know that eating could be considered aerobic exercise.

I glanced at Monica. She didn't seem to be angry at not being Daman's center of attention; in fact, she'd pressed her lips together trying not to laugh.

"Nicely done." Daman grinned. "I like a woman who eats."

"I didn't think you were going to make it, but you pulled through in the end." Monica slapped me on the back and then took the other croissant and nibbled it. "Impressive."

Monica might have called dibs, but she wasn't holding that against me.

"Shall we head to the gun range?" Daman's hand went to the small of my back again. There he was with the oversolicitousness. Again, not that I didn't like it, but it was weird.

First Ben, and now Daman? Was my body emitting some sort of I'm-single-and-slutty sex hormones? I started to discreetly sniff my armpit, but there was no way to discreetly sniff my armpit, so I just kept walking. We traveled through a huge living room with five-story-tall ceilings and no less than ten brown leather sofas in groups of two. I had no idea where someone would get ten matching sofas, or why they would want that many, but here they were. I don't think I own ten matching anything, including socks.

We walked down a short hallway and arrived at a bank of three elevators... because I guess one wasn't enough. If he was single and lived alone, why did he need three elevators? Riding all three at the same time must have been problematic... and time consuming.

We took elevator one—they weren't numbered or anything, this was just the first elevator on the right—down two floors to the subbasement.

Having lived in Texas my whole life, I'd never been in a home basement, much less a subbasement. Five stories above the ground weren't enough? He needed a couple of floors underground? This house made Tony Stark look like a pauper.

We walked past a set of double glass doors with "Cinema" spelled out in neon above them and took the second door on the left.

"This is my indoor pistol range. I don't think you ladies are ready for the rifle range." He smiled down at me like I was supposed to say something.

"Okay." I shrugged.

"I think we should keep it small caliber today. Nothing over a nine millimeter. I think a forty-five is too much for them to handle. What do you think?" Haley sounded like she was picking out flowers to plant in her front yard. Yes, let's plant the forty-five calibers in between the lantana and the mountain laurel.

"Yep, we don't know her at all." Monica shook her head.

I was beginning to see Monica's point. I thought that I knew Haley, but clearly there were aspects of her life that she kept to herself.

I felt the hand at my back drop. I missed the warmth.

He opened the door for me and held it open for Monica and Haley. The room was a long, rectangular, hall-type thing lined on all four walls with pointy gray foam that reminded me of egg cartons. Way at the back was a paper target of a white silhouette outlined in black clipped to a metal line that ran about five feet above our heads. Daman pushed a red button on the wall next to a tall podium with shelves that held other targets. The white silhouette whizzed toward us and stopped about ten feet away.

"The range is fifty meters, but we're going to start closer than that today." He walked over to a huge—big enough to be a bank vault—safe built into the wall next to the range. It appeared that the safe ran the entire fifty meters. He entered a combination, scanned his thumbprint, and then a large electronic motor turned several hammers and the door opened. He flicked a light switch and a contagion of fluorescent lights flooded the long, rectangular safe with a gray-greenish glow. Yup, the safe did run the entire length of the range, and it was filled with guns. Handguns, short rifles, long rifles, shotguns, and several bulky items that looked like rocket launchers were all neatly tacked along the walls. On a long, single set of horizontal shelves running down the middle sat ammunition—crates upon crates of bullets. And when I squinted to get a better look—yes, grenades lined a couple of the shelves.

I doubted that a military armory packed this much heat.

"Are you planning on taking over a small country, or is all this just for the neighborhood watch?" There I went prying into a drug lord's professional life. Maybe one day I'll grow a filter from my brain to my mouth, but chances are if I haven't grown one yet, I may be out of luck.

I couldn't take it all in. "You know, we really don't have much gang violence out here unless you're talking about the time that the Catholics and the Lutherans both tried to have their pancake breakfast on the same day. There was a little bloodshed, but nothing that would warrant this level of home protection." I waved my arm like a game show hostess showing what was behind door number two.

I looked around again and reconsidered. Okay, this might be overkill for Lakeside, but it seemed just right for a drug lord. Apparently drug lording required a bunker of weapons. Could he write these off his taxes? Surely they were a work expense.

I'd always wondered if strippers could write off bikini waxes as a work expense, too. And underwear. They couldn't strip out of it if it wasn't on.

I made a mental note to ask Lyle Grinchwalt, our un-esteemed PTO treasurer, the next time I saw him. Then again, he'd thrown a pencil at me the last time I'd asked him a tax-related question. All I'd wanted to know was if I could write off all of the Starbucks coffee I'd bought last year. Surely the caffeine was a medical necessity because Lord knows I needed it to stay awake at my boring day job. I have receipts. It was a valid question.

Probably Daman and strippers didn't pay taxes.

There I went prejudging people again. Daman might very well be a Catholic priest with a firearm fetish. I glanced his way. He eyed me like he was the Oreo and I was the milk—and he wanted to quadruple dunk.

"Firearms are my hobby. Don't you indulge your hobbies?" He grinned.

"I don't think sudoku requires a bunker." And I wasn't sure cupcake-eating qualified as an actual hobby.

He pointed to the wall of handguns. "Choose any gun from this point forward. We'll work up to the higher calibers later."

I didn't plan on practicing so often that I'd actually work up to anything. I chose a smaller gun that was purple. "I like this one."

Gently, Daman took it from me. "The Smith and Wesson Shield, a very reliable gun. Why did you choose it?"

"Because it's purple and that's my favorite color." I know, I know, I'm shallow. I judge things based on their appearance. It's both a gift and a curse.

"Cool." Monica took the gun from him. "I want a pink one... oh." She handed the gun to me and took a pink one off the wall. "Can I use this one?"

Daman nodded. "A Beretta Nano. Nice stopping power."

"I brought my guns, too." Haley pulled one gun out of her purse, rummaged around, pulled out another one, dove back into her giant Hermès, and pulled out two more.

All I had in my purse were some Tic Tacs, a wallet full of maxed-out credit cards, a couple of pens, and a crap-load of receipts. I was pretty sure that the receipts multiplied like rabbits when I wasn't looking. That was the only explanation for all those little scraps of white paper. It's not because I kept buying things, of course—how ridiculous.

"I'll set up at the podium." Haley pulled a huge pair of earphones out of her bag. She must have paid extra for the clown car version of that purse. Apparently, it held more than my van. "I brought my own ear protection."

Haley went to the podium, lined her guns up in some order that clearly made sense to her, pulled one... two... three... four... five boxes of bullets out of her purse, and lined them up, one behind each gun. So guns didn't all use the same kind of bullets... copy that.

"Before we begin, we should talk about gun range safety." Daman took the purple gun, popped out the ammunition clip, pulled the slide back, and turned to me. "First, take out the bullets."

He held the gun up for me. "There's a little button to the left of the trigger that releases the clip. See?"

He pointed to a little round button.

I took the gun, pressed the button, and the clip popped out of the bottom. The gun was heavier than I thought it should have been. And it was cold. I pulled the clip all the way out and could see that it was empty. So the drug lord didn't keep his weapons loaded. Or at least not the purple handguns.

"With the slide back and the magazine out, I know that you're not going to accidentally shoot me, so hold the gun with the barrel facing down." Daman took my hand and gently placed it at my side with the gun barrel facing the floor. "Like this."

His touch was warm and light, and there were callouses on his palms. Not that I spent a lot of time thinking about drug lords' hands, but I would have thought they'd be soft from lack of manual labor. Manicured and pampered even. Then again, maybe he was more of a hands-on boss. Killing people probably caused callouses.

"Walk your gun over to the podium and place it next to Haley's." He put a hand on my arm. "Wait, you'll need some bullets."

He turned around, grabbed six boxes of bullets, and handed them to me.

They were very heavy for such little boxes. I held the bullets mashed against my left breast and walked my gun over to the podium. Because Haley had taken up all of the space with her buffet of firearms, I put my gun and bullets on the shelf right underneath.

Daman walked Monica through the range safety and then she brought her gun and bullets over to the podium.

"You'll both need double ear protection. With an outdoor range, you can get by with just one level of ear protection, but an indoor range is several times louder. I've put in some serious noise reduction, but it's still very loud." He handed me a pair of small yellow foam stoppers to stuff into my ears and then a pair of earphone-looking things to put over my ears.

"Let me show you the proper shooting stance." Daman took my hand and gently pulled me from behind the podium. He picked up my gun and handed it to me. From behind me, he slid his hands down my arms to my elbows and lightly pushed at them until my arms were out straight. "You're right handed, right?" How did he know? Do drug lords have handedness powers? "So hold the gun in your right hand with your index finger out straight next to the trigger but not on it. Wrap the fingers of your left hand around the barrel over the fingers of your right hand. Then place your left thumb over your right so they sort of crisscross."

He leaned into me, slid his hands all the way down my arms, and checked my hand placement. His chest behind me was warm and solid and his scent wafted all around me. If I'd known that gun lessons came with lap dances, I'd have learned how to shoot a lot sooner.

"That's good." He stepped out from behind me and touched my elbows. "Don't lock them. Keep your elbows loose because the recoil is going to cause your arms to jerk."

"Okay." I couldn't help but wonder if all drug lords gave shooting lessons.

He put his hands on my hips. "Don't lean forward. Keep your hips over your feet unless you're more comfortable with one leg forward. I wouldn't advise that stance until you've learned the basics."

His hands dropped.

"My turn." Monica practically knocked me out of the way so she could have the drug-lord-lap-dance gun lesson. I didn't blame her. It had been fun.

I stepped behind the podium.

Haley leaned into me and whispered in my ear. "He's into you. I'm so jealous."

Two hours later, I was jealous of her. My hand was killing me and my shoulder burned.

"It's just gun fatigue." Haley clicked the key fob to unlock her Range Rover as Daman opened the front door. "It'll pass. The more you shoot, the less it hurts."

I rubbed my right shoulder as I followed Haley out. "I didn't realize that guns were so painful."

The wind ripped off of Lake Travis and I huddled into my sweater.

"Here, let me." Daman slid his hands over my shoulders and massaged. He had some very talented hands. I closed my eyes and melted back against him. He had an endless supply of carbs and magic massaging hands. If it weren't for that whole drug lord thing, he'd be the perfect guy.

I opened my eyes to find Monica glaring at me. She mouthed "slut" and then rolled her eyes.

Ten minutes later we drove down his long driveway.

"I don't get it." Monica shook her head. "Here I am throwing myself at him, and he knocks me out of the way to get to you. I called dibs and everything. Seriously, do I smell bad or something?"

Haley looked at her through the rearview mirror. "You smell wonderful."

"I know, it was weird. The only guys who wanted to date me before yesterday either lived with their parents or wanted the scoop on my ex-husband." I shrugged. "I have no idea what's happening."

I wasn't even wearing my red sweater today. My life had turned into *The Dating Game* meets *The Twilight Zone*.

"Did he ask you out?" Haley glanced at me. I'd called shotgun again, leaving Monica to sit in the back. She really needed to up her game.

"No, which is probably good, being that he's a drug lord and all." I reached down to the leather bag I'd brought with me this morning and left in the car. I pulled out everything I had on Molly. "Here's the picture Lakeside PD took at the crime scene."

I handed it to her.

"Let's pick up some lunch and meet the kids at the park. Maybe we can find a quiet table and take a look at the medical records." Haley turned into the drive-through line of a Chick-fil-A. Since her parents owned all of the Chick-fil-As in Central Texas, we ate for free. Fine with me.

She ordered our usual, and we followed the car in front of us to the second window to pick up our food.

"Her eyes are bloodshot." Monica held her phone up to the picture of Molly. "Why are her eyes bloodshot?"

I turned in my seat to watch Monica. "How can you tell?"

I didn't remember noticing that Molly's eyes were bloodshot.

"Magnifying app on my phone." She turned her phone around so I could see. "It has a light too. Very handy for the elderly and the nosy alike."

"Cool." I looked down at the picture through Monica's phone and saw that Molly's eyes were red and a little swollen. "Maybe she'd been crying?"

Had she been so upset about something that she'd pulled out a bunch of heroin and shot up? It just sounded so unlikely.

"The dog being dead is weird, too. Don't you think?" I pointed to the trail of blood. "Do you think she hurt the dog?"

"Never." Haley shook her head. "She loved that dog. She had this purse thing and used to carry him around. I saw her at Dillard's with him not two weeks ago."

"I agree. Paolo seemed to be her life." I looked down at the picture again. "We're missing something."

"I have the same feeling." Monica took her phone back and used it to scan every inch of the picture.

I turned back around. "We should check out the scene of the crime."

"I can't today. I have to take the girls to ballet." Haley smiled. "Sorry."

"I can't either. Landon has a swim meet this afternoon." Monica continued to scan the picture.

"I forgot about that. Max and I should come along and cheer him on. Is it at Nitro?" Max and Landon were both on the same swim team, but Max had no interest in competing in swimming. He was much happier crushing the competition at soccer.

"Sure. He'd love that." Monica sat back.

"Oh wait. Crap, I forgot. Max has a soccer game at four." I'd been so preoccupied with guns and Molly that I'd forgotten again.

"No worries. If you want, I'll take the boys to the swim meet while you check out Molly's house. We'll meet you at the soccer field at three thirty." She waggled her finger at me. "But I want a detailed explanation of what you find."

"Deal."

CHAPTER 6

I'd never actually been to Molly's house before. I turned Bessie onto the dirt road that led to the twenty acres where Molly had lived. If memory served, this had been her grandmother's house. Obeying my trusted iPhone, I took the second right and turned onto another dirt road with a gate.

Molly had said that her house was quiet. I looked around. When you lived out in the middle of nowhere, there wasn't anything *but* quiet. I bet her Internet speed sucked all the way out here.

This had to be it... mainly because it was the only road around. I put Bessie in park and hopped out. If there was a lock, I'd be doomed to climbing the gate and God forbid, walking to the house. If God had wanted me to walk, he wouldn't have invented cars.

God was smiling on me, because the chain holding the gate closed was just wrapped around the pole several times. I unwrapped it and the gate swung open on well-oiled hinges.

I jumped back into Bessie, pulled past the opening, stopped, and reattached the gate. In case someone did drive up, I wanted everything to look normal. I got back into Bessie and motored down the narrow, winding dirt road. The path twisted around trees, and I nearly bottomed out in a low-water crossing, but it brought me to a large clearing with an old farmhouse.

I don't know what I'd been expecting, but the white clapboard house with lots of windows wasn't it. It was charming and old-fashioned and very Molly. I was a little disappointed that no yellow crime scene tape hung across the front door, but maybe there was some inside.

I grabbed the leather work bag that usually held my computer. Today I was putting it into use as a murder-scene-photograph-holding bag and maybe something to collect evidence in.

On the front porch, wind chimes of all shapes and sizes hung down from the eaves. I opened my door and stepped out. The bonging cacophony wasn't charming or old-fashioned; it was just plain loud.

I didn't remember Molly being deaf, and I wondered how she'd managed to sleep through all that racket. I peeked in a window on the side of the house on my way to the backyard.

The interior was dark, and I could only make out shapes. Just for fun, I tested the window. Painted shut. I mashed my nose against the glass, but still couldn't see anything. I walked around to the back, unlatched the wooden gate, and let myself into the yard. A few large trees dotted the perimeter, but for the most part, the yard was a barren dust bowl... except for what looked like a clear plastic tent about twenty-five feet from the back door. As I got closer, I saw a tree inside the tent.

Why would anyone have a clear tent? I wasn't much for camping, but even I knew that you needed privacy at some point during a camping trip, and this tent reminded me of those clear plastic umbrellas—only a lot larger. Lost in those thoughts, I nearly tripped over a brown extension cord that ran from the back of the house to inside the tent.

I came across what resembled a doorway—little more than a zippered archway actually—and ran my finger along the interlocking grooved teeth until I found the zipper. I pulled the zipper up and around the doorway until the plastic fell free. Hot, dry air radiated out. The electrical cord I'd almost stumbled over was attached to a heater. Despite the unusually chilly October day, inside the tent it had to be at least seventy degrees.

I pulled my iPhone out of my back pocket and shot a couple of pictures of the tree.

This was a greenhouse? I walked around the perimeter. A greenhouse protecting one tree?

Yes, it was a giant, weird-assed, chrysanthemum-looking tree, but why did it have its own greenhouse?

I stepped out into the yard again and looked around. There were no flowers or bushes or potted plants. Besides the ancient oak trees that had probably been planted when Texas was still a republic and this one weird tree, housed by an even weirder plastic tent, Molly's backyard was a blank, dirt slate. It didn't appear that she was even able to grow grass. But she'd bought a plastic greenhouse to protect one tree.

I cocked my head in thought. At least she was trying. But it didn't make sense.

I could so vividly remember Molly proudly saying that she was a black-thumb-smith. But clearly she wasn't. The tree inside the greenhouse was thriving. Not that I was a master gardener, but it seemed to me that people who wanted to learn to grow things would start with something smaller, like a potted plant or some flowers.

I glanced at the back porch and stopped short.

The back door was wide open.

I looked around, suddenly feeling that someone might be watching me. I don't know why I thought there would be. This house was in the middle of nowhere. But something made me look around. Nothing.

I was totally alone in the middle of nowhere.

I knocked loudly on the open back door. I had no idea why. Clearly I was the only one around, but I couldn't help myself. I'd never barged into someone's house uninvited—well, except for Tommy Wilcox after he dumped me the day of senior prom. And I might have been wielding a butane curling iron, but in my defense that had been the only weapon I could find in the blind rage induced by too much hairspray and not enough sleep.

I would have given anything for that butane curling iron now. It's not that I was particularly afraid of the dark, but I wasn't that big on creepy situations, and walking uninvited into the home of my dead friend's head minus her body was high on the list.

"Hello," I said loudly in case anyone was inside and hadn't heard me knocking. "Anyone here?"

Did I really expect someone to answer me? I rolled my eyes.

I stuck my head inside and felt around for a light switch. My hand made contact with the switch and I flipped it. A ceiling fan light blinked on.

It took a minute for my mind to process the scene.

The large room was filled with white banker's boxes.

What was obviously meant to be a den was missing a sofa and television. Instead, long folding tables lined all four walls. On the tables were white banker's boxes neatly filled with envelopes. Large postal envelopes, small white envelopes, and everything in between. The weirdness factor was growing by leaps and bounds.

From the box closest to me, I pulled the first envelope out. It was a heavy brown one lined with some sort of shredded paper. The seal wasn't broken but it was opened and had obviously been through the postal system. I turned it over. The return address was a Mary Hargrove, Richmond, Virginia, with no street name. The addressee was L. M. Alcott. I picked up a small white envelope. It was from Anchorage, Alaska. The addressee was J. Arc. This label had been printed from eBay.

So Molly had bought something from eBay and had it shipped here to J. Arc? I flipped the envelope over. It, too, had been carefully opened so as not to rip the paper.

After a quick inspection, I realized that a good portion of the envelopes had labels printed from eBay. I looked at the front of the boxes. It looked like Molly had them categorized by date.

So Molly had a little eBay shopping addiction? I'd been known to partake in some eBay binge-shopping myself before the asshole ran off with his girlfriend. These days I binge window-shopped—it wasn't nearly as much fun.

Molly had always been the queen of orderly, but this was excessive, even methodical. Had she been some sort of envelope hoarder?

Was that even a thing?

None of this fit with her personality, but here was the proof.

I headed to the only doorway out of this room. A thought struck and I turned back to the envelopes. There were ten banker's boxes stuffed with envelopes, but where were the things that came in the envelopes?

In the kitchen, I flipped on the light and found nothing but a long, narrow, spotless galley kitchen. I opened every single cabinet looking for something out of placc, but all I found were pots, pans, dishes, and glasses. A small bistro table with two chairs sat next to the room's only window. A napkin holder filled with paper napkins and a generic salt-and-pepper set sat next to a small stack of unopened mail. I picked through it. There were two small, white, padded envelopes—one addressed to Sus B. Anthony and the other to Sandy D. O'Connor.

So Molly had felt so bad about her eBay addiction that she'd had her items sent to famous historical women? I ripped open Ms. Anthony's package. Inside was a small box of cinnamon-flavored toothpicks. Okay—so Molly loved toothpicks?

I ripped open the other one. A push-button drain assembly, according to the label. I couldn't even figure out what that was, much less come up with a reason why Molly would want one. I almost put the items and the envelopes back on the table and then thought better of it and shoved them in my leather shoulder bag. I needed to find out what these things had in common.

I stood back and studied the kitchen as a whole. It was warm and cozy, if slightly outdated, but it looked like any other kitchen. Reaching into my leather bag, I pulled out the crime scene photo. I could tell by the linoleum floor that she'd died in the kitchen. I held the picture up and used it to find the exact place where Molly's body had been found.

I glanced down. I was standing in roughly the same spot where Molly had died.

Someone had cleaned up the blood. I got down on my hands and knees, looking for anything that might be helpful. The floor was spotless and smelled faintly of bleach. Who had cleaned this up? The police?

There was absolutely nothing on the floor, not even the dust that always seems to gather on baseboards. Spotless didn't come close to describing this. Some considered me a neat freak, but this was beyond even me. Either Molly had been pathologically clean or someone had gone to great lengths to clean the floor.

I rolled back on my knees and then stood. I walked down a little hallway, passed the front door, then moved on into another den. This room had apparently been turned into a bedroom.

I looked back at the opening I'd walked through. There was no door or even a curtain. No privacy.

I walked farther into the room. It was large and had clearly been repurposed as a bedroom after the fact. A pink comforter covered a double bed, and a sturdy old wooden nightstand held a pink lamp and an alarm clock. Across from the bed, a set of double doors caught my attention. It was the kind of closet where a family kept board games for the weekly game night.

I opened the doors and stood back in awe.

Floor to ceiling, it was stuffed with clear plastic bins. I pulled out the one right in front of me and popped the lid. Inside were buttons... hundreds of buttons. Some in packages and some loose. Had Molly loved sewing?

I didn't remember her mentioning it.

I slipped that box back and pulled out another one. It was filled with electrical wall plates. Some had Disney characters, some were white, and then there were the abstract ones. There had to be hundreds of them. Was wall plate collecting a hobby?

I pulled out another box. It was filled with baseball cards. The one next to it had hundreds of anti-slip bathtub appliques. From the top row, I pulled out the center box. It held thousands of refrigerator magnets... everything from Lucille Ball eating chocolates to various metal bottle openers.

Okay, Molly was a hoarder? At least she was organized.

I was beginning to think that I didn't know my friend at all.

I slid that box back in and closed the cabinet doors.

I took the narrow, steep staircase to the second floor. There were two bedrooms separated by a bathroom. The first bedroom clearly had been Molly's. It held a brass queen bed covered with a flower print comforter. The bed was made, but the comforter was wrinkled, like someone had recently sat on the bed. There was a chest of drawers and a nightstand. I went to the double closet doors and opened them. Clothes hung neatly with shoes lined up on the floor beneath. Nothing out of the ordinary.

I went to the other bedroom and flipped on the light. I took a step back. The same kind of plastic boxes that I'd found downstairs were neatly stacked from floor to ceiling. There was a little walking path between the boxes, but the room was filled. I stood on my tippy-toes and grabbed one of the boxes off the top, careful not to disturb the ones it was stacked on. I pried the lid off and found patches. Different sizes and colors... some were Girl Scout patches, there were ski resort patches, and even those dark brown ones that were supposed to be sown to elbows of tweed jackets popular with snooty college professors.

I pulled another box down. It was filled with little paper seed packets. Another one held an assortment of lightbulbs.

Okay, I could accept someone's need to hoard incandescent lightbulbs, as they were no longer being manufactured, but I didn't get the patches or seeds. Or the wall plates or buttons or any of the other strange collections.

I pushed the boxes back into place, flipped off the light, and went to the bathroom. Nothing interesting in there. Just the normal girly bathroom stuff—flat iron, hair gel, toothbrush, toothpaste, face cleanser. I opened the medicine cabinet. Just aspirin, rubbing alcohol, Band-Aids, and fingernail polish. No heroin, no prescription medications. And that, in this house full of oddities, I did find odd. Everyone had a bottle of some prescription they hadn't finished and had tucked away in case they needed it later.

I closed the cabinet, wondering. Where does a person who lives alone in the woods leave her heroin? Out on the counter?

I walked back down the stairs and into the only room that I hadn't checked. The powder room under the stairs. And there was nothing there except a toilet and a sink.

I'd found no sign of drug use at all. And except for the organized envelopes and plastic bins filled with assorted crap, there was absolutely nothing out of the ordinary. Surely if Molly had been a big heroin user, I'd have found something. She lived alone, out in the middle of nowhere, so why hide her drugs?

There was only one more place to check—the detached garage.

I hustled out the back door, closed but didn't lock it, and headed for the garage.

It matched the white clapboard of the house. I checked the door—locked. I walked around to the front and tried to pull up the heavy garage bay door, but it was locked too. I went around to the back. There was a window, but as I looked closer, I saw that it had been blacked out.

I grabbed the lip at the bottom and pushed up. It opened about a foot and then stuck. I pushed, shoved, rattled, and even rocked it back and forth. Nothing. It was wedged in place.

Undaunted by a little half-open window, I stuck my head through the opening and inch-wormed my chest and then stomach, hips, and legs through, awkwardly landing on the floor in a belly-flopping splat. I'd expected concrete, but instead I felt the edges and grooves of tile.

Who tiled their garage? It was dark—the only light was from the opening I'd just inched through. Next time I broke into someone's house, I was bringing a flashlight.

I rocked back on my heels, out of the square foot of light, and flailed my arms in front of me trying to find the wall. I rolled to my knees and then stood, still waving my arms around in the blackness, trying to find something solid. I backed up and ran into the wall. Hand-over-hand, I worked my way around the perimeter of the garage until I found a light switch. I flipped the switch and found the most interesting garage I'd ever seen.

It was a startling white—everything white—the floor, walls, ceiling, and the furniture. The only window—the one I'd come through—had blackout paint all over the panes. But the most interesting thing was the sophisticated chemistry setup taking up three whole tables. Any high school chemistry teacher would have drooled over the bottles and beakers and Bunsen burners intertwined with tubes and clamps holding an array of glass and metal containers.

Had Molly been watching *Breaking Bad* and started cooking her own crystal meth?

This room seemed too clean to be a meth kitchen—not that I'd ever seen one. But if the first couple of seasons of *Breaking Bad* had taught me anything, weren't meth kitchens supposed to be crappy, old, singlewide trailers with the windows blacked out and scorch marks everywhere? At least the window was blacked out.

This was more of a clean room—stark white and meticulously maintained. Looking around, the only thing I saw besides the chemistry set were gallon-sized plastic bags full of what looked like beans. I picked up one of the bags. Sure enough, it was filled with dried, brownish beans—kind of like brown spotted lima beans.

I put down the bag and examined the chemistry set. The beakers were clean but well used. Some of the lettering had worn off and there were scorch marks on the bottoms, but the insides were clean. The hose running to and from the beakers appeared to be clean. I couldn't find any white powder or powder of any kind. Weren't all illegal drugs a powder? I really needed to research my illegal drugs so I could identify them. Maybe there was a YouTube video.

I spun around taking it all in. There had to be fifty bags of beans.

Maybe she hoarded lima beans? If so, what was the lab equipment for? Did she dissect the beans? Maybe she was trying to chemically alter the beans in some way? Molly had loved science. Maybe she was trying to create a new lima bean species?

Obviously, she'd loved her some lima beans.

I shook my head. I had nothing. Of all the things that I might have suspected would be in Molly's garage, a lima bean lab wasn't one of them. I turned to the side door and smiled.

Hanging on a nail pounded into the doorframe was a set of keys. God bless you, Molly. I snatched them up and shoved them in my pocket. Surely they would come in handy.

I flipped the light off, walked through the door, tried the keys until I found the one that locked it, and then threw the keys in my leather bag. I walked back around to the window I'd squeezed myself through and rocked the wedged pane back and forth until it closed.

I walked to the back door and locked it.

What did a plastic greenhouse, lima beans, electrical wall plates, envelopes from all over, refrigerator magnets, and a chemistry set all have to do with each other? Were they even related?

None of it made sense. And Molly certainly wasn't the person I'd thought she was. Instead of offering answers, her strange house only provoked questions.

CHAPTER 7

"Lima beans?" Monica nailed me with her baby brown eyes. "I don't understand."

"Me either," Haley said as she leaned back in my kitchen chair.

They'd all come over for dinner—Haley brought takeout from Don Julio's, thank God—and now the kids where playing in the living room while we discussed the case.

I glanced at Max, who was huddled against Landon as they played a game on Monica's iPad. The twins were building a fort out of sofa cushions and blankets.

"Lima beans and hoarding. That's all you found?" Monica looked like she was processing the information.

"Yep. There weren't any drugs, or drug paraphernalia, or anything suspicious—except for the lab and the hoarding." I didn't really think any of it was suspicious. Weird, yes, but suspicious?

"In the lab, did you see any chemicals or packages of cold medicine? Pseudoephedrine is used to make meth, I think. At least that's what the pharmacist told me when I asked why I had to show my driver's license to buy cold medicine." Haley sipped her wine. "I asked Daniel about it and he said that making meth is pretty easy. It's just basic chemistry."

Monica laughed. "I can see it now. The famous cosmetic surgeon Dr. Daniel Hansen making meth in his garage." She grinned. "In case you need some extra money."

"Gotta have a backup plan." Haley winked.

"I do believe that was a sarcastic remark." Monica put her hand over her heart. "I'm so proud."

"It won't happen again." Haley bit her bottom lip to keep from laughing. "I wouldn't want you to get a big head."

"I feel like poor, white-trash Eliza Doolittle before Henry Higgins got hold of her. Instead of teaching you how to speak properly, I'm showing you my lower class ways." Monica shrugged. "You know, only without all that singing."

Haley punched her playfully in the upper arm. "You're such a bitch."

Monica's mouth dropped open and she fanned herself. "Now she's cussing." She wiped an imaginary tear from her cheek. "My little girl is finally growing up."

I rolled my eyes at both of them. If eye rolling actually burned calories, I'd be a size zero. Maybe I should do more of it, just in case.

"Can we get back to the case?" I stood and went to the last set of kitchen cabinets, which were now secured with a small padlock. I pulled the key out of my pocket, shoved it inside the lock, and twisted it open. I took the lock off and set it on the counter. I pulled back the double cabinet doors. "What do you think?"

I'd Velcroed a dark green poster board up with the murder scene picture, and I'd stapled the two envelopes I'd taken from Molly's house to it. "This is our murder board. I got the idea after watching *Castle*."

Haley turned around and glanced at the kids. "Are you sure you should have this out here?"

"I keep it under lock and key. Besides, anyone who knows me knows that my kitchen cabinets are empty. I used to keep the extra sheets here, but I moved them to the actual linen closet to make room. And then I kept those extra toothbrushes you get at the dentist along with those tiny tubes of toothpaste they give you in here. But after today, I've decided I'm never going to hoard anything again, so I'm donating them to the Salvation Army."

"I don't think saving two sets of teeth cleaning supplies a year qualifies as hoarding, but okay. Cool." Monica eyed the poster board. "I think we need to add the facts we have now." She pulled out her iPhone. "Here's what I have: head removed cleanly from body—"

"Wait." I ripped the poster board down—the Velcro came unstuck with a loud "crrrrrrrkkkkk."

I brought it to the kitchen table and laid it down. I went to the silverware drawer and pulled out a black Sharpie. I wrote "Facts" in the upper left-hand corner. Under that I wrote, "head removed cleanly from body" and "missing body," and then I listed everything from the lima bean lab to the boxes of weird collections and the mysterious envelopes addressed to famous women.

"Did you find anything else at the house?" Monica propped her chin on her hand.

"No. Besides the sophisticated chemistry set, and tons more boxes that I didn't have time to look into, there were just the bags of lima beans." I hunched my shoulders. "I've never seen anyone who appreciated lima beans more than Molly."

Personally, I thought there were way too many lima beans in the world, so creating a new variety seemed like the dumbest thing in the world. I also thought there were too many beets and green peas in the world, but no doubt someone somewhere was trying to create a new variety of those, too. Some people had way too much free time.

"Did you get a sample of the lima beans?" Monica's gaze rolled up to meet mine.

They were lima beans. Why would I want to touch them unnecessarily? "Ahhh, no. I didn't think of that."

She shrugged. "Probably doesn't matter anyway."

"From the picture, I can tell that she died in the kitchen. I got down on my hands and knees and looked but didn't find anything." I shook my head. "It was clean... like super clean. Not a speck of dust even in the corners or on the baseboards."

Haley's brows bounced off of her hairline. "You'd know. You're the queen of clean."

"Thanks... I think." Remembering the photo I'd taken, I pulled out my phone. "And there's this." I pulled up the picture. "I'd forgotten about it. There was this tree she had in a pop-up greenhouse thing. The greenhouse was clear plastic like a tent, but, well... clear plastic."

I handed my phone to Haley.

She used her fingers to zoom in. "So this was the only thing in the backyard?" She handed the phone to Monica. "Nothing else?"

"Nope, just that tree and that plastic greenhouse. There was a heater in there and everything."

"That is strange." Haley glanced at the picture again. "That actually *is* a greenhouse. It's called the Flower House Conservatory. My next door neighbor, Mr. Earl, got one to protect his prized ornamental cabbage collection, but the neighbor on the other side of him, Mrs. Magee, called the city and complained that it was tacky, so they made him take it down. That was the beginning of what our street calls Tacky-Gate. Mr. Earl and Mrs. Magee have been at each other's throats since."

"Freaking Lakeside, they probably have an ordinance against tacky." Monica sat back. "I still can't believe they have an ordinance against cutting your own trees."

"Well, yeah, that's for oak wilt, and there's good reason for that particular rule, but otherwise, yes, it's stupid. Retirees have lots of time on their hands." Haley continued to stare at the picture. "I wonder what kind of tree that is? I can't really tell from this picture."

I'd intended to take a picture of the tree, but I'd gotten more greenhouse than anything. Freaking camera app. Me and that little focus box didn't get along.

"I might go back out there and take a cutting." Haley said as her gaze met mine. "I could take it to the Natural Gardener and see if they can tell me what it is, or I could just ask Humberto."

Humberto was Haley's gardener. She was constantly asking him to change this or that, and he always nodded and smiled and then did the same thing he always did. His English wasn't so good, but his wife made the best chicken tamales in the world. So Haley had learned to live without change, because you could only get the tamales by staying on Humberto's good side. I, of course, had been erased off the tamale list years ago. David had asked for the recipe, which had immediately made him and everyone he knew persona non tamale. Occasionally Haley snuck me a few, but only when Humberto wasn't around. Texas tamale politics is very complicated.

"Anything else?" Monica watched me, waiting for another revelation.

"Nope. That's everything. Molly was a hoarder and obsessed with lima beans. Other than that, her house was immaculate."

We stared at the poster board.

"I got nothing." Monica chewed on her bottom lip as she shook her head. "I can't think of a single way any of this is useful."

Haley drummed her perfectly manicured fingernails on the tabletop. "Me either. What do hoarding, lima beans, one tree, and a head with no body all have in common?"

She looked at me and then at Monica.

"No idea." Monica shook her head some more. "How about we take a look at those medical records."

I reached behind me to get my leather shoulder bag from the chairback where I'd looped it when I got home. I steadied the bag on my lap, unzipped it, and pulled out the stack of papers that was Molly's entire medical history. I plopped it down on top of the poster board and said, "Here's everything."

The files were in order by doctor. Each doctor's office was binder-clipped together. I broke the stack into three smaller stacks and handed a stack to each of my friends.

"I haven't been through all of the records, but I did find something strange when calling around to get the records. Molly used only doctors outside of Lakeside. Well, except for her pediatrician, but I guess she really didn't get to choose that."

"That is odd." Haley unclipped part of her stack. "She might not have wanted the small world of Lakeside to know everything about her. I can see that. She was the kindergarten teacher. Going to a doctor out here wouldn't be private. Sure, the government has cracked down on patient privacy, but gossip is gossip. I know Daniel's fired more than one employee for talking about patients."

"I can't blame her." Monica unclipped her top stack of papers. "It's not a bad idea. I wish I'd thought of it."

Haley drained her wine, grabbed the bottle, and poured more. "I wish I had, too."

An hour later, we were out of wine and hadn't found a damn thing. I stretched and yawned, then clipped the really boring ankle op report to its equally boring orthopedic note friends. I moved on to Enos Women's Health.

Unlike most medical records, Enos Women's Health's were backwards—meaning they went in chronological order from oldest to newest instead of newest to oldest—but they were computer generated, which made reading them easy. It was still amazing that in today's technology driven society, lots of medical records were still handwritten.

I started on page one and skimmed. Apparently Molly went to the gynecologist for her annual visit like clockwork.

Her paps were normal, her breast exams normal. I almost fell asleep. It was on the next to last page, and I almost missed it.

I checked the date... two months ago. Two months ago, Molly had a positive pregnancy test. I flipped the page. It was a blood test from Lakeside Regional. She'd gone to the emergency room with pelvic pain, so they'd run a blood test. Her hCG levels were very high. I flipped the page. That was it. There was nothing else.

I dropped the papers and sat back.

"Y'all aren't going to believe this." Why hadn't she told anyone? She would have been a little over two months gone. Had she lost the baby? It was too early for me to notice a baby bump. "Molly was pregnant."

Haley sat up. "What?"

I picked up the clump of papers from Enos Women's Health. "It's right here. She was pregnant."

"Homicide is the leading cause of death in pregnant women." Monica looked stunned. "It's something like 20 percent of women who die during pregnancy are murdered." Her gaze found me. "And most are murdered by their significant other."

"She was seeing Dick Stevensen." Or as the town liked to call him, Dr. Dick. He was our friendly neighborhood ophthalmologist, though blessed with pretty perfect vision, I'd never met him. "You know, I do need to get my eyes checked."

"I'm not so sure you should go alone." Haley looked worried. "He's not a very nice man."

"Hence the reason we call him Dr. Dick." The "you idiot" was implied by Monica's tone.

Haley shot her a dirty look. "I know, that's why I don't want her to go alone."

"So what do you propose? We go out to lunch and then run by to have my eyes checked?" I stared at her. "I don't think we can pull that one off."

The corner of Haley's blue eyes wrinkled. "That is kind of awkward."

She reached around for her purse, which was looped over the back of the chair. "At least take one of my guns. I don't think it's safe to be locked in the same room with him. He makes my skin crawl."

She pulled out a little gun with a white pearl handle.

"No thanks. I don't have a permit for that and I don't think it's a good idea to carry a gun in my purse." I had such bad impulse control that I'd probably end up shooting the next person who cut me off on MoPac.

Monica took the gun from Haley and slipped it back in Haley's purse.

"Ever see how mad she gets when someone cuts her off?" Monica eyed Haley.

"No." Haley studied me like I was a bomb that might go off at any minute. Hey, when someone cuts me off, they're taking their life into their own hands. I don't make the rules ...

"Yeah, well it's not pretty. Let's not put a weapon in the hand of someone with anger management issues."

That was a little harsh. I may not have impulse control but I could manage my anger with the best of them. Had I ever run over anyone who'd pissed me off?

No.

Had ever I tried?

Well... maybe once or twice... a week... for the last ten years, but I'd never actually hit anyone. Apparently I was very bad at it.

Maybe I didn't manage my anger all that well. I blame it on too much middle management—too many chiefs and not enough Indians. My anger wasn't sure who it reported to, so it was left to flounder about on its own. So sad.

A staccato of knocks sounded at my front door. I rolled my eyes heavenward just in case God cared that I was put upon. The only person who knocked like that was my landlady, Astrid Petrie. She was rich, nosy, and batshit crazy.

Another staccato of knocks sounded. She wasn't going away.

I stood, stretched, and answered the door.

My landlady swept in with a whoosh of orange velvet mumu and a clang of silver bangle bracelets. The red velvet turban wrapped around her head looked more like a bandage for a head wound, but it was the sterling silver cane I had to watch out for. She leaned on it whenever she was in an overly dramatic mood, and I'd come to know it as nothing short of a weapon she used to knock the crap out of people. Usually me.

"Girl, what took you so long to answer the door?" Today Astrid was using a terrible fake British accent. I was pretty sure that she only used fake accents to confuse and frustrate the world. I wanted to roll my eyes, but the last time I'd done that in her presence she'd belted me with her cane. It left a bruise. I was traumatized.

"I was busy and didn't hear you knock." I let out a long, hard breath and considered running away from home, but I was in sweats, and I didn't have on any socks, and it was raining.

She used her cane to point to me and turned her brown, cow-sized eyes on me. For a woman with so much money, I'd always wondered why she didn't just get Lasik instead of wearing those enormous, rhinestone, Liberace-esque eyeglasses. "Your presence is requested at my Monday evening séance. I insist that you be there."

She delivered those two sentences with all of the drama and flair of a Shakespearean actor.

"Of course." I was always there. It was in my rental agreement.

"Good." She nodded her head and the turban bounced. "You may bring your little friends if you wish."

For a second there, I thought she was talking about the kids, but following her line of sight, I realized she meant Haley and Monica.

"I will be contacting, and if the spirits allow, channeling, Molly Miars." Astrid threw her arms heavenward and spun around. "I feel her presence with us right now."

I was pretty sure the spirits that guided Astrid came from a bottle of Jack Daniels.

I glanced around the room in case Molly was here. I hoped she was in a better place than my living room, but I guessed I was okay with it if she wanted to hang around and show us who murdered her.

"Absolutely, I'd love to come." Haley smiled her best hostess smile as she kicked Monica under the table.

"Sure, whatever." Monica at the Monday evening séance? Since she didn't take crap off of people and Astrid was full of crap, this was going to be interesting.

"Perfect." Astrid lowered her arms and smiled triumphantly. "Having her friends with us will create a stronger force to call her over from the astral plane. If the dead cannot hear us, they cannot come to us."

I nodded and bit my lower lip to keep from asking whether, if Molly was with us, all we needed to do was crook a finger to call her over. Astrid was crazy, but my rent was cheap and included unlimited use of her hot tub. Focus on the positive.

"What are you doing?" Astrid zeroed in on our little murder poster board. "Is that a photograph of a dead body?"

I scrubbed my hands over my face.

"Yes, we believe that Molly didn't overdose." I walked over to the table. There was no use in hiding it from Astrid. When she wanted something she was relentless, and it wasn't like anyone would believe her if she talked about it.

"That sounds very industrious." She marched over to the table, leaned down, and picked up the large gold monocle that dangled from a gold chain around her neck. She held it over her left eye, which was awkward considering that she was wearing thick glasses. "Her eyes are red. She was poisoned through the eyes."

Monica looked at me like I should know what Astrid was talking about.

"In the seventies, we took LSD through eyedrops. Good times." Astrid's turbaned head nodded.

Astrid had taken LSD—so many things made sense now.

She knocked Haley on the shoulder with her silver cane. "Move over girl, I need to sit."

Crapola, now she would never leave.

Haley rubbed her arm and moved to my seat.

"What else have you found?" Astrid's cow eyes roamed over our murder board. "What's this about lima bean hoarding? Is that a real thing?"

"Apparently." I took the fourth seat.

"I suppose if my friend Trudy can hoard pantyhose, then your friend can hoard lima beans." Astrid continued to scan the board. "I intend to ask Molly about it on Monday."

I couldn't wait. This time I closed my eyes before I rolled them. Rolling your eyes with them closed is harder than you'd think.

"Now, who is up for a game of gin rummy?" Astrid reached into her voluminous pocket and pulled out a deck of cards. Not waiting for a reply, she shuffled them expertly and dealt us all in. She smacked the rest of the deck right on top of Molly's face.

If I were Molly, and if she was indeed here, I wouldn't have taken that. I'd have struck Astrid down with a bolt of lightning.

Just to be on the safe side, I scooted back from the table. You can never be too careful.

CHAPTER 8

When I woke up the next morning, my right hand was killing me. And the three Tylenol I took did little to dull the pain. Now several hours later, here I was holding another handgun.

At two on the dot, Ben picked both me and Max up and drove us to the Hidden Falls public gun range in Marble Falls. I kept calling it Hidden Valley and asking where the ranch dressing was, but both Max and Ben told me it was getting old and I needed to stop. Spoilsports.

"Don't lock your elbows." Ben tapped my left elbow.

Apparently I had terrible gun posture and was a chronic elbow-locker.

"Ever thought about nunchucks? I really think they're an underutilized weapon. Or a crossbow. That would work well for personal defense, don't you think?" And it wouldn't make my hand hurt so much.

"Nunchucks? Really? You'd probably hit yourself in the head and end up in a coma. And you can't fit a crossbow in your purse." Ben shook his head.

Oh yeah? Haley could fit a water buffalo in her purse. Then again, I couldn't afford Hermès.

"When the range goes hot again, I want you to concentrate on hitting the target." Ben was all business.

I'd learned a lot today. Primarily that public gun ranges took safety to a whole new level. When the red light was spinning, you had to put your weapon down so that people could retrieve their targets. That might have been explained to me beforehand. The first time the red light came on, I thought it was to set the mood—like hey, if you're running from the cops this is what you'll see. I'd almost shot the man in the stall next to me. If the angry death glares he was shooting me now were any indication, he was holding a grudge. Some people just couldn't let things go.

I had to say that I preferred Daman's private gun range, where all I had to do was push a button and the target came to me. Walking out onto a field where only seconds before people had been shooting just seemed like a bad idea. The man next to me was living proof of that.

"So you want me to hit the target." I rolled my eyes. "Got it."

I'd been trying... sort of. Shooting was incredibly loud and my hand hurt and I was cold and hungry. They should sell cotton candy or hot dogs like at the county fair. I looked around. Ehhh, this really wasn't a cotton candy kind of place.

A loud buzzer went off and the red light stopped flashing. I loaded the clip into the handgun Ben had provided, but since it wasn't purple I hadn't bothered to remember the name.

Ben put on his ear protection and nodded toward Max, who had on his own ear protection and was sitting at a picnic table behind us reading a book.

I wasn't much of a reader, but compared to this, books were starting to look good.

"Okay, chamber a round and remember not to lock your elbows," Ben yelled so that I could hear over my own ear protection.

If I shot someone, did I get to go home?

Probably not. With Ben being a cop, I'd get arrested.

I glanced over at the man in the stall next to me. He shot me the finger. I winked and blew him a kiss.

He wanted to kill me. I could see it in his eyes.

If I got shot, did I get to go home? I glanced at my watch. We'd been at this for exactly forty-seven minutes. What if I accidentally shot off my pinkie toe? Did I really need it? Obviously it would hurt, and I'd have to wear closed-toed shoes for the rest of my life. The pain would fade, but I'd miss out on wearing sandals. And that would suck.

I sighed heavily and brought the gun up. I aimed and squeezed the trigger. I hit the bull's-eye of the man next to me's target. I had crazy mad skills; if only I'd actually been aiming for his target. I did it again, just to be mean. And again just because I could. And once more because four times was way better than three.

The man growled so loudly that I could hear him with my earphones on.

I managed to make friends wherever I went.

Ben jumped between him and me. He flashed his badge and said something to the man that involved lots of pointing at me.

I nodded and waved graciously, letting him know that thanks weren't necessary and I'd be willing to hit the bull's-eye for him whenever he wanted. I'm such a humanitarian.

Ben walked back to me, took the gun, popped the clip out, and pulled back the hammer, causing the bullet in the chamber to fall out. He picked up the bullet, the clip, and the gun and motioned for me to follow him to the picnic table.

He set everything down, well out of Max's reach and yelled, "I think that's enough for today."

He loaded the handgun into a plastic box with a combination and then locked it. Max and I followed him back to his silver Ford F-150. Without a doubt, Ben's truck was the fanciest I'd ever seen. When he opened the passenger's side door for me, a folded-up running board automatically lowered. It was fantastic. I'd opened and closed the door for a good five minutes playing with it when he'd first picked us up.

Once we were all back in the truck, Ben turned on the engine and the heated seats came on. This beat the heck out of Bessie.

"I think we're done shooting for the day. Anyone up for a UTVing?" Ben took the path back to the Hidden Valley—um, Falls—main office.

Max and I looked at each other, and then I asked, "What's UTVing?"

"In addition to the gun range, Hidden Falls is an adventure park. I've rented us a couple of Cougar Cycle Thunderbolts. UTVs are kind of a cross between a dune buggy and a four-wheeler." He waggled his eyebrows. "Hidden Falls has three thousand acres of Texas Hill Country. Who's up for exploring it?"

I raised my hand before I figured out that it was a rhetorical question.

Fifteen minutes later, I was behind the wheel of a UTV. Ben was behind the wheel of another one, and Max was strapped in the seat next to Ben.

After the gun episode, I was beginning to think that Ben didn't trust me around other humans. Plus, I'd never driven a UTV, so Max was probably safer with Ben.

Two hours later, almost every muscle in my body hurt, but I'd had a hell of a good time. We'd ridden through the mud, climbed rocky hills, and I only flipped over once.

I smoothed the wrinkles out of my black pants as I walked out of the lady's restroom. Ben and Max, both cleaned up, were waiting for me outside.

"Now I know why you told us to grab some extra clothes." I pulled my denim jacket closed against the chill. The sun was low on the horizon and would be going down soon. After the sun went down, it was supposed to drop into the high forties.

Ben smiled appreciatively at the tight black turtleneck that showed under my jacket. I hadn't realized it had shrunk so much in the wash when I'd grabbed it earlier.

"I've got dinner reservations for us at the Overlook at Canyon of the Eagles." He grinned, clearly quite impressed with himself.

I returned his grin and nodded. I hoped it was enthusiastic enough, because I had no idea what the Overlook at Canyon of the Eagles was.

"They have a fantastic beef tenderloin with blue cheese butter." He put his hand in the small of my back as we walked toward his truck. "The view is fantastic. The restaurant is on the top of a hill."

I was starving. It didn't go unnoticed that he'd mentioned beef. I liked steak, but it needed some sort of potato product with it. Please let there be potatoes.

"Do you like steak, Max?" Ben opened the door for Max and then for me.

"Yeah, I love it. Can I get mashed potatoes with it?" My little guy was a man after my own heart.

"You bet. They have really good ones." Ben ruffled his hair.

So at some time in the past, Ben had been lured to the dark side by mashed potatoes. Good to know that there was hope.

"Unfortunately, I don't eat potatoes anymore." Ben closed Max's door and then mine.

And then the hope was gone again—just like that.

Well, I'd just have to eat enough mashed potatoes to make up for Ben's lack. Maybe I'd eat twice the dessert, too. I'm such a helper.

"Mom, can I borrow your phone?" Max asked from the backseat. "I like that new racecar game you let me download."

I pulled my phone and my earbuds out of my purse and handed them to him. Smashing racecars was loud business.

Ben opened the driver's-side door and sat. He closed the door and started the engine. I glanced back to make sure Max couldn't hear us.

In a voice slightly above a whisper, I said, "Thanks for the photo. It's been helpful.

Really helpful. Since Molly had been pregnant and possibly poisoned through the eyes and her sort-of boyfriend was an ophthalmologist, Haley, Monica, and I thought we had Molly's murder in the bag. Well, once we had some actual proof. Tomorrow, I'd call to get an appointment with Dr. Dick and see if I could get him to talk.

"I know that it's gruesome, but I thought it might give you some closure." Ben watched the screen above the radio that showed what the back-up camera saw. He backed out of his parking space and drove down the little road to the highway.

"Speaking of closure, your aunt is having a Molly-Miars-inspired séance tomorrow night. Apparently she's going to contact Molly and ask her why she died. Astrid came over last night and told me that Molly's spirit was in my house, so I guess it won't be hard to conjure her in the séance." I glanced back at Max, double-checking that he couldn't hear us. He was in game-land.

Ben shook his head. "Last Thanksgiving, she did this kind of pop-up séance at the dinner table. She started chanting and before we all figured out what was happening, she started talking in this really terrible Australian accent. It sounded a cross between Steve Irwin and Julia Child."

"That's Sebastian Sidebottom, her spirit guide. He died in some sort of horrible boomerang accident. According to her, the BAA, or Boomerang Association of Australia, celebrates his birthday with a reverence rivaled only by fans of Elvis Presley." I'd looked him up and—not surprisingly—he didn't exist. Either Sebastian was self-aggrandizing or Astrid was batshit crazy. I was going with door number two.

"It got really weird when she began interrogating my dead uncle Marvin about where he'd left his five-carat diamond cuff links." He sighed. "I didn't have the heart to tell her that he'd given them to me when I graduated from high school."

"Wow. All I got when I graduated was a diploma." I keep forgetting that the wealthy lead such different lives from the rest of us.

He laughed like he thought I was kidding. Yep, way different lives.

"You didn't grow up in Lakeside." Ben pulled out onto the highway.

"No, I grew up in northeast Texas—Longview. It's between Tyler and Shreveport." Most people outside of Longview have never heard of it.

"Sure, I know Longview. My family's oil company has an office there." He arched an eyebrow. "Good football team."

Okay, outside of the oil business and high school football no one had ever heard of Longview.

"So you were a Longview Lobo?" He glanced at me. "I bet you were a cheerleader."

"Nope, I was on the dance team. I was a Viewette. We had pom-poms though." Was he just making conversation or was he one of those guys who loved reliving his high school days? David had been a high school re-liver. There was nothing he liked better than talking about the good old days when he was quarterback of the Plano East Panthers. From what I could tell, under his leadership they'd almost won a couple of games... almost.

"I have a confession." His cheeks flushed and then he chewed on his lower lip. "I know the old chief was the quarterback, so that type of thing is probably important to you. I need to be honest. I didn't play football, I'm more of a soccer and chess club kind of guy."

Could he be any cuter?

"Honestly, I'm not that into football. The only reason I was on the drill team is that my best friend wanted to try out, so she convinced me to go with her. I made it and she didn't. I lasted a whole year before I turned in my pom-poms and hung up my white cowboy boots." Besides, drill team had been starting to cut into my hanging-with-my-friends time, and my BFF dumped me when I made the team and she didn't.

I'd learned a lot since high school. First and foremost, the smart guys were the ones I should have been chasing and not the dumb jocks. Smart guys ruled the world; just ask Melinda Gates. And I'd learned that ex-boyfriends, no matter how much they claimed they wanted to stay my friend, really didn't want to hear about my new boyfriend. And that having three dates to homecoming was one date too many. I'd also learned that calculus was a complete waste of time—no one used math that didn't have freaking numbers.

"So, how did you like Daman Rodriguez?" Ben tried to sound nonchalant, but he didn't quite pull it off.

Holy subject change, Batman.

"Um, he has a really big house... like overwhelmingly big." I had actually kind of liked him. He was hot, had pastries to spare, and massaged my shoulders. There was nothing not to like.

"How about that gun safe?" Ben nodded in appreciation.

That wasn't the first thing that came to mind when I thought about Daman. Usually it was the dimples or his hot ass. I cut my gaze over to Ben. I guess if he'd commented on Daman's dimples or hot ass, we'd have a problem.

"I guess. It was big." I shrugged. "Everything in Daman's house is larger-than-life."

"He has a net worth of over seven hundred million dollars. He's officially the richest man in Lakeside." Ben glanced over at me, presumably to gauge my reaction to his news.

"I noticed that we didn't travel in the same circles." Or the same worlds. I have a net worth in the seven hundred dollar range. Give or take six hundred and ninety-nine dollars.

"So you weren't impressed just a little bit?" Ben sounded a little nervous. "You know, his being so rich."

I would have been offended by the implication, but I was too hungry to be offended. I cut to the chase.

"Nope. If I was a gold digger, I wouldn't have married David." The fact that I'd been pregnant was the primary reason I'd married David, but since Max hadn't put that together yet, I wasn't going to point it out.

"I didn't mean to imply." He swallowed hard. "I just meant that lots of women seem to flock to him."

"I don't flock to anything. I'm not a big flocker." I didn't want to burst his bubble and point out that women flocked to Daman because of his hot ass and dimples. Yeah, his outrageous wealth didn't hurt, but it wasn't the only reason women were drawn to him.

"Good." He nodded to himself. "So he didn't hit on you. I thought he might, considering your family history... the diamonds."

"What are you talking about? Yes, he did hit on me, but we don't have any family history." Then the hair on the back of my neck stood up. "What diamonds?"

"You know... the diamonds." Ben's eyes turned huge like he'd just figured out that I really had no idea what he was talking about. "Never mind."

"Diamonds?" My stomach dropped to my knees.

"It's nothing." He blew out a long, labored breath.

"Either tell me what you're talking about or take me home." The edge in my voice had Ben glancing my way.

"The diamonds David stole from evidence before he left town." Sweat broke out on Ben's upper lip. "They were Rodriguez's. He's suing the city for a million dollars."

CHAPTER 9

"How come neither of you mentioned the diamonds?" I'd been chomping at the bit all day. We'd gotten home way too late last night for me to call either of my best friends, and then work today had just sucked to hell and back.

Ben had clammed up and refused to tell me anything else about my ex-husband, but he texted me several times wanting to know if I was mad at him. I wasn't mad so much as embarrassed. I'd texted him back telling him that everything was fine. He seemed relieved.

Haley studied the polish on her fingernails, and Monica gulped down her entire glass of wine.

We were meeting at my house for a pre-séance wine and cheese party.

"Someone needs to tell me. Ben blindsided me with it last night." I took a long, tall, hefty drink of my own wine.

Silence crackled through the room.

Haley took a deep breath and let it out slowly. "We knew you were hurting and we didn't want to add to it."

"I need to know the whole story." I poured more Shiraz all around. For me, wine and séances went hand in hand.

Monica scrubbed her face with her hands. "Okay, David took more than just the money from your bank account. He took some diamonds from evidence, worth 1.2 million and..."

She shook her head.

"What?" Crap, there was more? My heart kicked into overdrive.

Haley bit her top lip and then sighed long and hard. "It appears that he took some money from the city. Like close to a million dollars."

It took a full minute for my brain to process the information. Not only had David abandoned his child and his job, he'd stolen evidence and embezzled money. Well, if he was going to be a dick, why not be a huge one?

"Apparently Grand Cayman is very expensive." I knocked back the entire glass of wine and picked up the empty bottle, trying to ring one more drop out. "We're going to need more wine."

Knowing that David had embezzled money from the city sure did explain a lot. All those glances that I'd once thought were pitying... now I knew they were hostile. All those invitations for dinner and playdates that had dried up after David left? I'd thought it was just because I no longer had the status of being married to the chief of police. I shook my head. Clearly everyone in this small town had known the truth except me.

And just when I'd thought I couldn't feel any more betrayed by my ex, I find out this? I was a pariah in a town of gossip piranhas. It was a wonder the lynch mob hadn't beat down the door to get at me.

Maybe they couldn't find me because I'd moved.

I took a hand of each of my friends and squeezed lightly. "Thank you both so much for not shunning me. In this town, I'm sure it cost you."

"Like we care." Monica squeezed back.

"It's not like people think you took the money." Haley forced a smile. Oh hell, that's exactly what people thought. I looked around at my small guesthouse rental. The joke was on them.

There was a light knock at my front door and then Haley's nanny Anise opened the door. "Here's the food."

Anise was a short, plump girl with a British accent. When I'd first met her, she'd proudly told me that she was from Surrey... wherever that was.

"I took the liberty of having her pick up some dinner." Haley stood and took some of the sandwiches from Anise. "Tucci's subs."

Because Austin had outlawed plastic bags, even the ones used for takeout food, all of the butcher-paper-wrapped sandwiches were loose.

Anise would also be watching the kids this evening. Monica and I had insisted on paying her extra for the extra kids. At first she'd refused to accept it, but we'd been persistent.

Haley handed out sandwiches to the kids. "I got the kiddos all ham and cheese with nothing else." She walked over to the table. "I got the adults Italian Classics."

My favorite food on the evening that I'd just learned the worst news. Friends were amazing.

"Cool." Monica took her sandwich and unwrapped it. "I'm starving."

I took mine and did the same. "Thanks for telling me the truth."

I wish they'd done it earlier, but I understood why they hadn't. I'd had to deal with some pretty terrible things, and I don't know what I would have done if I'd known about David's thievery.

We ate in silence.

After we'd thrown away the dinner trash and I'd wiped down the kitchen table, Haley, Monica, and I put on our coats and headed for the main house. It was a good quarter of a mile down a winding gravel path, so we trudged in the dark, forty-degree weather.

"How long does this usually take?" Monica stuck her hands in her front jeans pockets. "I've got last week's episode of *Castle* DVRed and I'm dying to watch it."

"Oh, it's a good one." My breath clouded out in front of me. "The séance takes about an hour. Usually I turn my phone on silent and play solitaire. As long as I chant every once in a while, no one is the wiser."

"How many people come?" Haley pulled her coat tighter around her.

"Two or three. Mitzi Lange, Eloise Dunlap, and sometimes Donnalee Murphy if her son didn't hide her car keys well enough." I pulled my collar up to shield my ears from the wind.

"What do you mean if her son didn't hide her keys?" Monica shivered.

"Donnalee is as blind as a bat, but instead of taking away her Caddy like he should, her son just hides her keys. Spineless. Really, she's going to hurt someone someday." I looked back at Monica. "She can barely see over the dash."

A loud bang sounded from the direction of the garage. "Sounds like her son didn't do that great a job of hiding her keys. Donnalee just hit the retaining wall again."

A cloud of dust illuminated by headlights floated up over the garage.

"Damn, it's kinda hard to miss that wall, it being twenty feet tall and painted bloodred." Monica watched the cloud. "How blind is she?"

"It's hard to say. She comes when you call her, but she runs into the wall a lot. Astrid has that huge mural of a Tuscan village in her dining room, and Donnalee is always trying to walk through the painted doorway. She runs into the wall, backs up, runs into the wall, backs up, over and over again. It's kind of like watching a blind dog trying to find the door to the backyard."

"And she's behind the wheel of a car?" Monica shook her head. "Crazy rich people."

"Ms. Donnalee is a sweet lady," Haley said. "When she's not behind the wheel or handing out trick-or-treat candy. Last year she got confused and gave away all of her dog Buster's toys. I'm told that Buster died a couple of days later—she kept throwing Hershey bars for him to fetch. To be fair, the toys and candy were on the same table."

"A blind dog-murderer." Monica threw her hands up. "Fantastic, I can't wait to meet her."

"Buster was twelve years old, so it might have been natural causes." Haley sounded so hopeful.

Monica patted her arm. "You go on thinking that if it gives you comfort. I'm planning on driving Donnalee home and then throwing her car keys in the lake."

See, Monica doesn't wait for the world to take care of things, she jumps right on in there and confiscates the car keys of a woman she's never met. I admire that level of commitment.

"I should warn you... things can get weird." That was the understatement of the century.

Monica stopped and looked back at me. "We're headed to a séance. That by definition is weird."

She had a point.

"I'm just saying that Astrid takes this very seriously. She even dresses for the part. There will be lots of silver sequins, purple velvet, and crystal balls. Her headdress is supposed to be material from a voodoo priestess's old dress. There are lots of candles, as electric lights aren't conducive to communing with the spirits." I was doing my best to prepare them, but honestly, nothing I said could prepare them.

"Do the spirits actually come?" Haley was completely serious.

Monica and I shared a look. It's not that Haley was gullible, but she really wanted to believe this wasn't a waste of time.

"Not that I've ever seen. Well, once the logs flickered in the fireplace, but that was because I threw a wad of paper in there. While they were all chanting I'd been cleaning out my purse. I had to get rid of all those receipts some way."

Really, that was the closest the spirits had come to responding. Personally, I thought they were put off by all those silver sequins. There was nothing worse than an old woman dressed as a giant disco ball reflecting the light of a hundred burning candles. I'd often thought that Astrid could double as a lighthouse.

"I don't know about her trying to contact Molly. It seems so... I don't know... disrespectful." Haley was worried about absolutely nothing.

"The only way Astrid is going to talk to Molly is if she dies and goes to heaven and finds her. Since that's a one-way trip, I don't think we're going to get the message." Man, the things I did for cheap rent.

We made it to the back door and I knocked.

Dulce, Astrid's live-in housekeeper, answered the door.

"She's in the séance room." Dulce held the door and we stepped into the kitchen. "Miss Astrid is extra crazy today. This morning I caught her in the kitchen stirring something in my big Le Creuset pot. She claimed it was a voodoo recipe to summon the dead. I chased her out of the kitchen with my biggest chef's knife."

Her voice was monotone, like this was just an average day at the ranch.

I smiled at her. "Your burden is great, Kemosabe."

She held her hand up for a high five. "Wanna come over after she goes to bed tonight and turn all the living room furniture upside down again? She totally bought the living room poltergeist last time."

"It's a date." I high-fived her.

The only thing sweet about Dulce was her name. She survived Astrid's craziness by messing with her. Clearly that and her salary had been enough to keep her here for the last twenty years.

"Dulce, this is Monica." I pointed to Monica. "And this is Haley."

"Nice to meet you." Dulce shook their hands. "Wanna come over and help with the furniture?"

"I wish I could." Monica shrugged. "But it's a school night. I've got to get my kiddo to bed or I'd totally help with the furniture flipping."

"Me too," Haley said. "Another time?"

"You bet." Dulce winked. "You should see what I have planned for Thanksgiving. Last year the turkey came back to life and Miss Astrid became a vegetarian. This is the year of the vegetables. They're going to sing the Hallelujah Chorus. I can't wait."

"Her nephew is a prop guy in the movies." I needed them to understand how detailed some of Dulce's pranks were.

"He's getting into special effects—you know, the real stuff, where stuff gets blown up and not that digital crap." Dulce was very proud of her nephew.

An electronic bell rang, like the kind used at the theater when act two is about to start. Yes, I'm familiar with the theater. At the tender age of five, I played Gretl in *The Sound of Music* at the Longview Community Theater. As you might have noticed, I was not snatched up by Broadway or Hollywood.

There was a loud blowing noise coming from the whole house speaker system like someone was testing it. "The séance will be starting in five minutes. Please make your way to the séance room."

"It's just like Dillard's right before they close." Haley looked around like she was trying to find the person from whom the announcement had come.

"I've tried to disconnect the whole house intercom system, but she keeps having it fixed. I threatened the last repair guy with his life if he ever fixed it again. One day, I'm going to make it stop permanently." Dulce put one hand on her hip and shook her head. "It might take burning the house down, but I'm going to do it."

"I admire that level of commitment," Monica said. "If you're not prepared to go all the way, why do something at all?"

"Exactly." Dulce nodded in agreement. "If you're going to play, go all in."

The bell sounded again.

"You'd better go. Her Royal Weirdness doesn't like to wait." Dulce nodded in the direction of the living room. The séance room was just off of the living room in what the builder had probably intended to be a media room.

Astrid had wanted to convert her dining room into the séance room, but Dulce had put her foot down. Spirits weren't allowed in her dining room or her kitchen. The rest of the house was fair game.

"It's just through here." I led the way to Crazytown.

I opened the door to the séance room, stood back, and let Monica and Haley take it all in. What had once been a normal fourteen-by-fourteen room was now painted a dark red. Dozens of tiny octagonal mirrors had been glued to the wall at random intervals, and black zodiac signs dotted the red-painted ceiling.

"It's like the *Amityville Horror* blood room, only sparkly." Haley's gaze darted around. "And creepier."

"What's with the mosquito net?" Monica pointed to the large mosquito net canopy draped over the round séance table. "I wasn't aware that dead people attracted mosquitoes." She hunched her shoulders. "You know, after they're buried and everything."

"No idea." I walked around the table looking for the opening to the mosquito net. I finally found the ties that held it closed and untied them. "I've always thought of this room as Astral Safari Meets Crazy-Assed Rich Lady. Dulce told me that Astrid hired a séance consultant to help set up the room."

"A séance consultant is a real thing?" Monica followed me into the mosquito tent.

"If my neighbor can have a life coach, why can't she have a séance consultant?" Haley was right behind Monica.

"Mr. Earl has a life coach?" I couldn't see her crotchety next door neighbor, who was always out in his front yard measuring the grass with a ruler to make sure that all the blades were evenly cut, having a life coach.

"No, this is my neighbor down the street—Ava. You know, she's the one who was married to that drummer in that rock band before he divorced her to marry that eighteen-year-old groupie." Haley glanced up and noticed the black disco ball holding up the mosquito net.

"I thought she just married that strip mall developer." Clearly I was behind on the gossip. "Have a seat."

I pointed to the chairs on either side of me.

"She did, but he left her for his twenty-two-year-old receptionist." Haley took the chair on my left. "Her life coach told her that she needed to get a job."

"Crap, it must suck to be a washed-up trophy wife. It's not like that's a long-term gig. I bet her resume is a little on the empty side. Marrying well really isn't a saleable skill." Monica's eyebrows arched. "Or one she seems to be particularly good at."

"Is that a crystal skull?" Haley stared at the centerpiece.

"Yep. Astrid claims that it's one of the Mesoamerican crystal skulls from the British Museum and that she had to pay them some huge amount of money for it. I'm pretty sure she bought it off eBay." I sat and tried to make myself comfortable in one of the world's hardest chairs.

Monica sat on my right. "Where'd she get these chairs?"

"They're from some European monastery. I asked if they had to sit on the floor now that she'd taken their chairs, but she didn't think that was funny." Come to think of it, Astrid didn't think much of anything I did was funny, including my impersonation of a sprinkler head, and everyone knows it's hilarious.

"Were they the Order of the Uncomfortable Chairs?" Monica wiggled around trying to find a comfy spot.

"If I can sit on these for one hour a week, you can brave it for one night." I lowered my voice. "Wait until they start chanting and then grab a couple of handfuls of the mosquito net and bunch it up like a seat cushion. It works."

"What's with all of the candy?" Haley pointed to the large bowl of gummy cherries in front of her.

"Apparently the spirits like sweets. Astrid sets bowls of different kinds of candy out so the spirits can choose. Those are Haribo gummy cherries she imports from Germany. They don't have any high fructose corn syrup. It appears that the spirits are allergic to high fructose corn syrup." Obviously I'd been here too long, because that didn't sound so strange to me anymore.

"What about the Peanut M&M's in front of you. I'm pretty sure they have high fructose corn syrup and red dye number five." Haley gestured to the bowl right in front of me.

"Max and I really like Peanut M&M's. A couple of months ago when Astrid got on this anti-high-fructose-corn-syrup kick, I told her about this recurring dream I'd had since childhood about Nigel, my spirit guide, talking to me about my dead grandmother. Unfortunately he stopped coming to me when the Peanut M&M's disappeared. The next week they were back on the table." I pulled a quart-sized Ziploc bag out of my back jeans pocket and filled the bag with Peanut M&M's.

"Way to work the system." Monica held a fist up for me to bump. I gave her a bump back, zipped up the bag, and hid it under the table. Later, when the séance was wrapping up, I'd tuck it in my waistband and pull my shirt out to cover the bag.

"Silence." It was Astrid over the intercom. "The ceremony is about to begin."

"There's a ceremony?" Monica raised one eyebrow.

"Oh no, I forgot about the candle lighting ceremony." I rolled my eyes. Donnalee was here and I'd forgotten to grab the fire extinguisher.

"You know the Carols and Candles ceremony at First Baptist on Christmas Eve?" Until I'd moved in here, I'd looked forward to the Carols and Candles service. Watching the deacons walk down the aisles lighting all of the candles held by the congregation, and then they would turn off the lights—it was beautiful.

"Yes." Haley nodded. She was Catholic, but everyone went to First Baptist for the Carols and Candles service.

"It's like that, only there's no Christmas music, one of the candle lighters is stone-cold blind, and I'm pretty sure we're summoning the forces of darkness... but there's lots of candles." I leaned down, lifted up the hem of the purple and silver silk tablecloth to see if Dulce had hidden a fire extinguisher there like we'd talked about. Sure enough, there it was in all of its red glory. I grabbed it and set it down next to my chair. "I have a fire extinguisher."

"Thank God." Haley glanced up as the lights flickered.

"Here they come. A word to the wise. Close your eyes until after they are seated. All that candlelight radiating from the millions of silver sequins on Astrid's robe can cause seizures. After they are seated, do not look in her direction. Keep your head down or she might melt your retinas." I grabbed a handful of Peanut M&M's, shoved them in my mouth, and lowered my head. I could tolerate Astrid's robe as long as I didn't look at it head-on, but I still closed my eyes. Watching three senior citizens dancing around the table like they were druids at Stonehenge cracked me up. I'd been told on more than one occasion that laughter at a séance was inappropriate.

The lights went out and the door was thrown open.

"Spirits of the afterlife, we summon you. Your daughters of light are waiting. Come to us," Astrid chanted.

"Come to us," Mitzi, Eloise, and Donnalee chanted.

"Come to us." Astrid's voice got louder.

"Come to us," Mitzi, Eloise, and Donnalee returned.

There was a loud thunk over my left shoulder. I glanced behind me. Donnalee had run into the altar, which held an assortment of voodoo dolls, crystals, vials of holy water, and Jolly Ranchers. She was attempting to light the Jolly Ranchers. I jumped up and grabbed a couple of vials of holy water and poured them on the flaming candy.

"I got one!" Donnalee yelled. "There's a spirit in here pulling my arm. I'm being moved by the spirit."

"It's just Mustang." Astrid sighed heavily.

"Let me help you to your seat." She was an inch away from lighting my hair on fire—especially now that there was twice as much. Gently, I took her candle and blew it out.

"Okay dear." Her face turned up to me, and I noticed that she'd only drawn on one eyebrow tonight. Fortunately, it was directly in the center of her forehead. For her, painting on eyebrows was much like pin the tail on the donkey—as long as you got it on the board, it counted.

"Is your spirit guide the Hershey Skor bars, the Reese's Peanut Butter Cups, or the black licorice?" They all had named spirit guides, but I could only remember them by their junk food preferences.

"Skor bars." With all of the pomp and circumstance of Queen Elizabeth at her coronation, Donnalee allowed me to escort her. She got a little caught up in the mosquito net, but otherwise, we made it to her seat just fine.

At the rate Mitzi and Eloise were lighting the candles, we'd be here all night. Using the large lit candle next to the crystal skull, I relit the candle I'd taken off Donnalee and walked around the room lighting the remaining candles.

After all the candles were lit, I settled back in my seat.

"Join hands." Astrid grabbed Donnalee's hand before she knocked over the Skor bars.

We all joined hands.

"Sebastian... my dear sweet Sebastian. I feel you near. Come to me, old friend. Come to me." Astrid rocked back and forth, making the sequins flash in the candlelight. If she rocked with a little more force she'd be head banging, but since it was kind of slow she looked more like a little kid who had to pee but was holding it.

Monica let go of my hand to shield her eyes from the flashing sequins.

I mouthed, "Told you."

Astrid's voice got louder. "Sebastian, our circle of love is unbroken."

Monica waggled her I-broke-the-circle-of-love fingers.

"G'day, mate." Astrid appeared to be channeling Sebastian. "I was just off at a bottle shop with me bushie mates for a bit o' bundy."

I had no idea what that meant, but I was pretty sure that Astrid had only researched Aussie lingo through the letter C. We never got any Australian slang that didn't start with A, B, or C.

"It was a nice place too. Not like that bottle-o run by that cane toad." Or it might have been, "Nice people poop. Not in a pot though right on Cane Road." Neither made much sense. Her accent was so bad that it could have gone either way.

Haley glanced at me.

I shrugged. I don't speak crazy.

"Dear Sebastian, please help us find Molly Miars," Eloise said. Eloise had been given the great honor of speaking with Sebastian. Once, Astrid had tried to talk to Sebastian herself, but we'd all gotten so confused that we had to have a designated spirit driver.

"Molly Miars?" It sounded a lot like trolley cars.

"Yes, Molly Miars. Please find her. We need to talk to her." Eloise was all importance. "Her friends have joined us to help call her forth."

Monica squeezed my hand. "Oh, Troll—"

I kicked her under the table.

"—I mean, Molly Miars. Please come to us and tell us who murdered you."

"He did it." Astrid was fading into a Cockney Michael Caine. "Oh, me eyes. Me eyes. Help—me eyes are burning. He poisoned me eyes." She rubbed her eyes vigorously and coughed.

"Who is he? Could you be a little more specific?" Haley leaned closer to Astrid like that would help. "Perhaps a proper noun."

Astrid's coughing turned into a wheezing fit in which she grabbed her throat and convulsed from side to side. "Not lima beans... not lima beans."

There was lots of body twitching and gasping. After a full minute of hokey-pokey writhing where she put her right arm in and took her right arm out, put her right arm in and then she writhed it all about, she took one last, long, labored breath and then face-planted into a large bowl of assorted Lindt Lindor Truffles.

Astrid sat up and looked around like she'd just woken from a coma. "What happened?"

Eloise put her hand over her heart. "Sebastian is amazing. My spirit guide, Marvis, has never come through that clear."

"Is Sebastian still here?" Donnalee looked around and then yelled, "Sebastian?"

"He's gone." Astrid rolled her eyes. "What did he say?"

Like she didn't know. It was funny how the information that she'd seen on our murder poster board had been the only information that Sebastian gave us.

"He did it." Mitzi glanced at me. "Who is he?"

I shrugged. I had no idea.

"Sebastian said 'he,' and then his eyes started hurting. Isn't that clear enough?" Astrid pegged me with her beady little brown eyes.

Funny how we hadn't mentioned the eyes thing, yet she still knew what Sebastian said.

"It was the eye doctor? If Molly was poisoned through the eyes, it was her boyfriend, the eye doctor."

Haley and Monica turned to me. If Dr. Dick had murdered Molly, I needed to know... we needed to know. Tomorrow, I'd call and make an appointment.

CHAPTER 10

"You call me as soon as you get out." Haley was practically yelling. I pulled the phone away from my ear.

"Okey dokey, Mom." I was parked outside of Stevensen Optical, the office of Dick Stevensen, possible murderer and all-around A-hole.

"I meant it. He's a jerk and I'm worried about you." Haley rustled some papers. "I can't stand it. I'm coming over—"

"Stay home. I've got this. He won't know what hit him. I'll interrogate him and he won't be the wiser. I am female, hear me roar." I'd watched *Erin Brockovich* last night and was ready to take on the world. "I can handle one crazy ophthalmologist. Piece o' cake."

The earliest appointment I'd been able to get was Wednesday at noon. So here I was, sitting in the parking lot of the Randalls shopping center and waiting to meet a murderer. I had ten minutes to go before my appointment. You had to love a doctor's office squished between a Subway and a Papa Murphy's. Pizza sounded good, but the billing office didn't have an oven. Freaking take-and-bake. Subway it is.

I turned the screwdriver and Bessie's engine rattled a bit but finally turned off. I opened the driver's door and climbed out. Someone had painted the two windows on either side of the front door of Dr. Stevensen's office with giant eyeglass lenses. I opened the door, which was the nose, and walked in. The huge face with glasses was clever—stupid, but clever.

I headed to the L-shaped front desk, and an older lady with a flat-top haircut and tiny John Lennon specs looked up from the computer she was industriously pounding on.

"Can I help you?" It was more of an accusation than a question.

"I have an appointment with Dr. Stevensen." I checked my watch. It was eleven fifty-five; surely this woman had a schedule of appointments and should be expecting me.

"Let me check," the woman hissed out. Clearly the welcome wagon had run right over this dear woman on its way somewhere else. "You'd be..." She pulled her glasses down to the end of her nose and leaned so close to the computer I was afraid she might burn her retinas. "...Mustang Ridges. Is that your stage name or something?"

It's amazing what people feel is appropriate to ask a total stranger. Did I ask her why she looked like one of those little troll dolls? No, I did not. Next to this woman, I was a paragon of restraint.

I smiled so hard my cheeks hurt. "I'm Mustang Ridges, and yes, that's my real name."

"I'm going to need your health insurance card—that's for your office visit, your vision insurance card if you have one..." With her right pinkie fingernail, she picked a green particle out of the space between her two front teeth. "Oh, and I need to see your driver's license. Make sure you are who you say you are."

I couldn't help but wonder if everyone got carded or if she only wanted to check my name. It had happened before. I fished in my wallet for the cards.

The queen of good hygiene, she wiped the green particle on her pants before taking the cards I'd laid on the counter for her.

She felt around on the counter separating her from the rest of the world until her hand grazed a clipboard. Grabbing it, she checked to make sure something was clipped to it. "Here are your new patient forms. Because you haven't been in to see us in five years, you'll need to fill them out again."

I'd been a patient of Dr. Mueller, but when he'd retired and sold his practice to Dr. Stevensen, I hadn't bothered to come back. I didn't need glasses and could see just fine, so what was the point?

I took the clipboard and flipped through the pages clipped to it. The first page was a menu for the Great Wall of China restaurant. FYI, in Austin there's an adoption agency called the Great Wall of China. Once I called their number by mistake and tried to order takeout. They were not amused.

I unclipped the menu and stuffed it in my purse. Broccoli and beef sounded like an excellent lunch. Besides, the Wicked Witch of Stevensen Optical couldn't read it.

The next page was a list of phone messages for Dr. Stevensen. I pulled out my iPhone and snapped a couple of pictures of the phone messages so I could investigate those further. I was 99 percent sure that when I called these numbers no one would pick up the phone and say, "Great job killing Molly," but it could happen... maybe.

I walked back to the front desk with the good intention of telling her that these weren't the new patient forms, but since she held my driver's license about a millimeter away from her eyeball and was inspecting it like she was checking the molecules to make sure it wasn't plutonium, I decided that new patient forms weren't necessary.

"Ever thought about bifocals? That way you could see both up close and far away." I was just trying to be helpful. She did work for an ophthalmologist after all. Surely Dr. Dick had noticed that his receptionist couldn't even read the giant-lettered top line on the eye chart.

"I'm too young for bifocals. My vision is perfect." She pushed her glasses back up her nose and glared at me.

I seem to make friends wherever I go.

"I can see that." I didn't bother to smile because unless I backed up ten or so feet, she wouldn't see it. "Here are the new patient forms."

I handed the phone message list back to her.

"You filled them out quickly." She sounded skeptical but felt around the countertop for the forms.

Just to be a bitch I moved the clipboard just out of her reach. Every time she moved closer, I moved it a little more out of the way. I was the ex-wife of an embezzling diamond thief; cheap thrills were all I could afford.

"Where are those damn forms?" Her hand banged the edge of the clipboard, and I decided that she'd worked hard enough for it. "There, got 'um."

"Ma, is my next patient here?" A cloud of cheap men's cologne wafted in, announcing the presence of Dr. Dick. Molly had described Dr. Dick as a "mook," and I'd never really understood the meaning of the word until he stepped into the room. He was maybe six feet tall with slicked-back dark hair and a massive sternum bush sticking out of the unbuttoned top three buttons of his shirt. His fake-tanned skin made him look dirty rather than tan. His gaze went directly to my chest and a huge, happy smile curled on his face. "Hey there, sweetheart, I hope you're ready to spend the next twenty minutes alone with me in a dark room."

Without taking his eyes off of my chest, he pulled a small bottle of breath spray out of his front pants pocket and squirted a puff in his mouth. Yep, mook.

If I didn't love Molly so much, I'd have walked out right then and there.

"Dr... ." Don't say Dick, don't say Dick. "Stevensen." I held out my hand for him to shake. "Molly Miars spoke so highly of you."

I half expected her spirit to put me in a chokehold for lying, but this extreme situation called for extreme measures.

"What did you say, sweetheart?" His eyes stayed on my chest.

I could practically feel him picturing me naked. If he so much as laid a finger on me, I was kneeing him in the balls and punching him in the throat. And thanks to that self-defense instructor who bartered classes at the hospital to pay off his bill after he'd gotten mugged at a bar on Sixth Street, I knew how.

"She said, 'Molly Miars spoke so highly of you,'" the receptionist yelled.

"I got it, Mom," he yelled back, but his gaze never moved.

He had focus, I'd give him that.

So he let his mom continue to be blind as a bat even though he could fix it? It seemed that Dr. Dick was about as good an eye doctor as that self-defense instructor was at defending himself.

"Wait, Molly who?" This time his gaze darted briefly to my face and then back to my chest.

"Molly Miars." So he'd knocked her up, killed her, and forgotten her name. What was below mook in the asshole hierarchy?

He nodded. "Oh yeah... Molly."

He really didn't seem to know who she was. Then I got the full force of his lecherous smile. His bleached-white teeth had clearly been capped and were so huge that they barely fit in his mouth. "Sweetheart, I date lots of women. Hell, last week on my annual Bahamas singles cruise, I hit it with so many chicks I lost count." He winked. "Play your cards right and you just might be the next notch on my bedpost."

I threw up a little bit in my mouth, which was weird because I hadn't eaten anything today. I guess my body kept some vomit in reserve in case I ran into any worse-than-mooks.

Good to know.

Wait. Singles cruise?

"When did the cruise leave?" If he'd been out of town the whole week, he couldn't have killed Molly. Sure, he could have hired someone to do it, but that didn't feel right. This mook wasn't smart enough to have hired someone.

"Why?" His ferret eyes narrowed.

I looked around like an answer would pop out of midair. "It sounds like fun. I'd love more information. I might go next year."

It was a pathetic save, but it was a save.

"Yeah, that could be fun. I left last Sunday and got back this past Monday." He nodded. "Lots of broads on the ship go topless. What are you, a D cup? I could stand to see you topless."

I could have sued him for harassment right there but chose to ignore the last comment.

Molly was killed on Tuesday, and he wasn't in town. He could have been lying, but I didn't think so. I'm sure I could ask to see some pictures from his trip, but I wasn't sure I could stomach those.

I cleared my throat. "You know what, I just remembered that I have a roast in the oven." I had no idea where that had come from—I'd never cooked anything in the oven that didn't come frozen in a cardboard box. I headed for the door as fast as I could. "I'll call to reschedule."

I grabbed my license and insurance cards from the counter and practically ran out the door.

Dr. Dick was in fact a dick, a gigantic donkey dick, but my Spidey sense was telling me that he didn't kill Molly. He couldn't even remember her name, plus he'd been out of the country when it happened. After having met him, I couldn't see Molly, or anyone else for that matter, mating with him. Molly was smarter than that, and she had more self-respect. I was almost sure that Dr. Dick wasn't the father of Molly's baby.

I jumped into Bessie and glanced back at the giant glasses on the front windows of Stevensen Optical. I hoped Dr. Dick never fathered any children. Society as a whole had enough problems without his DNA peeing in the gene pool.

CHAPTER 11

"He didn't do it." I had called Haley, as promised, on my way to pick up Chinese takeout before I headed back to work.

"What do you mean, he didn't do it?" Haley was breathing heavily.

"What are you doing?" I turned onto Lakeside Boulevard and into the Founder's Village strip center. Great Wall of China was located in the crotch of the V-shaped strip center.

"I'm on the elliptical," Haley huffed out. "I have twenty more minutes."

"I don't know how you can talk and exercise at the same time." I couldn't do both, so I'd given up exercise in favor of talking. I play to my strengths.

"Years of practice." She took a deep breath. "You're sure it wasn't him?"

"He was out of the country on some singles cruise. There is the possibility that he hired someone, but honestly, I don't think he's that smart. Plus, I wonder why Molly ever dated him. Maybe she was lying about it."

I hoped.

"I was just thinking the same thing." Haley was breathing so hard that I could barely understand her. "I think we should go visit Molly's mother. I don't want to do it, but I think we need to."

"Sounds like a plan. I can't think of anything else to do." Question family and friends—that's what they did on

Castle. Hopefully, it was the right thing to do. Everything I knew about murder investigation, I'd learned from TV.

"I'll call Monica and find out if she wants to come with us. I think today after you get off of work is best. I'll have Anise watch the kids and we can go to Lakeside Living. I can't wait to see dear old Edna Miars." Haley's voice dripped with sarcasm. Monica would be so proud.

At six that evening, we pulled into the wide circle drive in front of Lakeside Living. The seniors living facility was four stories of opulence. It was part Tuscan villa and part Tara from *Gone with the Wind*. The outside walls were made of cut white Texas limestone, and a flowerbox with red geraniums hung under every window. A burnt-orange tile roof contrasted nicely against the giant white columns.

A uniformed man who was maybe eighteen flagged us down, so Haley pulled up to him.

"Hello, welcome to Lakeside Living. I'm Brandon, your valet." He opened the driver's door for Haley.

"Valet service?" Monica, who was riding in front this time, turned around to look at me.

"Apparently." Wherever we went, Monica and I were the fish out of water.

"The joke's on him. Haley will pay a thousand dollars for a good meal, but won't shell out ten bucks for valet." Monica grinned. "Rich people are so weird."

"I heard that." Haley stepped out of the car and handed Brandon ten dollars.

Brandon took the money gratefully. "Thanks."

"I stand corrected." Monica waited for him to open her door, and then she stepped onto the dirt-orange-stained concrete. If the builders of Lakeside Living were trying to make the concrete the color of crushed granite or red clay, they had failed miserably. It just looked like a cheap spray-on tan.

I waited for Brandon to help me out and then I followed Haley and Monica toward the huge, elaborate, cut-glass double doors. They were part Baptist church and part Vegas casino.

Brandon hurried past us to open the large right-hand door.

If I thought the outside was fancy, the inside was positively palatial. At the entry a three-story waterfall gurgled down and emptied into a huge ornamental fishpond. A sidewalk with small shops surrounded the pond. It reminded me of the boardwalk inside the cruise ship where I'd spent five terrible nights and six awful days on my honeymoon. By the way, morning sickness and motion sickness don't go well together. The honeymoon sucked; why didn't I take that as a sign that my marriage would suck too? Lesson learned.

On this boardwalk there was a hair salon, a yoga studio, an ice cream parlor, a storefront advertising therapeutic massage and physical therapy, several restaurants, and a Walgreens. This was better than downtown Lakeside.

"Wow." I looked up at the full-sized hot air balloon complete with basket hanging down from the ceiling. "Clearly, assisted living has changed since my Grammie Ida lived in one. Hers only had a cafeteria and a TV room with no cable."

"Tell me about it. My grandfather lived in a place that smelled like pee and applesauce." Monica took a deep breath. "All I smell here is money and vanilla air freshener."

"According to their website, Lakeside Living is a state-of-the-art-resort senior living center. They have two Olympic-sized lap pools, four restaurants, and two salons, and a different Vegas headliner does shows here each month. Last month it was Wayne Newton. There's actual video of seniors storming the stage and throwing their underwear at him. Trust me when I tell you that it was disturbing." Haley shivered. "One woman threw an entire box of Depends, but I'm happy to report that no one was seriously injured."

Haley led us to the front desk. Another uniformed man greeted us with a smile. "Welcome to Lakeside Living. I'm Charles Pennywhistle. How may I help you?"

On the intricately carved wooden counter sat a huge brass bell—like the ones cowboys dinged in old westerns to get the attention of hotel proprietors. Monica and I exchanged a look and my hand shot out to ring the bell first. Monica was quick, but I was quicker. I rang the bell. Then she rang it, and then I rang it again, and then back to Monica.

Charles Pennywhistle's hand covered the bell before I could ring it again.

"How may I be of assistance?" His glare all but said that if we rang that bell again, he was hiding our bodies in a shallow grave.

Maybe he killed Molly for ringing his bell?

"We're here to see Edna Miars." Haley, always the grown-up, didn't even bother to look our way.

"Yes, I'll just see if she's expecting you." Charles's jovial demeanor cracked around the edges. Apparently the mere mention of Edna Miars was enough to make him lose his cool, even though he'd kept it in the face of two crazy women playing with his bell. That spoke volumes about Edna. Perhaps she really was an evil bitch.

Five minutes later we stood in front of room ten-seventeen.

"Are we sure that we really want to do this?" Haley looked at me.

"Is she really that bad?" Monica cocked her head to the right and watched Haley. "Seems like a whole lot of drama for one crazy old lady."

"I'm sure that's what Queen Elizabeth said about Bloody Mary... well, before she was Bloody Mary." Haley rolled her eyes. "Okay, but I warned you."

She knocked on the door.

The door was tossed open like Mrs. Miars had been waiting on the other side. The old woman stood before us in all of her faded glory. She wore a baby-blue chiffon 1960s prom dress complete with puffy petticoat, a rhinestone crown, and a white sash draped from her left shoulder to just under her right hip proclaiming her as the first runner-up America's Junior Miss 1963. If the way-too-long dress was any evidence, she might have been five-seven or five-eight at one time, but the weight of years had hunched her over.

"Please come in," Edna said in a breathy Jackie-Kennedy-meets-Arkansas voice. She swept her arm grandly toward the living room. "I have tea laid out for us."

"How lovely," Haley said behind her huge fake smile. "This is Mustang, and this is Monica."

I glanced over at the living room table. It was covered in plates stacked with petits fours, finger sandwiches, croissants, cookies, and a silver tea set worthy of an afternoon at Buckingham Palace. My eyes drank in all those carb-laden goodies. How bad could she be?

I'd been so excited at the possibility of baked goods that only now did I notice all of the plastic-covered furniture. The sofa cushions were encased in clear plastic, as was the back and sides of the couch. So were the chairs, the table, and believe it or not, the TV. There was even a plastic walkway on top of the carpet. I suspected that microchip-manufacturing clean rooms weren't this dust free.

Monica caught my attention, and I could tell that she was thinking the same thing I was. What would happen if we stepped off the plastic pathway and onto the actual carpet?

Like she could read our minds, Haley turned around and shot us a "don't do it" look. She knew us too well.

"I see that you were the first runner-up in the America's Junior Miss pageant. Didn't Diane Sawyer win that year?" Monica loved her some trivia.

"Skanky-whore bitch, may she die of gonorrhea." The gracious smile never wavered off Edna's face.

I decided right then and there not to stray off the plastic path.

Monica's mouth dropped open. It took a lot to render her speechless, but there it was.

"Well, isn't this lovely." Haley nodded at the lavish tea setting. She had a master's degree in changing the subject.

"Yes, I like to throw a little something together when company is expected." Edna's dress got caught on the plastic, and she stumbled but caught herself on the edge of the plastic-encased dining room table. To her credit, she pretended like nothing had happened and commenced her regal march to the living room sofa.

As we got to the sofa before her, we stood there waiting.

Edna waved her arm graciously and said, "Please have a seat. Haley, dear, would you mind pouring?"

Haley nodded and sat, continuing to smile. With her right hand she picked up the highly polished teapot. With her left hand she held the lid down as she poured. A clear liquid splashed into the first of four ornate china teacups. The heavy scent of tequila filled the room.

"I prefer tequila to tea." Edna took her cup from Haley and knocked back the entire cupful.

Since alcohol would possibly make her more forthcoming, I motioned to Haley to fill her teacup again.

The plastic creaked loudly as Monica and I sat on the sofa.

"Help yourself to the goodies. They're fresh this morning." Edna knocked back another cupful.

She didn't have to ask me twice. I grabbed a china plate and picked up a finger sandwich. It was shinier than normal, and lighter. I thumped it. It was plastic, like the food often seen in model homes. I tested the other baked goods: all plastic. Edna loved her some plastic. What kind of sick bitch offers her guests plastic food?

My stomach rumbled and I risked the gonorrhea curse and shot her a dirty look. Since Edna was on her third teacup of tequila, I'm pretty sure she missed my death glare. Damn, I hated wasting a perfectly good dirty look on the oblivious.

Edna slurped down her fourth cup of tequila. I had to admit, the fact that she was still sitting upright was impressive. Clearly she had a high tolerance for tequila. Her liver must be bulletproof.

"Mrs. Miars, thanks for having us. I was hoping to talk to you about Molly." Might as well jump on in there before the old lady fell over.

Mrs. Miars's face crumbled and her eyes clouded over with tears. "I miss her so much."

So what if she was a little eccentric, she'd loved her daughter. That was obvious.

"She used to bring me Godiva chocolates. I really miss those chocolates." She stuck her hand down the front of her dress and pulled out a wad of Kleenex. Now her left breast was considerably smaller than her right. Evidently, she stored lots of Kleenex in her cleavage.

Like an elephant trumpeting, she blew into the wad of tissues. "That Godiva chocolate was the highlight of my day."

I take back the "she'd loved her daughter." Obviously, Molly had been nothing more than a vehicle to bring the old woman chocolate. No wonder Molly hadn't spoken often of her mother; this woman was tied with Attila the Hun for most huggable.

"To my sweet Holly... I mean Molly." Edna's words were starting to slur. She held up her teacup in a toast. "May she nest in peace."

Monica and I looked at each other, both willing the other not to make a rest-in-pieces joke. Sophomoric humor got a bad rap.

We all toasted Molly, but Mrs. Miars was the only one who drank. It's not that we didn't love Molly, but doing tequila shots right before we picked up our kids from school seemed like a bad idea.

Mrs. Miars turned to Haley. "I don't suppose you could start bringing me Godiva chocolates."

It was more of an order than a request.

Haley dropped her gaze. "I'll see what I can do."

Monica and I both stared at Haley. Over my dead body was she bringing anything to the woman who'd birthed Molly... or had she?

"Any chance Molly was adopted?" I smiled. Maybe Molly's real parents had been KGB agents on the run or perhaps serial killers—both were preferable to this woman.

"No." Mrs. Miars turned her faded blue eyes on me. "Could you bring me chocolates?"

Only if they were spiked with Drano, but that didn't seem like the best comment to make, considering that I needed information from her. "Sorry, but I'm allergic to chocolate; even the scent gives me hives. I'm so lucky that these chocolate cookies are plastic or I'd be dead right now."

"That's too bad." Mrs. Miars sighed heavily.

I'm pretty sure she was talking about the chocolates and not my fake allergy.

Her eyes drifted closed and her breathing turned shallow and rhythmic. It appeared that she'd started drinking before we'd arrived.

I picked up one of the plastic croissants and tossed it at her. It beaned her on the side of the head.

She shot up and looked around. "Yes, Hoover did borrow my pink party dress."

"Good to know." I leaned forward and propped my elbows on my knees. "About Molly. Was she seeing anyone?"

Edna's gaze zeroed in on me like she was trying to focus but couldn't quite manage it. "She saw lots of people. She had eyes."

She laughed at her own joke. Now that I saw it in action, I wasn't going to laugh at my own jokes anymore, even if mine were way funnier.

"Was she dating anyone?" I considered throwing another plastic goodie, but I needed her to not kill me. She was old and somewhat frail, but she had evil on her side, so I wasn't sure I could take her.

"Yes." She grinned from ear to ear and smoothed out an imaginary wrinkle in her dress. "She was dating a doctor... an eye doctor."

Haley and I exchanged a look. Had Molly been lying about a relationship with Dr. Dick just to appease her mother? That seemed like the most likely scenario, but the thought of her really dating him made my skin crawl.

Monica sat back and crossed her legs, plastic crunching under her. "Was there anyone else? A special friend or something?"

Edna stared off into space. Since her eyes were out of focus, I couldn't tell if she was thinking really hard or if she'd had a stroke.

"No, no one I can remember." Slowly, she put her index finger to her lips and tapped. I didn't know if she was shushing us or that was her thinking pose. "She did have a friend... she was named after a car. Let me think a minute. It might have been Maverick or Mercedes..."

"Could it have been Mustang?" I offered. I guess the introductions all the way back ten minutes ago had skipped her mind.

"Yes... that was it." She pointed to me. "Her name was Mustang. Have you tried talking to her?"

Sadness stumbled into my heart. Molly had thought of me as a dear friend. I missed her. This was the first time that I'd admitted it. After I found out what happened to her, then I'd allow myself to grieve.

"Yep." Monica nodded. "She was no help."

I did that thing where I pretended to scratch my eyebrow and flipped Monica off.

"Did anything out of the ordinary happen around the time that Molly died?" I needed answers. "Did she meet anyone new or do something that she didn't normally do?"

Like try heroin? Then again, would she really admit that to her mother?

"My cup's empty, dear." Edna held it out for Haley to fill.

"I beg your pardon." Haley couldn't help her good manners. They were part of her DNA, like eye and hair color... well, eye color. She filled Edna's cup one more time.

Edna sipped her tequila. "Now that I think about it, she did have to cancel our weekly Saturday lunch date to help a sick friend." The slightest bit of coherence flashed in her eyes. "Why are you asking me all of these questions?"

Haley topped off Edna's cup. "No reason. We were just going through Molly's... um..." I had to give her credit for starting out solid, but she'd lost it in the follow through.

"Calendar," I picked up. I was an excellent liar, where as Haley couldn't even make it through one sentence. "We wanted to make sure that there was nothing she'd left unfinished. I know that she did lots of charity work for the Baptist church and for the food pantry."

I took a mental bow for that marvelous save. Monica winked at me in appreciation.

"Oh." Edna drew the word out for several beats. "Okay."

She thought some more, or possibly had another stroke. "No, she didn't do anything... " The finger went back to the lips. "There is something."

Slowly, she inch-wormed her way off of the sofa and tried to stand, but fell back against the sofa. I reached out and righted her.

"Thank you, dear," she said in the same gracious voice she'd used to wish a social disease on Diane Sawyer. Edna staggered around the coffee table and went to a china hutch that was—you guessed it—encased in plastic. She unzipped a side panel and opened a drawer. I couldn't help but notice her vast collection of clown figurines behind the plastic and glass of the china cabinet. She shuffled some papers around, a handful of receipts dropped to the floor, and then she came up with something.

"Here it is." Edna held her hands up in a Rocky victory pose. She staggered back to the sofa and, like she'd just run a couple of marathons, sank down onto the plastic. "Here you go."

She dropped a key into my hand. It wasn't a normal-sized house key, but smaller and lighter. I had no idea what I was supposed to do with it. "What does it go to?"

"No idea." Edna's head wobbled back against the sofa back. "She said that I might need it if something happened to her."

I wanted to say, "Next time lead with that," but she was asleep again.

Monica took the key and held it up to the light. She turned it over and over. "There's not so much as a number on this sucker. It's so small, it looks like a key to a locker or a small padlock." She shook her head. "It could be anything."

It was smaller than the keys I'd found at Molly's house.

"How are we supposed to find the lock that it fits?" Haley stood. "I think we should leave before she wakes up."

I stood too. "I agree."

Monica stood. "One thing first."

She sauntered off the plastic pathway and walked right onto the deep, orange carpet. She dug her heels in, stomped a couple of times, and made her way to the front door. "That was bothering me."

Haley bit her bottom lip, eased out the sofa cushion next to Edna, flipped it over and unzipped it, took the teacup that was resting in Edna's lap, and poured the tequila on the underside of the cushion. Then she zipped it up and replaced it. "Everyone needs a sofa cushion with a stain on the bottom."

Monica nodded. "I'm so proud of you, Hales. It wasn't the top of the cushion, but it's progress."

"Good one." I patted Haley on the shoulder. "I say we stop off at Home Depot on our way back to your house and see if this key looks like it fits anything on the padlock aisle.

Edna Miars had been more help than I'd thought she would be. I couldn't see her as the killer—for one thing, Molly's death had been messy. I didn't think the princess of plastic could have taken all of that blood. For another, Molly's death had seriously impacted her Godiva chocolate fix. If Edna was Molly's killer, then my middle name was Rufus. Thank God I didn't have a middle name.

CHAPTER 12

Two evenings later, after Max and I had spent a half hour comparing the key to every lock in Home Depot and had come up with nothing, I drove up to my little guesthouse. As I turned into my private drive, my headlights reflected off a black boxy car parked in my parking space. I pulled up beside it. The car looked kinda like a fancy Hyundai. I didn't know anyone who drove a black Hyundai except my arch enemy Satan, a.k.a. Salina Atan, and I was pretty sure she wasn't here to thank me for signing her up for Cell Mate to Soul Mate—"where love shackles our hearts, not our hands"—an online dating site for prison inmates. I genuinely hoped she found true love, and just to up her odds, I'd signed her up for both men seeking women and women seeking women. People really shouldn't leave their Facebook password taped to the inside of a locked desk drawer—anyone with a vendetta and a sharp letter opener could have found it.

The Hyundai's driver-side door opened, and a tall figure stepped out.

"Who's that man?" Max pointed to the figure.

"I don't know, but stay in the car until I find out." I opened my door and slid out onto the pavement. I hadn't meant to slide, but what with Bessie's vinyl seats and my black silk-blend trousers, I'd been sliding all over the place today.

"Mustang?" The Spanish-accented voice was vaguely familiar.

Now I saw that the car was a Rolls-Royce and not a Hyundai. Thank God I didn't comment on his nice Hyundai. Rich people get so mad when you mix up their expensive possessions. One day in the parking lot at work, I'd complimented a lady's huge topaz ring. Her eyes got all big and she informed me that it was a whiskey diamond. When she came in a couple of weeks later to pay her husband's hospital bill, I complimented her on her Kool-Aid diamond, just to piss her off. It worked; she was pissed off. Sarcasm is just another service we offer in Lakeside Regional Hospital's billing department. Pissing people off and price-gouging the idle rich by charging fifteen dollars for a Band-Aid are really the only entertainment sources I have. It's the simple things in life.

"Yes?" I got closer and saw the killer dimples. "Mr. Rodriguez?"

I couldn't remember if I was supposed to call him Daman or not.

"It's Daman." He slid his hands into the front pockets of his jeans.

Well, that mystery was solved. I tried to think of a nice way to ask why he was here, but nice isn't my natural state of being. "What can I do for you?"

"Mom, is he here to kill us or can I get out of the car?" Max yelled from the passenger's-side window.

When Max had been a baby, I'd thought it was a good idea to teach him to speak. Now I regretted that decision.

"I think we're good." I waved for him to come on over. I was like 90 percent sure Daman wasn't here to kill us... okay, 85 percent.

Max jumped out of the car as I unlocked and opened my front door, flipped on the lights, and stepped aside, letting Daman go first. "Would you like to come in?"

I'd never had a drug lord in my house before; then again, I'd never had a rodeo clown or a tent revival preacher or WWF wrestler either. I did have a transvestite once, but that had been at Halloween, so I still didn't know if he was really a cross-dresser or just pretending for the evening. Either way, he'd rocked that gold bikini.

Daman held the door for me and Max, and then he walked into my tiny guesthouse. While Daman wasn't a giant, he was well over six feet and muscled. He made my little house seem even smaller.

"Have a seat." I gestured to the sofa in front of the fireplace, then turned to Max. "What's the homework situation?"

We had company, but homework came first.

"Taken care of." Max grinned. "Mr. Battus let us do our math homework in class. What's for dinner?"

"I've taken the liberty of ordering some dinner for us." Daman sat on the sofa.

He wanted to have dinner with us? And he'd ordered it? I hoped it involved carbs. Every time I turned around, there was a handsome man bringing me food. I hadn't popped a frozen pizza in the oven for days. My electric bill should be pretty damn low this month.

"I ordered pizza from Franco's. When I gave them your address, they asked if I wanted your usual. So I got that plus a meatball pizza." Daman shrugged one shoulder. "I hope that's okay."

I really thought Max was going to kiss him. "Yeah. We love Franco's."

I'm almost ashamed of the fact that we love it so much that Jimbo the delivery driver felt like family. He was over so much that Max had invited him to his last birthday party, and Jimbo had actually come.

"That sounds wonderful." I looped my work tote on the back of a kitchen chair. "Thank you."

Why was he here? Sure, it was nice, but it just didn't make sense. We didn't run in the same circles, have the same friends—well, except for Haley—or have much in common.

Max sat on the sofa beside Daman. Max's eyes turned huge. "I just figured out who you are... you're D-Rod."

I walked the five feet from my kitchen to the sofa. How did my son know a drug lord? "How do you know Daman?"

"Mom, He's D-Rod, the best striker in the history of soccer... well, Mexican football. He was on the Mexican team when they almost won the World Cup in 2006." Max looked at me like I was crazy for not recognizing D-Rod.

So Daman went from a pro-athlete to a criminal. That seemed to happen a lot in today's society.

"Mom, are you sure you don't want to go put on that red sweater?" Max jerked his head toward my room. Daman was a famous soccer player and had ordered pizza from Max's favorite place on earth. My little boy would probably have me married to Daman before dinner arrived.

There was a pounding on my door.

Or not. Marriage would have to wait until dessert. "I'll get it."

I walked to the door and opened it. Jimbo's smiling face, and more importantly, the large, square thermal holder with hot pizza inside was here. "Mrs. R., looking good."

I moved to the side and gestured for him to come in. "Put it on the table."

"Okey dokey." Jimbo propped the thermal box holding the pizzas on the table and slid them out. He nodded to Max. "How's life M-man?"

"Good." Max pointed to Daman and said in a stage whisper, "This is D-Rod."

Jimbo looked to me for an explanation.

"Famous soccer player." And drug lord. I mentally patted myself on the back for leaving out the last part. My self-control was becoming legendary, at least in my own mind.

"Thanks for setting up that interview in Radiology for me. I got the job. I start next week."

Jimbo was going to schedule Radiology appointments, and all I'd had to do was wear a low-cut dress and lean over the Radiology reception counter to ask Dr. Haverman if he'd do me a favor. "It was the least I could do since you feed my family on a regular basis."

"Ahhh, you're my favorite customers." He offered me a fist bump and I bumped back.

I grabbed my purse off the chair and unzipped it. At least I could take care of the tip. Daman had paid for the pizzas and saved us from the frozen fish sticks I'd planned for dinner. Yes, there are still frozen fish sticks. Don't judge me, I had a coupon.

"The tip has already been taken care of." Jimbo grabbed the thermal container and looked over at Daman. "Thank you, Mr. D-Rod, you were very generous. I gotta run."

He headed for the door. "Catch you later, M-man." Jimbo waved to Max as he opened the door. He walked out and closed it behind him.

"Max, please set the table." I shot him a look that said he better not bring up the fact that we usually eat pizza on the sofa and directly out of the box.

"Let me help." Daman stood and stretched.

"We've got it. You bought dinner, the least we can do is set the table." I still had no idea why he was here, but I was willing to wait around until he got to it only because he brought really good pizza. I grabbed plates from the cabinet next to the sink.

"I insist." Daman was at my side. "I'll get the glasses."

He eyed the cabinet with the small padlock that held the murder board. "I'm guessing you don't keep the glasses locked up."

The strangest thought hit me. What if he was here to search for his lost diamonds? I'm sure a padlocked kitchen cabinet looked more than a little suspicious. I was pretty sure that as a drug lord he had mad lockpicking skills, but I really needed to stop jumping to conclusions. Then again, conclusion jumping was really the only exercise that I got. Maybe I should do it more so I could eat more cupcakes.

"No, that's where I keep all of my stolen diamonds." I clamped a hand over my mouth. Did I mention that I don't have a filter from my brain to my mouth? While it's gotten me in trouble in the past, I was pretty sure that tonight it was going to get me killed. I choked out some forced and somewhat hysterical laughter, so possibly he would think I was kidding or crazy. At this point, either one was better than dead.

I was a terrible mother. I'd just gotten my son murdered before he got to eat his favorite pizza.

Daman threw back his head and laughed. I looked around in case that was the signal for his squad of hit men to storm the place. No one repelled down from the roof, crashed through my windows, or knocked down my front door.

I looked down to find that I was hugging the plates to my chest like a Kevlar vest. Carefully, I peeled the plates from under my left breast and laid them out on the table.

"You're very funny." Daman shot me those dimples again. "I like that."

I didn't know whether to fake laugh again or continue setting the table. I settled for a single shoulder shrug and setting out the napkins.

"If you think I'm here because of the diamonds—"

"Max, why don't you go put your backpack in your room and then wash up for dinner." I shot him another mom look that said he didn't need to mention that we'd never washed up for anything.

Max rolled his eyes and headed to his room.

I waited until the door was closed.

"He doesn't know about the stolen diamonds. I just learned about them a couple of days ago. We don't know where your diamonds are. Trust me, if I had a million dollars worth of diamonds, would I live here?" I spun around to drive the point home. "The only diamond that David ever gave me was the itty-bitty one he slipped on my finger after he proposed." Which I'd hocked ten minutes after he'd left so I could buy my son a new pair of athletic shoes. I almost made enough to cover the shoes.

His dark chocolate eyes stayed on me. "I'm not here about the diamonds. That's between me and the City of Lakeside."

"Just out of curiosity, what does a million dollars in diamonds look like? I'd guess it's a whole bunch of diamonds... like pounds." I thought about it for a second. "I guess diamonds aren't weighed in pounds."

He hunched his shoulders. "Nowhere close to pounds or even ounces. The bag that went missing from police evidence was a small, black, velvet drawstring bag with 132 diamonds. All different sizes."

"That's not nearly as impressive as pounds of diamonds. I'd rather think of a million dollars in diamonds as one giant diamond the size of a baseball." Hmmm, would a baseball diamond—pun intended—weigh more or less than an actual baseball?

"You're good at changing the subject." His boyish smile was downright dangerous. "But I'm still curious about what's in the locked cabinet."

Don't say "murder board," don't say "murder board." I crossed my arms and matched his smile. "Cleaning supplies."

"Somehow, I don't believe you." He opened the cabinet next to the murder board, found the glasses, and grabbed three. "I could pick the lock and see."

Totally nailed it on the lockpicking skills.

"Cool, can you teach me how to pick a lock?" It seemed like a good thing to know how to do.

He stared at me for a full beat and then shook his head. "You're the strangest woman I've ever met."

"Around here that's saying something." I was perfectly normal, no matter what the Rorschach test said.

"Tell me about it." He set the glasses down on the table, one by each plate.

At the risk of offending a drug lord, I asked, "So why are you really here? Not that I'm not grateful for dinner, but it's a little unexpected."

Do I have a talent for understatement or what?

"You're all business, I like that." He scratched the back of his neck and looked around. "I'll be honest with you, I've wanted to meet you for a long time."

My bullshit meter clanged in my head. "Why?"

He held his index finger to his lips in the universal "be quiet" gesture. He slid his hand into his back pocket and pulled out a small rectangular black device about the size of a fat cell phone. It had a grid of red lights on the front. He switched it on and moved it over my kitchen table and then moved on to the kitchen cabinets.

"What the hell?" Lately my life had taken a turn for the weird. Sure, it had been weird before, but Daman was taking it to a new level.

He stepped into my personal space, leaned down, and whispered next to my ear, "Your house has a bug problem. You're under surveillance."

CHAPTER 13

I stood there while the verbal grenade he'd just tossed out in front of me exploded. Someone had bugged my house? I looked around like the listening devices would jump out and run around.

"What?" I understood his words, but it didn't make sense to me.

He leaned in even closer and his lips brushed my earlobe. "Just act normal and let me sweep the place."

I almost pointed to the broom, but I didn't. Queen of self-restraint, right here.

"Why would I be under surveillance?" I whispered. I knew I should be scared, but honestly, the first thing that popped into my mind was that surveilling me must be so disappointing. Some people really had too much free time.

"Molly Miars." His lips tickled my earlobe again.

Adrenaline slammed through my system. This was about Molly? Holy crap, what had she been into? For that matter, what had she gotten me into?

Max wasn't safe here; I wasn't safe. We needed to move. I glanced in the direction of my bedroom. Our suitcases were under my bed. I needed to pack. We would go... where?

He gripped my shoulder and pulled me into him. "You look like you're about to lose it. Stay with me. Focus on the sound of my voice. I'm going to take care of this problem for you."

"Why?" I didn't know him that well, and he was possibly a drug lord.

"Looking into Molly Miars's death has put you on the radar of some very dangerous people." His breath tickled the side of my cheek and sent little tingles up and down my spine.

"Why are you helping me?" I needed to get out of here. The only problem was, I didn't have anywhere else to go, and I had like thirty-five dollars to my name. Payday wasn't until next week. If I was on the run, would I still need to pay my electric bill?

"Calm down." Daman hugged me against his chest. "You're shaking."

Gently, he rocked me back and forth.

Man, he smelled good. Usually I didn't like men who wore cologne, mostly because they tended to think that more is better, but Daman wore something that mixed perfectly with his body chemistry and produced a deliciously sinful smell. Once, in college, I'd followed a guy across campus because he smelled so good. Unfortunately I lost him in the quad—my life could have been way different if I'd been willing to run after him, but I was wearing heels. C'est la vie.

There was something I'd been worried about before my ovaries sidetracked me... oh yeah, my house was bugged.

"Molly died of a drug overdose... ask anyone." Except me or Monica or Haley. "There's nothing to look into."

It's not that I didn't trust Daman, it's just that, well... I didn't trust him. Up until five minutes ago, I was sure that he was here to kill me, and now he was holding me and patting my back like I was a frightened child.

"Mom, what's going on?" Max leaned against the sofa back and crossed his arms. He might want me to put on my red sweater to impress D-Rod, but the reality of seeing me in Daman's arms was a different story.

Daman dropped his arms and I stepped back.

“Nothing. Daman just, um...” I let my voice fade to keep from telling him that our house might be bugged.

“Max, how about some pizza?” Daman moved in for the save. “After dinner, I’ll tell you all about the World Cup.”

Max shrugged and headed to the table. Apparently, pizza and soccer were way more important than why he’d found dear old Mom in the arms of a man he didn’t know. Chalk one up for stranger danger.

Dinner was largely a quiet affair, as I wasn’t sure exactly what to say now that I knew my house was bugged. Every time Max opened his mouth to talk, I offered him another piece of pizza. After the pizza was nothing more than a pile of half-chewed crust, I closed the boxes, stood, tucked them under my arm, and headed to the door. “I’ll be right back. I need to throw these away in the big can outside.”

Daman took the boxes from me. “I’ll help.”

Max rolled his eyes.

I couldn’t get outside fast enough. As soon as Daman closed the door, I leaned into him. “Are there any bugs out here?”

He shook his head and whispered, “Only the insect variety. Too much wind noise, but cameras could be a problem.”

I looked around for something like a traffic cam. How hard could those be to find?

“Stop looking around. Just lean in close and laugh like I said something funny.” He tossed the pizza boxes in the trash and then hugged me into him.

“Why?” I leaned into him and tried to laugh. It came out as more of a cackle, but he’d said there weren’t any mics out here, so it didn’t matter.

“Because if they do have cameras trained on us right now, it will look like we’re just on a date. Two people enjoying each other's company, out stargazing." He pointed to the sky.

"You don't go on very many dates, do you?" I pretended to stare up at his hand.

"Why do you say that?" The dimples were back.

"People haven't stargazed on a date since electricity was invented. Now we meet at chic bistros and order flights of wine and weird cheeses from a menu written on a large sandwich board that the server wears strapped to his back." I watched as he traced the big dipper. That was kind of neat.

"That sounds really uncomfortable—the sandwich board thing." He pointed to the stars in Orion's belt.

"Who's bugging my house?" And why? What had Molly been into? "How is this related to Molly?"

I shivered. I was freezing. It had to be in the forties tonight. Daman shrugged out of his black leather jacket and hung it on my shoulders. It smelled like him, and I drew in a long breath. Drug lords and chivalry—did they have a code of honor or something?

"Yep, we're on camera." He nodded his head slightly to the left and pointed up at the stars again. "On your six o'clock. Don't look."

Had Daman been in the military? I actually knew that "on your six" was a military term, based on all of those war movies David used to haul me to.

"Copy that." I decided to speak military too. We had a theme going, best not to change it.

"Kiss me." He was all serious.

"Why?" It sounded a lot like "no." He was hot—there was no arguing that—but he may or may not be a drug lord. He'd brought dinner though, and I kind of wanted to kiss him. Indecision, this is why it takes me an hour to pick out something to wear in the morning.

"Because all of this pointing is making my arm tired." He cut his gaze toward me. "Does all of that thinking hurt?

It looks like you're trying to recall the first million digits of pi."

"Oh... I like pie, especially à la mode." It's not that I didn't want to kiss him, but he had the whole bad boy thing going. And I'd given up bad boys around the time I'd gotten divorced.

"Seriously, I'm a terrific kisser." He nodded.

"Is this the part where you pull out the breath spray and squirt it in your mouth?" Because I'd already been through that with Dr. Dick.

"I would if my arm wasn't shaking from pointing up at the night sky." His shoulders shook with laughter. "Do you have any breath spray? Feel free to squirt it at any time."

Crap, did I need breath spray? The pizza sauce did have a lot of garlic. Was there a way to discreetly smell my breath?

Daman lowered his arm, turned to me, and slid both of his hands around my waist. His head lowered. Gently, he kissed one corner of my mouth and then the other before his soft lips settled on mine. Oh yeah, he could kiss. His tongue slid past my open lips and did some swirly thing that sent pleasure tingling all the way down to my toes.

He ended the kiss and pulled me into his chest for a hug. That's when I noticed that my hands had fisted in his shirt like I was trying to crawl up him. I let the shirt go and smoothed it down. Underneath, Daman had some hard, nice pecs. He gave me one last tight squeeze and then let me go.

I glanced behind me, checking my six. There was nothing. I shrugged off his jacket and handed it back to him. "There is no camera."

He grinned like the cat who'd eaten the canary. "No ma'am, I just wanted to kiss you."

"Oh my God." I punched him on the arm. "You made that up? Did you make up the bugs too?"

I reached for the doorknob, but he got there first.

"Nope. Your house has more microphones than the SETI listening station," he whispered. "Don't worry. I've got a jamming device that you can use when you need a little privacy. I can't remove the bugs, because then whoever bugged you will know that you're on to them. You can't use the jammer all the time, or again, they'll know. Just use it when you're talking about Molly Miars. I'll bring it over tomorrow."

I touched his arm. "Why are you helping me?"

"I like you." He let the full meaning of that fall between us. "A lot."

What does it say about me that I was suspicious? A hot guy stumbles into my life to teach me gun safety and sweep my house for bugs? All because he spent a couple of hours with me one Saturday? I didn't believe it for one minute. Daman knew something about Molly's death, and I aimed to find out what it was.

CHAPTER 14

The next morning my cell phone thundered out "All About That Bass." Letting people pick out their own personal ringtone for my phone was a bad idea.

I rolled over and picked up my phone. It was six thirty-two. Hadn't we talked about Monica not calling before noon on Saturdays? Freakin' morning people; there ought to be a law against awakeness before noon.

"You better have found the real reason for daylight savings time and are rooting out the evil that keeps it alive." I might be yelling, but it was too early for my brain to work.

"The key belongs to a safety deposit box." Monica sounded triumphant.

"Key?" It took a nanosecond for my brain to process her words. I sat up. "The key. A safety deposit box to which bank?"

The only thing Lakeside had more of than old people were banks. There were four on every corner—banks, not old people.

"No clue." All of the air went out of Monica's sails.

"How did you figure out the safety deposit box part?" I yawned and stretched. Morning people were right up there with phone solicitors and carb-haters on my list of evildoers.

"It turns out that there's an app for key identification. I used the picture I took of it and the program identified it as a safety deposit box key. I think we need to go to Molly's house and find out where she banks." Monica returned my yawn. Apparently they were contagious even over the phone.

"I didn't find a bank statement or anything like that before, but I wasn't really looking for it." My phone buzzed with another call. I pulled it away from my ear to find Haley's face on my screen. "Hang on, Hal's on the other line. Let me conference her in."

I put Monica on hold and answered Haley's call.

"Daman kissed you last night, and you didn't call me?" To say she was accusatory was putting it mildly.

"Hang on, Monica's on the other line. She figured out that the key is for a safety deposit box." I conferenced them in. "Okay, we're all on the line."

What if my cell phone was bugged? Crap. My brain was working now.

"Y'all hang on. Give me a minute." I threw off my pink comforter, the only extravagance I'd allowed myself after David left. I'd burned all of the bedding and everything of his that I couldn't sell. With the proceeds of the David's-stuff yard sale, I'd bought yummy, soft, pink, thousand-thread-count sheets and a matching comforter. A girl had to have some vices.

With my phone tucked between my ear and shoulder, I stumbled into the kitchen. Did I mention that I'm not a morning person? I grabbed the bug detector device I'd dubbed the bug zapper and flicked the power switch to on. I held it next to my phone. The lights on the front lit up like the Christmas tree in Zilker Park.

Well, double crap.

Whoever was listening now knew we had a safety deposit box key.

I put the phone back to my ear. "I can't talk right now. Are y'all up for pancakes at Kerbey Lane?"

"I could eat some pancakes." Monica was in.

"Okay, thirty minutes?" Haley dropped the phone and then picked it up again. "Sorry. I'm back. Yes, we can do

Kerbey Lane. Wait, make it forty-five minutes. I need to get the girls ready. Today is Anise's day off."

"Forty-five minutes at the Lane." I hung up and headed to the bathroom. Now whoever was listening knew we were going to Kerbey Lane. That was probably bad. Would they be waiting at the Westlake restaurant? Was my bathroom bugged? Besides the toilet flushing and shower water hitting the drain, why would anyone bug a bathroom? I turned around and picked up the bug zapper. I wasn't comfortable with someone listening to me shower. It made me feel dirty, and since the shower was the only way for me to feel clean, it would be very bad if someone bugged my bathroom. What if I burst into song or decided to recite the facts we'd found in Molly's case aloud as I lathered, rinsed, and repeated?

Was I being overly paranoid?

I watched the bug zapper like a hawk. Not once did it light up in my lavatory. So the people on the other end of my listening devices weren't perverts? Well, that's a relief. Funny, it didn't make me feel any better.

Forty-three minutes later, Max and I walked into Kerbey Lane. The upscale diner with its white and chrome color scheme and occasional pops of lime green looked more South Beach-y than Westlake-y. At least this was what I thought South Beach would look like, but I'd never been there.

Haley, her girls, and Monica and her son Landon, were seated at two tables that had been pushed together in the front left corner of the restaurant. Besides the staff, we were the only ones here. Well, at seven thirty in the morning, I guess so. The rest of the world was sleeping.

As soon as Max saw Landon, he dropped my hand and ran to his friend. I followed behind him, walking of course. I'd left my phone in the car on purpose. I watched TV. Bad guys could use the microphone in my phone to hear our whole conversation. And Hollywood was always 100 percent accurate—really.

Daman had said that I couldn't remove the bugs, so I'd have to start doing things without my phone.

I leaned down and hugged Haley from behind. I whispered close to her ear. "My phone and house are bugged. Hand me your phone and let me see if yours is too."

She looked at me like I'd lost my mind and then shrugged and gave me her phone.

"What's going on?" Monica called from across the table. "Haley looks like she's just seen a ghost."

"Nothing." I shot her a shut-up look.

It must have worked because she shut up.

I pulled the bug zapper from my purse and held it up to Haley's phone. It didn't go off. I walked around to Monica and whispered, "My phone and home are bugged. Let me check your phone."

"Really?" She didn't look convinced, but she handed me her phone. I held the bug zapper against it. Nothing happened.

"Both of your phones are clean." I sat at the head of the two tables, which meant that Monica and Haley were on either side of me. The kids sat around the other table talking Minecraft.

Monica and Haley both stared at me expectantly.

"Spill. Now." Monica was losing her calm. Not that she'd ever had that much to begin with, but it was definitely on the decline.

I glanced at Max. He wasn't paying attention to anything but the iPad where he and Landon were building something in Minecraft.

"Last night, when we got home, Daman was waiting for us. He invited himself to dinner, but in all fairness he brought pizza, so I was okay with that plan. I told him that I didn't know anything about his missing diamonds, in case he was there about those."

"Good thinking, because a drug dealer is so honest and trustworthy." Monica's tone implied an eye roll, but I was watching Max so I missed it.

"He's a drug lord, not a dealer. He's management," Haley whispered as she watched her girls. "That's better, right?"

Slowly, Monica and I turned our heads to stare at her.

"Yeah. That's so much better." Monica was the queen of sarcasm. This time I got to see her eye roll in all its glory.

"Management is always good," Haley said under her breath.

"Anyway, he told me that he thought my house was bugged, and he brought this." I held up the bug zapper. "He was right. There are bugs in every room except the bathroom. My phone is bugged too."

"Why?" Monica crossed her arms and leaned back.

"Molly. Apparently she was into something bad... very bad. Our looking into her death is getting attention." I felt a little overdramatic.

One corner of Monica's mouth curled up. "Aren't you being overdramatic?"

Nailed it.

"That was my first reaction when Daman suggested it, but once he swept my house for bugs, it was clear that he knew what he was talking about." It was still hard to believe that anyone cared enough about little ole me to listen in on my conversations.

"Has it ever occurred to you that he might have planted those bugs?" Monica put the skeptic in skeptic. "Let me guess... he told you not to remove the bugs because the," she threw up some air quotes, "bad people would know that you're on to them."

That certainly made more sense than Molly being into something shady. "You mean so he could find his stolen diamonds? Crap. I feel like an idiot."

He'd plied me with pizza and then played me like a pair of aces on poker night. Was "idiot" stamped on my forehead? I almost went to the bathroom to look.

"Think about it. If he wasn't in on it, how would he know that your house was bugged? It's not like house bugging is a common thing. I've certainly never had a friend come over and say, 'Hey, I think your house is bugged.' It's weird." Monica picked up her Diet Coke and sipped.

I knew it was Diet Coke because that's all she ever drank. I'd heard somewhere that Diet Coke has so many preservatives that it keeps your body from decomposing after you're dead. I'm pretty sure that in a thousand years, Monica will look exactly like she does now. Maybe Diet Coke was the fountain of youth?

"He's going to be pretty bored listening to my house." I felt like a fool.

"Unless... he was telling the truth." Haley wanted to believe that all was good and kind in the world. "There's a simple way of telling if he's being honest. Let's see if our houses are bugged too. If all he wants are the diamonds, why bug our houses?"

"He may think that we might know where they are." Monica's voice wavered. "That is a stretch. I'm game. After breakfast, let's head to my house and see."

It seemed like a lot of extra work to bug their houses on the off chance that I'd bring it up while visiting them. If this was related to Molly, then it was reasonable that their houses would be bugged too. Part of me wanted their houses to be bugged because I liked Daman... all his drug lording aside.

"Now to the kissing part..." Haley—ever the romantic—wasn't going to let this go.

"How did you know about that?" I was constantly amazed by Haley's ability to glean information. She had Lakeside wired as well as my house was.

"Dulce told her sister Marisol that she'd seen you kissing him out by the recycle bin last night. Marisol plays bridge with Becky Sims, who told her personal chef Gabriel. He also cooks for Nat and John Holder, who live three houses down from me. Nat and I are both on the performing arts board, and she mentioned the kiss to me while we were hashing out the refreshments for the next board meeting."

"Damn, that's complicated. I'm going to need a flowchart." Monica nodded like she was trying to connect all of the dots.

"Nat told me that it was a very passionate kiss." Haley's eyebrows rose as she sipped her coffee.

"I'm not going to lie, sparks did fly, and he's an exceptional kisser, but in light of new evidence," I glanced at Monica, "the spark has died out."

"Too bad," Haley said all dreamily. "I was counting on your dating him so I could live vicariously."

"Me too." Monica matched her dreamy expression.

"He's a drug lord... Okay, so he's hot, but he's a bugged-my-house drug lord," I whispered. "Okay, I'm a little bummed."

"Damn." Monica sat up. "Your phone is bugged, and I told you about the safety deposit box this morning."

"Don't worry. I've got a plan for that. I think you need to call me later today and tell me that you were wrong. The key goes to a padlock or something. We'll go look at her house and pretend it's for a padlock." I propped my chin in my hand. "If the bugs are about Molly, we need to assume that her house is bugged too." But we wouldn't know for sure until we checked Monica's and Haley's homes.

An hour later, Monica and I pulled into her duplex's driveway. The Arapahoe Shores Duplexes took up one whole street next to the water treatment plant and were Lakeside's equivalent to inner city public housing. The rent was fifteen hundred a month, which by Lakeside's standards was pocket change. By my standards, that was pie-in-the-sky high. Since I couldn't afford Arapahoe Shores, what did that make me... aspiring to poverty?

Monica put her silver Honda Civic in park and turned off the engine. We'd taken her car after we dropped Haley and the kids off at the Hill Country Galleria. They were getting hot chocolates and checking out books from the library. I loved that our library was in the mall. It was right across from Barnes and Noble. I'd go into Barnes and Noble, find the book I wanted, and then go to the library and check it out. Poverty has made me thrifty. No wait, that's a lie. I totally did the same thing before I had to give up my not-so-strapped-for-cash lifestyle.

Monica opened her car door. "Think we need to check the garage?"

She was all fancy-schmancy with her garage. "I guess."

She reached back into her car and clicked the button on her garage door opener. The metal door rolled up. We walked into her garage. Monica liked to refinish old furniture. Well, that's not true. She liked to start refinishing old furniture. Her garage was stacked with half-finished projects. My fingers itched to clean up this mess, but the last time I'd suggested it she'd growled at me, so I pulled out the bug zapper and walked around the room. I hadn't gotten two feet when it lit up like the disco ball the Knights of Columbus used on bingo night. I'll admit it, I'd tried playing bingo to supplement my income, but those little old ladies were vicious and they scared the crap out of me. Gangster rappers have nothing on the rabid old ladies at the Knights of Columbus bingo night.

Inside Monica's house, every single room had at least two listening devices.

Monica looked at me and shook her head. She picked up a yellow legal pad and black Sharpie that were sitting on her kitchen table. She wrote something and then turned it around for me to see. "Let's go outside."

I nodded. I hadn't thought to scan her car for bugs, so I ran the bug zapper around the car. It was clean. We got into the car and closed the doors.

"I can't fucking believe it. Who the hell would want to bug my house? I never do anything exciting." Monica's brown eyes were enormous. "This is ridiculous."

She put her hand on the lever to open the car door. "I'm going in there and destroying them all."

I put a hand on her arm. "That's exactly what I said to Daman, but he said it's a bad idea. Think about it. We know about the bugs, so now we won't say anything useful. If we take them out, they're just going to put in new ones or do something worse."

This was a conversation I never thought I'd be having. Now if I could just have a conversation where someone tells me that I've won the lottery, I can get another never-thought-I'd-have-that conversation out of the way.

Monica slumped back in her seat. "I can't believe it. I feel so violated."

"You're preaching to the choir. I've never been so quiet in my own home. Max asked me what was wrong. I told him I had a headache." I couldn't tell Max about the bugs. It would freak him out, and he needed to feel safe.

"I wonder if there's a way to find out who's doing this." Monica never took anything lying down. She was a fighter. I totally loved that about her. "On Monday, I'll ask a couple of the private investigators we have on staff. They should be able to help." She turned to me. "What was Molly into?"

"No idea. I think we do need to go to her house and find out which bank she used. The safety deposit box key is the only lead we have. Now more than ever, we need to know who has us under surveillance. Do you think Daman had anything to do with this?"

I wanted her to say no, but I knew that was a stretch.

"If he isn't involved, how would he know that your house was bugged?" She shook her head. "Then again, why would he tell you? Doesn't that defeat the purpose of bugging your house?"

"Yeah." I took a deep breath and let it out slowly. "I think we can assume that Haley's house is bugged too, but I'll check later today. It feels like we've stepped into an episode of *Covert Affairs*."

"Tell me about it. I keep waiting for the punch line, only there isn't one." She shook her head like she just couldn't believe this was happening to her. "Why would anyone go to the trouble to bug my house? I'm a nobody. I have no life."

"Daman said that it had to do with Molly's murder. He could be lying, but really, besides the PTO that's the only thing that links the three of us... besides friendship." I hunched my shoulders. "I can't think of any PTO business that's bug worthy, apart from the heated discussion the moms go into over the fourth grade spirit shirts." I rolled my eyes. "Some people take pink rhinestones way too seriously."

Monica turned the engine over and backed out of her driveway. "It's too weird. Now I don't know what to say in my own home."

"I hear ya. I don't think we can get rid of the bugs, but I do think we should use them to our advantage. From now on, we only say what we want others to hear. If someone is listening in, let's mess with them."

If there was one thing I was good at, it was messing with people. This was game on.

CHAPTER 15

Monday morning, I called in sick, and Haley and I went to Molly's house. I felt guilty for calling in sick for a whole ten seconds, and then I was over it. I'd never used a sick day, and I had several of them saved up. Occasionally I do take off work early, but other than that, I'm a model employee most of the time... okay, some of the time.

Armed with my set of keys, the bug zapper, a legal pad, and a black Sharpie, I marched up to Molly's front door and unlocked it.

"Wait for me." Haley slid out of her Range Rover, grabbed her own legal pad and marker, and followed me into the house. The second I stepped inside Molly's house, the lights on the bug zapper went red. Her house was bugged too.

This confirmed that the "bugging," as Monica had come to call it, was definitely related to Molly Miars. Clearly that was bad, but I had to admit that I was relieved our houses weren't bugged because Daman was trying to find his diamonds. He was still involved in the bugging, but this wasn't about stolen diamonds.

Haley and I had worked out a script of sorts in case Molly's house was bugged.

I started.

"Since the key wasn't a safety deposit box key, we need to look for a padlock," I read from the first page of my legal pad. I am willing to admit that my voice was louder and a little more mechanical than normal.

"Yes. That is correct." Haley sounded like a fifth grader reading from a script for the Valentine's play.

We both sucked as actors.

Wait a minute. I was a fantastic actor. I'd faked hundred of orgasms throughout my marriage. I could do this.

"The key is little, so it goes to a little padlock, or maybe a bike lock." I threw in that last bit as improv.

Haley looked at me and mouthed, "Bike lock?"

I shrugged. Didn't she understand artistic license?

"Okay, I will look for a small padlock or bike lock." Haley continued the elementary school monotone. "How about a book on tape to pass the time while we search?"

"Sure. Sounds good to me." I added in all the emotion of a Mexican soap opera. One of us needed to ramp up the emo if we were going to pull this off.

"Okay, here goes." Haley pulled out her phone. She touched the iTunes icon and piano music thundered out. James Earl Jones began, "James Earl Jones reads the Bible, the New Testament, King James Version. The Gospel According to Matthew..."

On my legal pad, I wrote, "The New Testament?"

I turned it around so Haley could read it.

She scribbled something on her legal pad and then turned it around for me to see. "I thought the people bugging us could use a heavy dose of Jesus."

She had a point.

James Earl Jones droned on. I kept hoping he'd say, "Luke, I am your father," but sadly Luke Skywalker hadn't made it into the Bible.

We searched our way through the front-parlor-turned-bedroom and found nothing. When I opened the closet to show Haley all of those plastic bins full of crap, she wrote on her legal pad and turned it around to me. "I thought you were kidding. What's with all of this junk?"

I wrote, "No idea, but she liked her some junk. At least she kept her hoarding organized."

We searched the kitchen, the weird envelope hoarding room, the upstairs, and then we headed out to the garage.

I leaned into Haley and whispered, "If you thought the envelope filing was weird, wait until you see this."

I tried the keys on the ring until I found the right one. I pushed open the door, flicked on the light, and found a totally empty garage.

"What the hell?" I said it out loud. I couldn't help it. "Where's the chemistry set?"

Haley smiled at me like she was assuring her daughter Riley that she really could see her invisible friend. "I'm sure it was very nice."

"It was here. I swear." I figured that since the people who'd bugged the place already knew about it and had taken it, our talking about it wouldn't make a difference.

I walked around looking for any hint that the chemistry set had been here. There wasn't so much as a scuff mark on the tiled floor. The floor and walls were clean as a whistle. I couldn't help but be impressed by Molly's killer's level of commitment. If I couldn't find fault with it, the room was sterile enough to do surgery in. Maybe the killer owned a cleaning service? If so I'd give them a reference, because they did good work. Well, apart from the whole murder thing.

James Earl Jones barked out, "He saith unto them. How many loaves have ye? Go and see. And when they knew, they said, five and two fishes."

My stomach rumbled. The loaves and fishes always made me hungry.

"It looks like we've come up with a big fat zero on a padlock." I was reading from the script again.

"Yes, we found nothing." Haley's voice was even louder than James Earl Jones. "I guess we will just go home empty-handed."

Acting clearly wasn't her forte.

I turned off the lights, closed the door, and locked it.

Haley turned off James Earl Jones, and we headed back to the car. As my hand touched my door handle to open it, Haley tapped on my shoulder.

She showed me her legal pad. "Where are the lima beans? What about the tree?"

Since I tend to stop listening after someone mentions lima beans, it took me a second to register what she was talking about. I crooked my finger in the universal follow-me gesture. I led her to the backyard.

The plastic tent and tree were missing. Whoever had taken them had done a good job, but the ground where the tree had been was slightly higher than the surrounding dirt.

"It was here, I swear." I pointed to where the tree had been. It seemed like I'd been saying "It was here, I swear" a lot today.

"Okay, whatever you say." Haley turned her pad around. She'd written, "Don't mention the pics you took."

"Whoever is behind this is smarter than me." I rolled my eyes. "I give up."

I didn't think that would deter them, but hey, it was worth a shot.

"Me too. I am tired of wasting my time." Haley grinned, very proud of herself for going off script. She wrote, "I'm getting into this."

She did sound less like a robot.

"Let's get out of here." I walked toward the backyard gate. "Hold up. Let me make sure I locked the back door."

I trotted up the steps to the back porch and checked the door. It was locked.

As I turned away, I tripped over the corner of the black welcome mat and stubbed my toe. "Damn, that hurts."

I reached down to massage my toe.

Sunlight reflected off the back window and hit something metallic on the wood slats of the porch. I leaned over. It was silver and shiny. I got down on my knees and snapped my fingers to get Haley's attention. She ran up the steps.

"Crap. I think I left my flashlight inside." I heaved an I'm-so-stupid-but-what-can-I-do sigh and pointed down. "I just stubbed my toe. Can you go find my flashlight for me?"

I handed her the keys and scribbled "Find me a hammer" on my legal pad and showed it to her.

She nodded and took the keys. "Be right back."

The shiny, silver thing that had drawn me down on my knees was a nail. A brand-new nail. I pulled the welcome mat back and glanced around. All of the other nails were age appropriate to the century-old farmhouse. This could have just been a loose board that Molly had nailed down, but my gut was telling me otherwise. This house was pier and beam, not concrete slab like houses were now. If I were going to hide something, this would be an excellent place.

I tried to yank the board up, but it didn't budge.

"Here's your flashlight." Haley handed me the hammer.

"Thanks." I took the hammer. "Do you have a Band-Aid? My toe is bleeding."

Her gaze went to my toe and she shot me the what-are-you-talking-about look.

I pointed to the phone in her hand. "I think I'll just sit here until it stops throbbing."

I wrote, "Turn on the Bible."

She nodded and touched the iTunes icon again. James Earl Jones said, "And Jesus went unto this place..."

I used the nail-puller part of the hammer and loosened the nail. It squeaked a little, so I started coughing to cover it up. I was pretty sure Mr. Jones at full volume would cover the noise, but I was playing it safe. After working the hammer back and forth, the nail finally popped out. The board had an old rusted hinge on the opposite end so the whole board folded up. Apparently, this had been the family hiding place for many decades.

Haley held the board up while I pulled my flashlight out of my back pocket. I flicked it on and shone it at the hole in the porch. There were two long, narrow metal boxes sitting side-by-side on the dirt under the porch.

They were safety deposit boxes.

Bingo.

I threw both of my fists into the air and yelled a silent, "Yes."

Haley and I quietly high-fived.

I handed the flashlight to Haley, got down on my stomach, and told myself not to think of all the critters that probably lived under this porch. I reached down and my fingertips grazed one of the boxes. I worked the box until it flipped on its side. I grabbed it and tried to lift it. It weighed a ton... well, not really, but it felt like it. I used both my hands and finally hauled the box out of the hole. I reached down and worked the other one on its side and then brought it out of the hole.

Haley had to use both hands to lift the first box. "Your toe looks really bad. I'm going to check the first-aid kit in the car for a bandage."

She winked as she walked down the stairs and carried the safety deposit box to the car.

"Good call," I yelled after her.

I was really impressed with her last statement. Not only had she made it up on the fly, it almost sounded like a real human had said it.

A couple of minutes later she returned.

"You know, I think my toe is broken." On my legal pad, I wrote, "I need to nail this back in, so we need to pretend to set my toe so my screams will hide the hammering."

She gave me an okay sign and then held up one finger. She wrote something really fast on her pad and then turned it around. "I'm louder, so I'll scream while you bang."

I bit my bottom lip to keep from laughing. Yet another sentence I'd never thought to see.

I gave her a thumbs-up.

"I'm going to need to set it before the swelling gets bad." Haley nodded like she had this. "Don't worry. I'm not a doctor, but I sleep with one so I've seen this done many times."

If the people listening could hear us over James Earl Jones, I was pretty sure they'd be wondering why I didn't go to the hospital since I worked there and all.

"On the count of three." Haley pointed to the hammer.

I moved the board back in place.

Haley mouthed, "Ready?"

I grabbed the hammer.

Haley said, "One, two, three."

She yelled at the top of her lungs while I pounded that nail back into place.

All in all, I think it worked. Between James Earl and Haley, I couldn't even hear the hammer. I moved the welcome mat back into place and stood.

"Let me tape that broken toe to the other toe," Haley said loudly.

"Okay," I said just as loudly. Not sure why.

"And thanks for setting it for me. While I have free medical care at Lakeside Hospital, I am supposed to be sick today, so that would have been weird." Now I was starting to sound like I was performing in a fifth grade play.

"You bet." Haley said.

I mouthed, "You bet?"

She hunched her shoulders and mouthed, "All I could think of."

I picked up the other safety deposit box and stumbled under the weight. Haley grabbed my elbow and helped me up.

"Let me help you to the car." She grinned.

I mouthed, "Bitch."

"You know, working out would strengthen that toe." Haley practically pulled me down the steps.

I stuck out my tongue.

We loaded the second safety deposit box in the back of Haley's Rover and got in.

"I can't believe that we found something." Haley was talking so fast, I could have sworn she was high on caffeine.

"I know. It was a total accident. If I hadn't tripped over the welcome mat, I would have never seen that shiny nail." I glanced in the direction of the safety deposit boxes. "Maybe now we'll find out what Molly was into."

"Let's call Monica. She needs to be here when we open them."

"I agree, and we need to find a quiet, bug-free place to open them."

"That's easy. My neighbors across the street just left for their home on Bonaire. I have the keys. Their house is private and hopefully not bugged." Haley was about to break and enter—sort of. Monica would be so pleased.

"Bonaire?" I'd heard of Grand Cayman but not Bonaire. I was pretty sure it was in the Caribbean.

"It's next to Aruba." Haley stopped at Molly's gate.

I got out to open the gate. I hated to disappoint her, but I didn't know where Aruba was either.

CHAPTER 16

Thirty minutes later we pulled into the driveway of the Bonaire people. I'm sure they had an actual name, but Bonaire people worked for me. Monica pulled in right behind us.

We'd stopped at Target and bought a prepaid cell phone—Haley's idea. I'd used it to call Monica's work and had left a message with the receptionist that she needed to call us at this new number. She'd used her administrative assistant's phone to call us back.

Haley pulled all the way up to the garage, pulled out her cell phone—the old one, not the new one—touched an icon, and the garage door rolled up. "Garage door app. I have the code."

"There's a garage door app?" Wow, I didn't even have a garage door, but I was totally going to download the app.

We pulled into the four-bay garage, and Monica pulled right in next to us. Haley touched the icon again and the garage door rolled closed.

Yep, I was totally downloading that app. Could you open any garage door? It would be really fun to drive down the street and randomly open and close other people's garage doors. I'm poor, remember; cheap thrills are my only source of entertainment.

Monica opened her car door and stepped out. "I can't wait to see what's inside the boxes. This is just like the time Geraldo Rivera opened Al Capone's safe on live TV."

"Yeah, but that safe was empty." I stepped out. "Let's hope these two safety deposit boxes aren't."

"Where do you think she got two safety deposit boxes? Surely they're hard to come by." Haley stepped out of the driver's seat and joined us at the back of the Rover.

"EBay." I cocked my head to the left. "That's where she bought all of that other junk."

"Oh yeah." Haley slipped her left hand into her jacket pocket and pulled out ten dollars. "Here you go." She handed it to Monica.

"Yesss." Monica stuffed it into her front jeans pocket. "We made a bet on whether there really was a bunch of hoarded stuff or you were just exaggerating."

I put my hand over my heart. "Me... exaggerate?" I swooned and fake cried. "I'm hurt."

I really was channeling a Latin soap star.

"I should have bet on the chemistry set." Haley touched a button on the handle of the Rover's back door and the door opened on its own. "Someone took the chemistry set. The garage was spotless."

"If I didn't know better, I'd say it was me who cleaned it. It was that clean." I couldn't get over it.

"That's saying a lot, coming from you." Monica watched as the Rover's back door rose and then stopped. She ducked underneath the hatchback door and sat on the bumper. She tried to pick up one of the safety deposit boxes. "Damn, this is heavy. I say we take them inside to open them."

She adjusted her grip and picked it up. Haley grabbed the other one.

"Hand me the house keys." I glanced at Haley.

"Don't need them. I remote unlocked the door from my phone." Haley heaved a breath like she was carrying a thousand pounds.

"What's the name of that app? I'm totally downloading it." I could open garage doors and house doors? Life was good.

"I'm not telling you. You'd use it for evil." Haley held the box balanced on her hand and shoulder like a waitress with a large tray of food.

"Would not." She knew me so well. I opened the only door in the garage and walked into a huge hallway with benches and coat hooks. It looked like a waiting room in a doctor's office. "What's this?"

Haley walked through the open door. "The mud room."

"What the hell's a mud room?" Monica followed her in.

"A place to take off your muddy shoes and hang your coats." Haley kept on walking down a hallway lined with glass-fronted cabinets.

"I don't get it. This is Central Texas. It hardly rains here, so there's no mud, and it's not like we have tons of coats that need hanging." Today it was in the sixties. I followed Haley down the hall.

"If I've said it once, I've said it a million times, rich people are weird," Monica said from behind me.

"Here we go." Haley laid the box down on a huge kitchen table. It had to be ten feet long.

These people must have like twenty kids. Or did the husband and wife sit at opposite ends of the table and play shuffleboard to pass the salt?

Monica laid her box down next to Haley's.

I felt like we needed a drumroll, but there weren't any drums lying around. Surely if they had a mud room, there'd be some drums. Rich people were so weird.

I pulled the small key out of my front jeans pocket and slid it in the lock. I tried to turn it and it wouldn't budge. I pulled it out and tried the other box. This time the key turned a tiny bit.

I slid it in again and turned. Still nothing. I jiggled it around and it still wouldn't open the lock.

"Are you kidding me? This is crazy." I slapped the key on the table. "We have two safety deposit boxes and one safety deposit box key and it doesn't work on either box."

"I love it when she states the obvious," Monica said.

"Maybe she collected safety deposit boxes like she collected stamped envelopes?" Haley liked to try and make sense out of stupidity. That's probably why she's my friend.

"This is stupid. I need a hammer or a crowbar." Monica headed back to the garage.

"You're not going to find one in there," Haley called after her. "Marshall Huddlestone is a trust fund baby. The only thing he knows how to do on his own is walk. His wife, Brenda, is worse. She calls a handyman anytime she wants to hang something on the wall. Home maintenance isn't their thing."

"Of course not." Monica turned around. "When the zombie invasion comes, they are definitely going to be the first ones eaten."

"There's got to be something around that we can use to open these boxes." I looked around. The décor was black and red and white. Lakeside's school colors are black, red, and white. This was way too much school spirit for me.

The kitchen walls were red, and the floor and countertops were black. In the living room part of the great room, the walls were black and the floor was red. It was a lot of black and red. In the corner was a chrome hand that seemed to have sprouted out of the floor. There was a red velvet cushion on it, so I guess it was a chair. "I got nothing."

"Haley, grab the other box." Monica hefted the box she'd carried in. "I vote we run over these with the Rover."

"What if it breaks whatever's inside?" Haley glanced at me for backup.

I shrugged.

"Because Molly stored her priceless collection of porcelain duck figurines in two safety deposit boxes under her back porch?" Monica didn't even bother to turn around.

"She has a point." I tried to pick up the box, but dropped the corner I'd managed to get off of the table. "That's really heavy."

Haley rolled her eyes. "Fine. I'll try it."

She picked up the box and stomped to the garage.

I followed after her.

She shoved the box under the passenger's-side tire as Monica shoved hers under the driver's-side.

Haley walked around the back of the Rover, closed the hatchback, and stomped to the driver's door. She opened it, climbed in, and started the engine. Without closing the driver's-side door, she put the car in reverse and rolled over the boxes.

I crouched on the concrete next to the driver's wheel. "They didn't crush, only dented. Pull forward and roll over them again."

After several roll overs, back ups, and roll overs again, the box lids finally caved in.

Haley put her car in park and turned off the engine. "Let me get the tire iron out and see if we can pry the lids off."

She hopped out, checked the safety deposit box damage, and walked to the back of her Rover. She opened the door, rummaged around, and came up with a tire iron.

With a loud scraping noise, I pulled the driver's-side box out from under the car.

"Here." Monica held her hand out for the tire iron. "I think I can work those back hinges loose."

Haley handed her the tire iron.

Monica rammed the chisel end of the tire iron in between the two box hinges. She worked it back and forth until the hinges popped. Haley and I each took a corner of the newly released lid and pulled back hard. The lock didn't give, but we bent the lid back.

"Holy shit." Monica stared down into the box.

Holy shit was right. Stacks of hundred dollar bills were crammed all the way up the sides of the box. Each was held together with a white paper band with ten thousand printed on it. Haley reached in and picked up a stack.

"Ten-thousand-dollar bundles. These are new." She handed it to me. "See, it's the new hundred dollar bill."

"I don't understand." I put that stack on the floor, and one by one I pulled out the first layer of bundles. I kept going. All in all, there were three layers of hundreds amounting to thirty-five bundles of money. "Molly was as broke as I am. Why does she have three hundred and fifty thousand dollars under her back porch?"

We all glanced at the other safety deposit box. Monica walked around the front of the Rover to it and dragged it over to us. Again she wedged the tire iron between the hinges until they popped open. Haley and I peeled back the lid.

"Holy shit." Haley's eyes were huge.

"I'm so proud." Monica smiled and then the smile froze on her face. "Fuck."

I glanced down. The box was filled with gold coins, and a black velvet bag sat right on top. I reached inside and grabbed the bag. I pulled the drawstring at the top apart and poured the contents into my palm. A shower of diamonds spilled out. I did a quick count. One hundred and thirty-two diamonds in a black velvet bag. Daman's diamonds.

Oh, crap.

What in the hell had Molly been into?

CHAPTER 17

"How long will the unhandy trust fund family be out of town?" I sat back in my chair at the kitchen table and stared at the bundles of cash stacked up around the safety deposit box full of gold.

"Until spring. They claim the winters here are too much." Haley shook her head. "Tomorrow it's supposed to get up to the seventies, but whatever."

"I love it when you think rich people are weird, too." Monica patted her arm.

"I vote we leave this here until we figure out what's going on." Absently, I started picking gold coins out and stacking them. They were heavier than you'd think and definitely not those ridiculous gold dollars you get as change at the post office when you plug in a twenty for a book of stamps. When the machine spit out the gold dollars, Max had thought we were rich. I still hadn't told him that they had absolutely no gold in them.

"Think I should tell Ben about all of this?" I placed the stacked coins on the table. The gold was shiny. I knew real gold didn't tarnish, but I was having a hard time convincing myself this was real gold.

Monica shook her head. "No. Think about it. He's been to your house and your house is now bugged. Put two and two together and you get that he might be the person who planted the bugs."

I didn't want to believe it, but I'd thought of that myself. He claims to have this longstanding crush on me but doesn't call me in the six months that David's been gone? I may be a sucker, but I wasn't born yesterday. "I can't tell him."

I pulled out three more coins and stacked them. The box was so overfilled that the space I'd made was quickly taken over by falling coins. For a split second before the other coins had slid down to cover the bottom of the box, I'd seen a scrap of white. Since the box was gunmetal gray, there must be something at the bottom.

"I think there's something on the bottom. Help me move these out of the way." I grabbed a handful of coins and dumped it on the table. I grabbed another and dumped it on the table.

Monica and Haley shoved coins out of the way. At the bottom of the box was a white legal envelope bulging to over an inch thick. I picked it up and pulled back the flap. Inside were five little navy-blue-bound books that looked a lot like passports. I upended the envelope, and the contents spilled out on the table. Five passports landed in a heap.

"Look." Haley picked up something black that had been under the envelope. "It's an old cell phone." She flipped it open. "It's dead."

Monica took it from her. "It's a Motorola Razr. This is old school, from back when phones didn't do much of anything but call people."

"Why would she have an old cell phone? Especially with all of this money." Haley shook her head. "She didn't use this phone. She had an iPhone."

"This phone has no SIM card. It's harder to track." Monica set it down and reached around me, picking up the passport on top. She flipped it open. "This just keeps getting weirder and weirder." She held the passport up so we could see it. "Meet Jessica Lynne Martin."

Molly's smiling face stared back at me from a passport with a different name.

I grabbed the other passports, opened them, and lined them up on the table. Each one held a picture of Molly with a different name.

"Are y'all thinking what I'm thinking?" Monica looked at me and then Haley. "Molly was a spy."

I shook my head. "That's ridiculous. She was the kindergarten teacher at Bee Creek Elementary. When did she do her spying? Weekends and spring break?"

Now that I thought about it, maybe she could be a part-time spy. I looked down at the diamonds, gold, and money on the table. Clearly, part-time spying paid well.

I continued to shake my head. "Molly was a rule follower—well, except for her blatant use of glitter in violation of the district's strict no-glitter policy. Other than that, she followed every rule and obeyed every traffic law. She led a really boring life."

"Sleeper agent?" Haley sounded like she thought that was as ridiculous as it sounded.

"What about a thief? Maybe she stole all of this?" I was grasping at straws. "That sort of fits."

"Do you really believe that she was a thief? I saw her run back into Don Julio's a couple of weeks ago because she'd miscalculated the tip and went to leave more money." Monica exhaled long and slow. "What does this have to do with her pregnancy? Maybe the father gave her all of this for the baby?"

I grabbed a handful of gold coins and held them up. "Because her baby daddy wanted to pay her off with gold coins?"

Monica nodded. "Okay, that's pretty stupid, but I can't help thinking that the pregnancy had something to do with this. Maybe she found out she was pregnant and tried to get out of her life of crime." She pointed to the table. "And this is the retirement plan?"

"Maybe." Actually, that was just as logical as anything else we'd come up with.

"Blackmail?" Haley picked up one of the stacks of hundreds. "Maybe she was blackmailing someone?" She shook her head. "That doesn't explain the multiple passports."

It hit me and I didn't want to say it out loud. "Drugs. That's the only thing that makes sense. She had the chemistry set in the garage—she was making designer drugs. That explains the money and the passports. Maybe she wanted out after she found out that she was pregnant, and she was murdered because once you're in that's the only way out."

"Drugs just seems so contrary to her personality. She didn't even drink. Then again, maybe she was smarter than to use the stuff she was making." Haley rubbed the muscles at the back of her neck. "That also explains Daman's interest and possible bugging of our houses. That explains how his diamonds were found in her safety deposit box. Maybe they were in it together? She made the drugs and he distributes."

It was a lot for Haley to even think of incriminating her friend.

I didn't want to believe it. Daman seemed like such a nice guy. I liked him and wanted to know him better. The drug lording didn't fit with what I knew of him personally, but I'd learned many times that people often had two faces. Take David. I'd had no idea he had a girlfriend or that he was capable of stealing from the city and running away with her.

"Where do we go from here?" I looked at Monica and then Haley. "Ideas? Anyone?"

"It would have been so much easier if Molly had left us a note in one of these boxes that said, 'If I'm dead and you find this, blank is the killer.' I can't imagine there was a line of people wanting to kill Molly, but then again, I wouldn't have taken her for a drug maker either." Monica watched the stacks of cash like she half expected them to get up and walk away. "Think the money is real? It could be counterfeit or something."

"I have no idea. How do you even tell?" I picked up a stack.

Haley picked up a bundle and thumbed through it. "They seem to be nonsequential. I don't know if that matters."

"Do we take a hundred dollars and try to buy something? What if it's marked? Or what if the people who bugged our houses are tracking the serial numbers. I don't want to get caught with stolen or counterfeit money." Molly was into something bad, and it had gotten her killed. Any sane person would stop, but no one had ever accused me of having an overabundance of sanity.

"I've got an idea." Haley ripped off the white wrapper from around the bundle she was holding and pulled out a single hundred dollar bill. "I'll take this to my husband's office and trade it out for one of the hundreds in the daily deposit. If it's fake, the bank will call."

Monica shook her head. "If the serial numbers are being tracked, it will lead back to you. We need a way that if the bill does raise red flags, it can't be tracked back to us, but that we can still track it."

"Banks are out and so are convenience stores—surveillance cameras. We can't just go use it at the grocery store because even out here, who pays for things in hundreds? Everything is credit or debit these days. We need to spend this some place that handles large amounts of cash so the hundred will go unnoticed but we can still keep track of the bill." I couldn't think of a single place to spend it.

I did think of casually dropping it outside of Salina Atan's door, but if she spent it and was arrested, it wouldn't be hard to connect her to me. It was almost worth it, but more than likely Molly's death was linked to this money. I wasn't willing to die even to have Salina arrested.

"I've never had such a hard time figuring out a way to spend money." Monica sat back and waved a stack of hundreds around. "A food truck?"

"True, they don't have cameras and probably do a pretty good cash business, but how many people pay with hundreds. Besides, how would we track it? We need to know if the people who bugged our houses are looking for this money." Every single way I could think of to get rid of the money, but still track it, would be linked back to us.

Haley pointed to the money. "What about this... a donation to the Salvation Army? A girl I went to summer camp with a million years ago is married to the bank manager where funds for the Salvation Army Central Texas are deposited—"

"Do you have any contact with her via the Internet or your home or cell phones?" Monica was good. She was a thinker.

"Only Christmas cards through the mail. I send her one every year and she sends me one. They live in Waco. We could drop the hundred in one of the red barrels after Halloween, and I'd drop by her house a couple of weeks later. That way the contact is face-to-face." Haley brightened.

"You still send Christmas cards through the mail?" Monica glanced at me. "Why do we like her again?"

"I'm more appalled by her willingness to gyp the Salvation Army out of a hundred dollars." Really, it was appalling. True, it was sneaky and would probably work, but it was still appalling.

Haley rolled her eyes. "Like I don't donate thousands to them every year." She bit her bottom lip. "What do you think?"

Monica shrugged. "I'll do the drop-off if you want. There's always a red barrel set up down the street from my office."

"I don't know. It sounds risky and complicated. I'd hate for this to get us killed. Let's just sit on it for a while." Nothing made sense. "I wish we could see what's on that phone. Molly had to have been using it. It doesn't seem possible that she held onto it for no reason."

"Let's dump out all of the gold and see if Molly left us a power cord." Monica scooped out handfuls of gold onto the table. "Think about it. She had a secret phone, wouldn't she have a secret cable to charge it? If she left it out, someone's going to ask why she has this old phone cord."

Monica was always on top of things.

I lifted a handful of coins and sure enough, a black charger sat at the bottom of the safety deposit box. Haley picked it up and plugged it into the wall. She shoved the charger end into the bottom of the phone. After about a minute, it lit up. Now we were onto something.

We all stared at the tiny screen.

"Check the call log." I pointed to the option.

Haley used the arrow buttons to scroll to the call log. It felt like she was on an old-fashioned computer with dial-up that took forever to load. Man, today's touch screens were so much better.

She clicked on the call log. There was nothing.

"Try voicemail." Monica leaned over Haley's shoulder.

Haley pulled up voicemail. Nothing again.

"Who has a phone but no voicemail?" Monica shook her head like it made no damn sense.

"Look in email." I pointed to the option.

Haley pushed the arrow buttons a bunch of times. Email came up.

"Finally." Haley nodded at all of the messages. She selected the first one.

It was from anon123456@anonymous.com. The title was blank. The body of the email said, "Mustang Ridges."

"My name? Why is my name in an email on Molly's secret phone?" I looked at Monica in case she had any ideas.

She hunched her shoulders. "No clue."

Haley clicked on the next email. It was from the same person and had no title either. The body of the message read, "Jonathan Swerling."

"Who's that?" Haley clicked on the next message. "It looks like all of the emails are from the same person."

The body of this email read, "Alicia Mangris-Fuentes."

One by one, Haley pulled up all seventeen emails, and every single one of them had a different name.

Haley grabbed the envelope that had held the passports and wrote down the names.

"Why would Molly have emails with random names? And why is your name on this list?"

"I don't understand. This doesn't make any sense. Who are all of these people?" This took creepy to a whole new level.

Monica grabbed the envelope. "I'm on it. Not the list—the finding out about the people on the list." She stood and said, "Does Trust Fund Baby have a computer?"

"I don't know, I guess. Who doesn't have one these days?" Haley pointed to a hallway on the other side of the living room. "The study is down that hallway. Check in there."

Monica disappeared down the hallway.

Haley and I stood to follow her.

I gestured to the windows behind the kitchen table. "Should we leave all of this lying around? Even with the blinds closed, it feels weird."

"I agree. I'll take care of it." Haley headed to a red and black striped room that could only be the dining room. She opened a white lacquered buffet and pulled something black out. She waved it at me as she walked back to the kitchen table. "Tablecloth."

"Who besides a practicing satanic priest has a black tablecloth?" I looked around. "There's not an altar with a dead chicken on it in the bedroom, is there?"

"Not that I know of, but we can check just to make sure." Haley grinned. She was cussing, eye rolling, and being sarcastic. Our little girl was growing up to be a bitch just like her best friends.

"Bingo, I found the computer," Monica called from the end of the hall. "Damn, I think it's older than I am. I don't understand. You have a second home on some Caribbean island that no one's ever heard of, but is probably very expensive, and you own a piece-of-shit computer. Priorities, people."

Haley and I followed the sound of her voice.

I walked into the study, and I could feel my eyes almost bleed. "Holy crap..."

I just didn't have any more words to describe the black and white block tile that, instead of being on the floor, covered the walls and ceiling. The floor was covered in bloodred carpet. On the wall opposite the desk was a giant three-dimensional red dot—like a clown nose minus the clown. It had to be three feet across. I looked at Haley for an explanation.

"Don't look at me. Wouldn't you hate to see the clown that left his nose on the wall?" She pulled up a chair next to Monica.

I did the same.

"I'm pretty sure this iMac is first generation circa 1998. So after forty-five minutes and it boots up, we can get started." Monica shook her head like she couldn't understand how someone would own this.

The log-in screen came up asking for a password.

Monica looked at Haley.

"I have no idea. Just hit return. Maybe they don't have one." Haley reached over Monica and hit return on the silver and white keyboard.

The computer thought about the command for a moment and then the main screen came up.

"See." Haley pointed to it. "No password."

"Wow. People continue to amaze me." Monica handed me the list as she clicked on the Safari icon. "What's the first name after yours?"

We all held our breath as she clicked on the WiFi icon. Three wireless networks showed up and none of them were password protected. She chose the one with the strongest signal.

I read, "Jonathan Swerling."

After a full minute, Safari finally came up. Monica typed "Jonathan Swerling" into the Google search window.

Safari thought about the request, and thought about it, and thought about it.

"We probably have faster processors in our smartphones than this old thing." Monica tapped her fingers against the desk, biding her time.

Safari finally pulled up the results, and we got 2,609,000 hits. The first one was an obituary. Monica clicked on it. A few seconds later it finally opened up. "Jonathan Swerling, entrepreneur and philanthropist, died unexpectedly in his home on Sunday of respiratory failure..."

"That's the *Times* out of London." Haley pointed to the upper-right-hand side of the story. "I wonder how Molly knew him."

"This one's a dead end. I guess we're not going to find out how he knew Molly." Monica laughed. Again, I was giving up laughing at my own jokes.

"The next name is Alicia Mangris-Fuentes." I showed Monica the correct spelling of the last name.

She typed it in the Google search window. It came up with 700,292 hits. The first one was an obituary from the *Miami Herald.*

Monica clicked on it. "Cuban rights activist Alicia Mangris-Fuentes was found dead in her South Beach home of apparent respiratory failure..."

"Both dying of respiratory failure? That's weird... right?" Haley bit her bottom lip. "The leading cause of death in the U.S. is heart disease."

"Let's check another one." Monica looked at me. "Who's next?"

"Peter Flannery." I watched as Monica typed in his name.

This time only 400,016 hits came up. The first was an obituary from the *Plain Dealer* out of Cleveland. "Peter Flannery, age fifty-six, died Monday from respiratory distress..."

"This is officially spooky." I looked at Haley and then Monica. "Respiratory distress?"

We ran through all of the names on the list, and every single one—all seventeen, except me—had died of respiratory distress within the last two years.

The people were from all over the world and had very different jobs, but all had died from the very same thing.

Was I next?

CHAPTER 18

To say I was freaked out was an understatement. Why was I the only one on the list who was still alive? I'm not complaining—alive was a whole lot better than dead, but still ...

I was on my way to pick up Max from school and then take him to soccer practice.

Would I be the next one to die from respiratory failure? I took a deep breath. I didn't feel like I was coming down with a nasty case of respiratory failure. Or was I? I fake coughed. Nope, I'm good.

But I was on the list. Why me? Had Molly stumbled onto some terrorist plot to kill random people by somehow inducing respiratory failure? What did I have to do with all of those names? I'm just not that important to anyone but my friends and family. And no, I'm not being modest, I'm the billing manager for a small hospital. In the grand scheme of things, I'm background noise. If I'd died in Pompeii, I wouldn't have been one of the flash-fried cement corpse things, I'd have been the one trampled to death so that the person on top of me could be one of those flash-fried corpse things. Always in the right place at the wrong time.

I rubbed my right temple, where a headache of massive proportions was building. As I pulled into the Bee Creek Elementary parking lot, I glanced at the clock. I still had ten minutes before school let out. I pulled out the printouts Monica had made of all the people who had died.

One was a human rights activist, two were philanthropists, one was a Russian ballerina, one was a Catholic priest, and there was a plumber from Johannesburg. I flipped to the next sheet. There was a housewife whose husband and three children had been killed by a drunk driver, an oil company executive with no family, the Egyptian undersecretary of antiquities—no info about his family—and a New York City high school principal who had grandchildren.

I didn't know these people, and I certainly didn't have anything in common with them. In fact, they didn't seem to have anything in common with each other except for the way they had died.

I'd never really thought of myself as a conspiracy theorist, but I was quickly leaning in that direction. Now that I really thought about it, an international conspiracy theory was the only thing that made sense. Had all of these people seen something they shouldn't have and been killed for it?

I didn't recall seeing anything I shouldn't, but I'd seen lots of things I regretted—hippos having sex on the Discovery Channel, leg warmers, the time I walked by the OR and saw a doctor removing a Wesson bottle from a man's rectum, the movie *Glitter*, and chocolate-covered garbanzo beans. Some things you just can't un-see. And in all fairness, the garbanzo beans I didn't see so much as taste, but each one was a new level of horrible.

Why would Molly have a cell phone with a list of dead people? Maybe it wasn't hers and she'd found it or was keeping it for a friend? If so, why would she keep it under her back porch? What was the deal with all of that money? Now I wished I'd let Molly pick up the tab every time she'd offered.

Maybe she'd stolen the phone and was using the names to blackmail someone? But who? And why?

The more I found out, the less I knew. There was no denying it, Molly was involved, but how? Had she stumbled onto some information that had gotten her killed, or had she willingly participated in the deaths of these people? How did my name end up on that phone?

My questions were piling up like vodka bottles at a frat house. Besides Monica and Haley, I didn't know who to trust. My house was bugged, my life was in danger, there was a fortune in money and gold hidden under a black tablecloth in the tackiest house I'd seen in my whole life, and the two men who'd suddenly popped into my life were probably involved—not with each other but with what had happened to Molly. My life was just plain craziness.

Not my best day... not my worst either.

This was a puzzle, and every new piece I found didn't fit into place. I couldn't help thinking that there was something I was missing... something obvious. Tonight, after Max went to bed, I planned to pull out the murder board and see if something new jumped out at me.

I checked my watch. It was two forty-seven and parents were getting out of their cars to walk to the gym to pick up their kids. After I picked up Max, we'd have an hour before soccer practice, so a trip to the library for a little research sounded like a fantastic idea. I didn't feel comfortable using my own computer, but I could search the Internet all I wanted at the library. I'd written down the aliases Molly had used on her passport and wanted to find out more.

Twenty minutes later, I pulled the heavy door to the Lakeside library open for Max and followed him in. The library was small, but what it lacked in size, it more than made up for in amenities. A bank of state-of-the-art computers each had a private cubicle. An espresso machine complete with real heavy cream in an ice bucket stood ready to meet my caffeine needs. It sat right next to the librarian's station. Of course there were rows and rows of books, but the library also had audio books on MP3 players and DVDs that could be checked out.

"Hey, Max." Carol Tatum, the librarian on duty, looked up from the book she was reading. Did I mention that not many Lakeside citizens frequent the library? Living in a wealthy town had its advantages. First, there was plenty of money to keep the library in espresso, and second, every one of the "haves" bought their books, because being seen checking anything out of the library was a sure sign that your tens of millions were dwindling down to a mere seven figures.

"Hello, Mrs. Tatum." Max's cheeks turned a nice shade of rosy. He had a little crush on Carol. He thought I didn't know. It was so cute.

"I just got a brand-new book on airplanes and thought you might like it. I've been saving it for you." She rolled to the other side of her circular desk, leaned over, and pulled out a huge hardbound book. She rolled back over to us and slid the book over to Max.

No wonder my son had a crush on her. In addition to being petite, blonde, and curvy, she always managed to have a special book that she knew he would love.

"Thanks." His gaze drank in both the book and Carol. He slid the book off of the counter and glanced at me. "Can I go sit in the chairs and read it?"

"The chairs" were what we'd always called the bank of overstuffed chocolate leather chairs next to the espresso maker.

"Sure, buddy." I ruffled his hair as he walked past me.

"Sorry, I don't have that new *People* magazine yet, but maybe tomorrow." Did I mention how wonderful Carol is? She knows I love me some *People* magazine so she had the library buy a subscription, because she knew I couldn't afford it.

"That's fine. I actually came to use the computers." I knew that she had to turn on the Internet from her computer first.

She rolled over to her computer, typed furiously, and then stopped. "Take number two." She gestured toward the computer cubicles. "The Internet is up and running for you."

I made an espresso and headed to computer number two. I set my espresso down, pulled the printouts from my tote, and sat. I logged into the computer using the log-in and password taped to the top of the monitor and pulled up the browser.

I typed in "respiratory failure." Before I could come up with a viable conspiracy theory, I needed to know exactly what respiratory failure meant.

Eight million hits. This could take a while.

I clicked on the Wikipedia site first. It had a bunch of scientific mumbo jumbo that involved chemical names for gases. I got crossed-eyed trying to figure it out so I clicked on MedlinePlus—a service of the U.S. National Library of Medicine. It stated that respiratory failure happens when not enough oxygen gets to the brain or when the lungs can't remove carbon dioxide from the blood.

I clicked on causes. There were several: lung disease, conditions like spinal cord injuries that affect the nerves and muscles that control breathing, an injury to the chest that damages the tissue around the chest, drug or alcohol overdose, or inhaling harmful smoke or fumes.

Okay, so unless someone used lung diseases to commit murder, which seemed like an inefficient way to kill someone, as it would take a long time, that was out. Spinal cord injury maybe, but wouldn't the death be attributed to the spinal cord injury? The same for the chest injury and the drug or alcohol overdose. The only thing left was the harmful smoke or fume inhalation. That didn't seem like a very good way to kill someone because the murderer ran the risk of inhaling the fumes or smoke too. Okay, say the killer wore a face mask or something that prevented the fumes from killing him—or her. When the killer forced the noxious fumes on the victim, wouldn't there be burns or something around the nose, or wouldn't the air around the victim leave some clue that they had inhaled something toxic? I didn't really know, but it seemed like a strong possibility.

It just seemed like there were better ways to kill someone.

What about poisons?

I typed "respiratory failure and poison" into the Google search window.

Only three hundred thousand hits this time.

The first article was about pesticides causing respiratory failure in third world countries, but according to the article, death wasn't immediate. It took years' worth of repeated exposure to kill someone.

The next article was about poison hemlock ingested by a toddler. He had abdominal pain and muscle weakness that resulted in the respiratory failure. It took hours though, and once he was intubated and could breathe, he was out of danger. It took twenty-four hours for the hemlock to work its way out of his system.

So maybe poison hemlock as a murder weapon?

I wrote that down.

There was an article on acute barium poisoning caused by barium salt, which is a heavy metal used in radiography. That seemed like something that would be really hard to get your hands on, unless you were a psychotic radiologist, which I guessed was possible. After all, radiologists are locked in dark rooms all day looking at X-rays. That sure would make me psychotic, but then I don't like dark rooms. Presumably radiologists do, since they chose that profession. On the off chance Molly was blackmailing Dr.

Haverman, our local radiologist, I wrote barium poisoning down on my list.

The next article was on cyanotoxins, which are produced by blue-green algae. It seemed like a lot of work to grow, harvest, and then refine them to be used as a poison, but I wrote it down.

The next article was about poisoning using household items. I had already found hemlock could be deadly, but so were oleander, rhododendrons, azaleas, arsenic, cyanide, strychnine, methanol, some mushrooms, and toxic venom from reptiles. The last one made me shiver. I hate snakes and would probably die of fright before I'd be able to harvest the toxic venom, so I definitely couldn't use that as a murder weapon.

It just seemed like all of these murder methods would be spotted in an autopsy.

Maybe these people hadn't been murdered at all and really were just a random list of people who all happened to die of respiratory failure.

That was it.

Just to make sure I wasn't being poisoned, I was no longer eating food that didn't come from a drive-through window. No one was slipping hemlock into my salad. If food was going to kill me, I wanted to take the slow road to coronary artery disease, one Big Mac value meal at a time. It was the American way—downright patriotic. If being on Molly's list meant that I was going to die, I'd do it with a Big Mac in one hand and an American flag in the other.

My stomach rumbled. In the frenzy of finding gold and mucho moolah, I hadn't eaten lunch.

I clicked on the Google search window to clear it and typed in all five of Molly's aliases. Lots of people came up with those names, but none of them was Molly. Had they been names she'd picked at random? It seemed like it.

I glanced at the clock on the computer screen. I had fifteen minutes until Max had to be at soccer practice. That was exactly enough time to run through the Mickey D's drive-through and still make practice.

"Buddy, it's time to go." I turned around to look at Max. "Why don't you check out whatever books you want so we can get to practice."

I clicked on the computer's browser history and cleared it in case the FBI monitored library Internet usage. It could happen. Probably not, but a week ago I wouldn't have thought my house could be bugged either.

CHAPTER 19

I dropped Max off at practice and decided to run home and grab the murder board and Molly's medical files. Keeping them both at Trust Fund Baby's house seemed like a better plan than having them at mine. What with the bugging and the men showing up to bring me food, my little house had seen more action in the last two weeks than in all of the rest of the time I'd lived there.

I grabbed the murder board and medical files and headed back to Trust Fund Baby's house. We really needed a better name for it. From now on, it would be named TFBH. I was halfway there before I remembered that I didn't have a key or that handy-dandy phone app that unlocked everything. I couldn't call Haley because my phone was bugged. Bugging people's lives was very inconvenient for them. I wanted to shout it, but I was pretty sure the people listening didn't care.

I glanced at the clock on the dash. I didn't have time to stop by Haley's house and make it back to the soccer fields in time to pick up Max. So I made a U-turn in the middle of Lakeside Boulevard and headed back to the soccer fields.

An old guy in a Cadillac Escalade flipped me off and laid on his horn. I pretended not to hear him and didn't make eye contact. I'd found that it was pointless to get into a screaming match with seniors. They couldn't hear me, so all of the good one-liners I liked to bounce off them were lost. Nothing's worse than a perfectly good comeback gone unheard.

Red and blue lights flashed in my rearview mirror.

Crapola.

I pulled over and the old guy in the Escalade slowed down, rolled down his window, and blew me a kiss. I really hated that old man.

I looked in my rearview as the cop pulled his black and white Chevy Tahoe in behind my car. Quickly, I gathered up the murder board, folded it as best I could, and crammed it and the medical records in my leather work tote. I zipped it up tight and rolled down my window.

Ben leaned down. "Ma'am, you just committed an illegal U-turn."

He flipped the cover open on an iPad-looking thing. "I'm going to have to cite you for that. There's a No U-Turn sign right there."

He pointed to the white and black sign not two feet away from my front bumper. Where had that come from?

"Okay." Had Ben hit his head and forgotten we'd been out on a date a little over a week ago and had been texting back and forth every single day? I guess he took his job way more seriously than I'd thought. "Would you believe I can't read?"

Slowly his hand stopped typing and his gaze met mine. "You had no trouble reading my texts."

"It comes and goes." I smiled.

He started typing again and said without looking at me, "I heard the strangest thing today. Like seven people told me that you kissed Daman Rodriguez a couple of nights ago. I seem to remember you telling me that we couldn't get together that night because you were too tired."

When he said it like that, it sounded really bad. Honestly, it had never occurred to me to tell him. Daman and I weren't dating and certainly didn't have a thing going. "He showed up at my house with pizza and he kissed me. That was it."

He continued typing. Apparently U-turn tickets required a *War and Peace* length novel.

"So you're angry because a man I barely know showed up at my house with pizza, invited himself to dinner, and then kissed me? Why?" If Daman had brought cake I might have slept with him. To be fair, I'd have slept with Ben if he'd brought cake, provided that it wasn't gluten-free, carb-free, or sugar-free. Did that make me a carb slut?

"You might have mentioned it." He kept typing.

I was beginning to think that he was fake typing just to intimidate me. Well, the joke was on him. He could type until his fingers fell off. I wasn't afraid.

"The thought never occurred to me. I didn't mention it because honestly, I'd forgotten about it." I glanced down to make sure my pants weren't on fire from all of this lying.

"So you're not dating Rodriguez?" This time he looked at me.

"Not that I'm aware of." Then again, I occasionally miss social cues and misread men who bring me food. So far, two men had shown up on my doorstep with dinner, and I was pretty sure one of them had bugged my house. Was there a nonchalant way of asking if Ben had bugged my house?

"How do you feel about Chinese food?" He smiled down at me. Did this mean he wasn't going to give me a ticket?

"I'm in favor of it. Generally, I like anything that involves egg rolls and fried rice." I returned his smile. If he was bringing over Chinese, it better have carbs. Was there such a thing as carb-free Chinese food? Inwardly, I cringed. God, I hope not.

"Six o'clock, your place." He leaned closer. "I'll bring extra egg rolls and double fried rice."

"Wait, tonight is your aunt's Monday night séance. She requires me to be there. It's in my lease." And I was running low on Peanut M&M's.

"I'll call her and get you out of it. She'll give you the night off. I'm her favorite nephew." He leaned even closer. "Now would be an excellent time to kiss me."

"So romantic. What with the cars whizzing by and all that exhaust." I moved a hair's breadth from his mouth. "What did you have in mind?"

He cupped my chin and pulled me into him. His lips were demanding, and I'd forgotten that he knew how to kiss. Oh man, he'd had a lot of practice.

He pulled away. "You taste like McDonald's fries."

"Guilty." I glanced at his ticket-writing iPad thingy. "About the fries."

"I miss those." He leaned in and kissed me on the cheek.

"Come over to the dark side, we have french fries." I used my exorcist voice. I'm willing to admit that it was more creepy than cute.

"I'll give it some serious thought." He straightened. "I'll see you in an hour or so."

He walked back to his car. There were so many lights flashing, it was like a mobile disco wagon.

Every time I turned around, there was a handsome man plying me with food. It was nice and I'm not complaining about the free food part, but I still wondered why. Not until I'd started investigating Molly's murder had these guys shown up. Me and my newfound conspiracy theory brain were wondering, what's the deal? Not that two handsome men being interested in me was a problem, but the timing was a little odd.

Six minutes later, I pulled into the parking lot by the soccer fields and saw Max talking to Daman.

Crapola.

Daman was wearing shorts, a soccer jersey, and cleats. He was cute, damn it. I should feel guilty about dating two men, but I didn't. Men did this to us all the time, right? I was dating both of them for womankind—it was our turn to poly-date.

Max and Daman seemed to be deep in conversation and were the only two people left at the soccer fields. The light was fading, and here I was late to pick up my little boy. I'm a terrible mother and should be prosecuted for... lateness?

I pulled right up to the pair, who were standing under a stadium light in the parking lot. "Buddy, sorry I'm late."

"It's okay." Max nodded to Daman. "D-Rod came to practice and helped us work out."

Max was brimming with excitement. Daman might be a drug lord, but he'd made my son happy today.

Daman turned his dazzling smile on me. He walked right up to my door and placed his hands on the open window. "I went by your office today to see if you wanted to have lunch, but they told me that you'd called in sick for the first time ever. I was worried."

"I'm fine." I glanced at Max, who was too busy loading his soccer bag into the van to pay much attention to the adults around him. I hadn't exactly told him that I'd called in sick. I didn't want him getting the idea that he could blow off school. "It was more of a mental health day."

Oh, and I also found your diamonds, but I can't tell you how or where.

I had no idea how to work that into the conversation.

He opened my door. "I brought something for you."

I guessed that I was supposed to follow him. I slid out of the van. He waited for me and then put his hand on the small of my back and led me to the trunk of his car. I know it was bad, but for a split second I wondered if he was going to throw me into the trunk.

He leaned in close to my ear. "Is your phone in the car?"

I nodded. Surely if he tried to knock me out and load me in the trunk, I could get away. I glanced down at his muscular legs. Instead of trying to outrun him, I'd kick him in the balls and then make a run for it.

Here's the thing though, I really liked him. And I was having dinner tonight with another guy that I really liked. I didn't get it. After months of no dates—or worse, weird dates who lived with their mothers—suddenly two nice guys wanted to spend time with me. Something was definitely going on.

Daman clicked his key fob and the trunk lid glided up. My next car was totally going to have one of those trunk opening thingies.

He reached in the front pocket of a black gym bag. Holy shit, was he going for a gun? I braced myself to bring my knee up and hammer him a good one when his hand came out of the pocket with—a small gold cylinder.

It looked like ...

"Lipstick?" I tried to picture him wearing something in a bubblegum pink, but my mind was having a problem putting that picture together.

"Stop picturing me as a cross-dresser." The dimples were back.

I know it was wrong, but I didn't feel as threatened as I should. His lashes were so long that they were tangled. It took all I had not to reach up and untangle them.

"It looks like lipstick, but it's a signal jammer." He twisted the bottom. "Turn it like this and it will jam any signal for two hundred feet, so whoever bugged your house only gets static. You can't use it all of the time or whoever is listening will figure it out, and they'll know I gave it to you."

How would they know that he gave it to me? That was strange... the knowing that he gave it to me.

"Just so we're on the same page, are you a drug lord?" Mentally, I slapped my forehead. I was so determined to get murdered.

He shook his head and laughed. "That's what you've heard, huh?"

He did a three-sixty scan of the area. Was he looking for witnesses?

I backed up. This was bad. "Is this where you throw me in the trunk and take me to your private torture chamber?"

"Really?" He looked down at me. In the fading light I could see the hurt in his eyes. "You think I'm a monster."

I'm guessing that a *Fifty Shades of Grey* joke about the torture chamber wouldn't go over so well right now. Maybe he hadn't read it or seen the movie.

He bit his top lip.

"That's just it. I don't. I've been told by several sources that you're this badass drug lord, only you don't seem like one." I hunched my shoulders. "Or look like one."

"How many drug lords do you know?" He looked relieved.

"Including you?" I was serious. "One."

"And what does a drug lord look like?" Tentatively, he touched my arm.

"Danny Trejo." That guy had the drug lord look down.

Daman's chest shook with laughter. "I'm going to tell him you said that."

"You know Danny Trejo? That's awesome." I knew someone who knew a famous person. That was almost like knowing a famous person. Once, at city hall, Willie Nelson gave up his seat for me when we both went to vote and had to wait. It was still warm from his butt. That was my total brush with fame.

He scanned the parking lot. "If I show you something, you have to keep it a secret. You can't tell anyone, not even your friends Haley and Monica."

"Okay. I can keep a secret." Sometimes. I hadn't told him about finding his diamonds, so I could keep a secret.

He unzipped the main pocket of the black bag and pulled something gold out and set it on the black felt-lined trunk next to the bag. He pulled out his iPhone and turned on the flashlight feature.

I knew my eyes were the size of York Peppermint Patties. My heart lodged in my throat. "You're DEA?"

CHAPTER 20

"I'm undercover and my life depends on no one knowing that I'm DEA." Daman reached for the badge and tucked it back in the main pocket of the black gym bag.

"Why are you here? This is Lakeside. Nothing bad, except for Molly's murder, happens here." This was the last thing I'd expected. He was DEA? Of course he could be lying, but why? I already suspected he knew more about Molly's death.

He pulled out a small business card from inside the black bag and handed it to me—the business card, not the bag. "Here's my supervisor's card. Call him and confirm if you want, but don't do it from a phone that's bugged."

I guess my I'm-convinced expression needed some work.

"Look, I'm here because Lakeside isn't what it seems. On the outside, it's all *Stepford Wives* perfect, but there are some really bad people who live here, and really bad things happen here that go uninvestigated. The police department looks the other way. Your husband was investigating something big before he... ah... left." He handed me the golden lipstick jammer.

"What bad people? What bad things? Wait a minute, my ex-husband was involved?" Should I tell him that my name was on a list of people who'd all died from respiratory failure? Until I called the number on the card and verified that Daman was really a DEA agent, I really shouldn't tell him anything. Then again, the card could be fake, and so could the boss man. My capacity for conspiracy theories was astounding. In fact, I was becoming a champion conspiracy theorier... theorist? Would Googling that word clue the people who'd bugged my phone into the fact that I was on to them?

"Yes, David was knee-deep in bad business before he disa... um, before he left." Daman watched me very closely. My guess was, he was waiting for me to call his bluff. Or maybe, he was expecting me to attack him in defense of my ex. We'd be having the Winter Olympics in hell before that would happen. David was a shit; nothing about him surprised me anymore. The man had a public face that was all charming and amiable, but I'd seen the real David... the mean David.

"A lot of money moves in and out of Lakeside." He looked at me like I was supposed to know what he was talking about.

"So, most of the people who live here have a minimum of seven-figure incomes. Out here, excess is the norm." I was the exception to the rule. My idea of excess was splurging for dessert at Chili's.

"This is dirty money. Lakeside does a nice business in cleaning money for terrorists, the Russian mob, drug lords, the triad, and every other illegal operation you can think of. Lakeside is the capital of taking black money and turning it into white money. Something like eight out of every ten dollars that leaves here came from some illegal means. There's more to Lakeside than just country clubs and banks. Did you know that every major terrorist group has an account that leads back to Lakeside? Every single one." He watched me very carefully, gauging my reaction.

"Black money into white money?" What the hell was that?

If people were going to talk to me in code, they needed to provide me with a decoder ring.

"Taking black money that comes from illegal sources and turning it into white money that's clean is basically money laundering, but the only people who call it money laundering live in Hollywood."

"Okay, so white money is clean money?" I'd had no idea being a criminal was this complicated. I'd lived long enough not to swallow whole every tale I was told, but part of me believed this. Something about Lakeside had always been off, and I always thought it was just me.

"Yes, white money is clean money."

"Okay, for the sake of argument, let's say this is true. You've been able to trace the money, why not just arrest the people in charge?" Was this why Molly had been killed? Because she knew too much? That would explain the large amount of cash. Should I ask about the gold? Did gold need to be laundered... um, whitened? Was there such a thing as dirty black gold?

"It's not that simple. Even though we have the account information, we need to know how they're cleaning the money and where it's going afterward. That's why I'm here. We think they use the Mexican drug cartels to smuggle the income out of the country somehow. While we're interested in the people here who are cleaning the money, we want to know who the mastermind is. All we have is a name... Cervantes."

"Cervantes?" The name didn't sound familiar, but I really didn't run in the same circles as criminal masterminds. Hell, I didn't run in any circles period. "So they set you up here with the fancy house and money to flash around, hoping to attract the right people."

If all of this was true, the plan made sense.

"Sorry to disappoint you, but the money and houses are all mine." He grinned. "I'm a trust fund baby. My parents own all of the McDonald's restaurants in Latin America and several in Europe."

Well, *that* was reason enough to like him. Who cares about the trans fats, his family was responsible for the making of some fantastic fries.

"That's disappointing. I liked you better five seconds ago when I thought you were only a DEA agent." I hunched my shoulders. You win some and you lose some. "You're the second trust fund baby I've met recently." Well, I hadn't actually met the other trust fund baby, but I'd met his house, and it was so horrible that I really didn't want to meet the people who lived there. "Is Molly's murder connected to all of this white money... or black money... or whatever?"

Not that I didn't care about the seedy underworld side of Lakeside, but well, I kind of didn't. All I cared about was finding out who killed Molly and why.

Daman looked around again, making sure that no one was watching us. "Yes. I don't know how or why, but it's connected. I didn't know Molly Miars, but from what I've been told, she wasn't the person you thought she was."

"What do you mean?" After all I'd found at Molly's house, I too was beginning to believe that she wasn't the person I'd thought she was.

"Her mom lives at Lakeside Living. Molly bought her mother's condo in cash. That is a huge red flag." My blank look caused him to cock his head to the left. "Most law-abiding citizens store their money in a bank, but Molly's bank had no record of any large deposits. Only her teacher's paycheck, and that wasn't anywhere close to the million she paid Lakeside Living."

I leaned against the open car trunk. "It's drugs... she was manufacturing or selling or something."

It was the only thing that made sense. She'd probably used the phone we found in her drug business. Should I hand it over to Daman? The tiny law-abiding part of me thought I should, but luckily, that was only an itty-bitty little part. The rest of me said no way.

"Yes and no. We don't have much information on Molly, but what we have doesn't suggest that she was making or distributing. She was involved in some other way." His dark brown eyes were all sincerity.

"How?" What about the massive chemistry set in Molly's garage? Maybe she was transitioning into making the product instead of just working behind the scenes?

"We think she was involved in the black-to-white operation. No one knows how, only that she had a lot of cash. Not that she flashed it around, but she did start investing in gold and other precious metals." He crossed his arms. "Making large purchases in cash and converting large sums of cash into precious metals or precious stones raises lots of red flags. Both are ways of turning black money into white."

"What about gray money?" It was a fair question. Not everything was black and white.

He stared at me for a couple of beats. "I don't understand."

"If there's white money and black money, why can't there be gray money? You know, kinda dirty and kinda clean?" Hopefully Molly's money was on the gray to whitened side, but I didn't think so.

"And what about diamonds?" I was trying for nonchalance, but my voice came out high and squeaky. "Are they a way to whiten money?"

Was there a possibility that the diamonds weren't his? Maybe Molly had bought exactly 132 diamonds, which coincidentally was the exact number that he'd lost. It could happen... maybe.

Daman's eyes narrowed and five straight lines dented his forehead. "Mustang, watch your back. Like I said the other night, you've made it onto the radar of some very bad people. They're watching and listening. Don't piss them off."

I was pretty sure I'd already done that. I seem to piss people off without really knowing that I'm doing it. Everyone has a talent, and that's mine.

His face screwed up. "What do you know about diamonds?"

He continued to stare at me. Was this some interrogation tactic he'd learned in the DEA?

"Okay, um... what if I told you that I'd found some diamonds?" Notice I didn't say his diamonds. They could have been anyone's. Since he was probably being honest, I thought I'd throw him a bone. "They might be yours, I can't be sure. Can you describe the diamonds you lost?"

His mouth dropped open, and I could swear he was thinking, "You idiot." "They're diamonds... they look like diamonds." He closed his eyes and shook his head, and then his eyes opened. It was like he was taking a moment to keep from strangling me. David had done that... lots of times. "Where exactly did you find these diamonds?"

I looked down. Studying the pavement at my feet seemed like a great idea. "Molly's house."

This might be revealing too much, but I didn't think he'd let me leave until I told him.

"Ay dios mío." He tunneled his fingers through his hair. "Put them back and walk away. You have no idea what you've stumbled into."

That pretty much summed up my life. I'm a stumble-into-er.

He grabbed my shoulders and pulled me into a tight hug. "I can't protect you all of the time."

"Since when do I need protecting? I've been doing a wonderful job all by myself." Okay, so wonderful was stretching it, but he'd pushed my biggest, hairiest button. I'm not a feminist per se, but I'm not *not* a feminist either. I believe in equal rights and pay for everyone, but I'm fine with men opening doors for ladies and picking up the tab at dinner. Call me old-fashioned, but real men don't go dutch. And what does that mean anyway? Are Dutch men known for being cheap?

"Calm down." He stroked my back.

I'm not going to lie, it was nice. Daman's chest was warm and hard. Every time he took a breath, his pec bumped my ear.

His hand stroked my hair. "I'm not saying that you can't protect yourself, I'm only saying that..."

Yeah, there was no way out of this for him. I respected that he'd come to that conclusion all by himself. Most men would have kept on arguing in the hopes that I'd get tired of it or I'd get so confused by their asinine logic that I'd give up. My ex had preferred the asinine logic method. It never worked for him, but since he believed his own asinine logic, he'd never realized that it didn't work. I have a theory that Y chromosomes are incompatible with common sense.

"Daman, I appreciate your concern, but why in the world do you feel the need to protect me? We don't know each other all that well." I wasn't trying to antagonize him, but that goes back to my ability to piss off people and not know it.

Daman took a deep breath and let it out slowly. "David asked me to take care of you."

David? My ex-husband? It took me a couple of seconds to let that sink in.

I shook off his hands and stepped back. "What the hell? Was that before or after he ran off with his girlfriend?"

A bucket of ice water dumped on my head couldn't have been more shocking. "And wait, how do you even know David?"

"We were friends at Texas A&M. After I tore my ACL and couldn't play soccer anymore, he was the one who encouraged me to join the DEA. He was my friend." He turned large, brown, puppy dog eyes on me, imploring me to believe him.

Suddenly things fell into place.

"Oh my God, you're Rod... D-Rod. He called you Rod... Rod, his friend from the DEA." David had spoken about his friend in the DEA. I didn't want to tell Daman, but David had spent a good deal of time laughing at his sappy friend in the DEA. Here's the thing, and Daman clearly didn't know it: my ex-husband wasn't a nice person. He used people to get what he wanted, and when they were of no more use to him, he found bigger and better friends.

I clamped my hand over my mouth. "What do you mean 'was'?"

Daman opened his mouth to say something and then closed it again. He looked like he was weighing what he was going to say very carefully.

"Spit it out." My heart was pounding a mile a minute. What did "was" mean? They were no longer friends? Or did the "was" mean something else... something awful. Yes, it had taken me a while to see David for the person he really was, but he was still the father of my son. I didn't want him dead... well, I might have pictured it in detail a time or two, but I was pretty sure that I didn't really want him dead.

"Mom, what's taking so long?" Max opened the passenger's door and hopped out. "I'm hungry."

He started walking over to us.

Before Max made it to us, Daman leaned over and whispered, "I haven't heard from David since the day he... left." Daman shook his head. "Mustang, he isn't on Grand Cayman. David disappeared."

That was a hell of a thing to say one second before my son walked up. There was no chance that I could get any more info, but I had so many questions.

Max looked up at me with worried eyes. "Are you okay? You look funny."

I cleared my throat and plastered on what I hoped was a halfway sane smile. "I'm fine."

Daman leaned down so that he was on Max's level. "I was just about to tell your mom, I have to go back to Mexico for a couple of days on business, but I'd love to have dinner with both of you when I get back. Would you be available on Saturday? You could bring your swimsuit.

I have an indoor pool. How about two o'clock? We could swim and then have dinner."

David hadn't run off, he'd disappeared? Nothing made sense. Daman thought that David had disappeared. What did that mean? Was David dead?

I hadn't heard from him since the day he left the note and cleaned out our checking account. I'd been blindsided.

There was a tugging on my T-shirt hem.

I glanced down.

Max was asking me something.

"What?" Usually I could carry on several conversations at once, but I was nothing short of shell-shocked. "What did you say?"

"Can we go?" Max was using the pitiful puppy dog eyes. "Please?"

I looked from him to Daman and back again. "Where?"

Max heaved an oh-my-God-adults-are-stupid sigh and said, "To Daman's house to swim and have dinner on Saturday."

Two handsome men were setting a trap for me. Like there was any way out of it.

"Sure." I couldn't think of anything else we had planned for Saturday. Wait a minute. Hadn't Daman said that he was going out of town? "When do you leave?"

"I'm on my way now. I just wanted to give you that lipstick before I left. My pilot is gassing up the plane as we speak." He sucked in his bottom lip and held my gaze. I could see in his eyes that he had more to tell me.

"I guess we can finish our discussion on Saturday." As much as I hated David, I didn't want to hear that he was dead. Even after everything, Max idolized his father. Kids don't always know the truths about their parents; most of the time they just love them no matter what. It's both sad and sweet.

Daman straightened. "Max, do you mind if I kiss your mother good-bye?"

Max scowled up at Daman. "I guess not. I'm going back to the car."

My little boy shot me a parting questioning look, turned around, and walked back to Bessie.

"Saturday, I'll show you everything I have on David since the day he left." He tucked a lock of my hair behind my ear. "In case someone is watching, I'm going to kiss you so it makes sense that we'd be standing out here talking... flirting."

He took the lipstick from me, turned the jammer off, and placed it back in my palm. Gently, he stroked my cheek and leaned into me. His lips were soft on mine, like he was tasting something new and delicious. His hand slid into my hair as his tongue parted my lips and dipped inside my mouth. Heat pooled in places that I'd almost forgotten I had. My hands went to the front of his soccer jersey and fisted, pulling him closer to me. The weight of his body pressed against me, sandwiching me between him and the trunk. His knee worked its way between my legs and I moaned. At least I think it was me—I'm like 80 percent sure the moaning was me.

Daman dropped his hands and stepped back. He looked as dazed as I felt.

"Well, then..." I clasped my hands behind my back to keep from pulling him into me again. I'd practically climbed up him like a beginner on open pole night. Here he was kissing me to keep up appearances, and I'd groped him. I'm fairly certain that my hands had slid down his back and squeezed his butt. For the record, his ass was hall-of-fame fantastic.

"I have to go." There was something I was supposed to do tonight, but I couldn't remember what it was. "I need to go home because... I live there and Max lives there. We live there together." Oh my God, I was babbling. I shook my head. "I'm not sure why I said that... okay... um... bye."

I waved inanely and did an about-face, banging my hip on the side of the car. Pain shot out from my hip, radiating down my leg.

Daman grabbed my arm to steady me. "Are you okay?"

"I'm fine." I patted his hand and then stepped out of his grasp. Could this be any more embarrassing? I limped toward Bessie.

"I'll see you on Saturday at two," he called after me. "Remember, you can't trust anyone."

The only people I trusted were me, Haley, and Monica. Everyone else, including Daman, had ulterior motives. At least now I was fairly certain that he wasn't the one who had bugged my house.

I waved without turning around and limped all the way to Bessie, opened the door, and climbed in.

My life had just gotten way more complicated.

CHAPTER 21

Was I supposed to volunteer the fact that I'd kissed another man not thirty minutes ago? Technically, I'd kissed Ben and then Daman. I hadn't told Daman about Ben, so that part was fair—I think—and I wasn't about to mention to Ben that I'd kissed Daman again. Fair is fair.

I wiped my mouth with a paper napkin that Ben had unloaded onto my kitchen table along with three bags of Chinese food. True to his word, he'd brought mountains of fried rice and extra egg rolls along with broccoli and beef, Max's favorite, General Tso's chicken, my favorite, and a whole bunch of other stuff that I didn't recognize because Max and I always ordered the same thing. When you're on a budget, it's risky to stray from what you know unless you have a coupon for something specific like, say, moo shu pork. Only, because I don't like moo shu pork, I would have thrown that coupon into the trash right next to the one for off-brand sandwich cookies. Even on a budget, real Oreos and Charmin toilet paper are necessities.

"Your mom's awful quiet, Max. What do you think's on her mind?" Ben elbowed Max playfully.

Don't mention Daman. Don't mention Daman. I shot Max my best mom glare.

"Probably the fried rice. She loves it. Once, she tried to make it and Dad and I both got sick. Mom didn't eat any so she was fine." Max grinned. He was keeping quiet about Daman, but I could tell that it was going to cost me.

Both boys looked at me.

I shrugged. “I don’t care what that emergency room doctor said, y’all both had a touch of the stomach flu.”

Rule number one and, well, the only rule—when you’re a bad cook, never eat the food you prepare. I shoveled in more fried rice that I hadn’t made. I loved the stuff.

“Am I safe in assuming that cooking isn’t one of your... um... talents?” Ben was trying to be nice.

“Nope, I’m willing to admit that my cooking is terrible, that’s why I don’t do it anymore. Some people were meant to cook and others were meant to order takeout. It’s the way of the world.” I bit into a crunchy egg roll. Cabbage, shrimp, and whatever else they put in there rolled around my tongue. Yum.

“Besides the fried rice, what was her worst dish?” Ben was having way too much fun with this.

I tried to make myself smile, but the numerous events of today weighed heavy on me. Not only had I found that Molly was probably whitening money, but Daman was DEA and he thought my ex-husband was probably dead. I wasn’t going to let my mind jump to any conclusions; I’d mull that one over when I had more facts. The hardest part was that I couldn’t tell anyone. I couldn’t reveal anything Daman had told me to Haley and Monica. As my best friends, I counted on them for advice and support. I’m a woman, we don’t carry burdens alone, that’s what friends are for.

I glanced at Ben. How did men carry burdens? I was pretty sure they didn’t confide in each other, and I was also sure they didn’t stew over things either. Did they hide troubling issues in that 90 percent of the brain that humans don’t use? If so, how could they ever find them again? Let’s face it, if men can’t find the milk in the refrigerator when it’s three inches from their nose, how could they recall important things they’d filed away?

Or maybe everything is equally important to them. So finding their car keys is right up there with finding out who murdered their best buddy. I had noticed that the men in my life didn't seem to have a sense of urgency about anything. They certainly didn't think unloading the dishwasher or taking out the trash was all that important.

"Next to the fried rice, I'd have to say it was the lemon chicken." Max made gagging noises. "It had chocolate in it."

"I can't help that the pages of my cookbook stuck together. How was I supposed to know that it wasn't a lemon chicken chocolate soufflé? It sounded exotic." In my defense, my monster-in-law was coming over for dinner. I'd thought it would be nice to make something that sounded as crazy as she is. Besides, she'd given me that cookbook as a wedding gift. I burned it along with all of David's stuff that I couldn't sell on Craigslist or at the garage sale.

Maybe I shouldn't have burned David's things? No, burning them was the right thing to do. Just because David wasn't on Grand Cayman didn't mean that he'd suddenly turned into a nice guy. He'd still cheated on me with just about every woman in Lakeside between the ages of eighteen and sixty. Except for Haley and Monica; they just might hate David more than I do.

"That sounds terrible." Ben's nose screwed up.

"It was nasty." I'm the first one to admit my faults. "That's when I decided to hang up my apron and pick up the phone."

"Lucky for you, I know how to cook." Ben wiped is mouth and leaned back in his chair. "Give me a grill, and I can make you just about anything."

I didn't want to look a gift-griller in the mouth, but it sounded like he only cooked low carb. I shoved in another forkful of fried rice. I don't think you can make rice on a grill. Then again, I can't make rice on a stove, so what do I know?

"Hamburgers would be nice." Max nodded. "You know, the kind that someone doesn't hand us through the window of our car."

"Traitor. Now Ben's going to think I'm a bad mother because I only feed you fast food." For the record, that's not true. Sometimes we eat at Chili's, and their food is anything but fast.

"I don't judge." Ben winked at me. Under the table, he patted my knee.

I flinched, not because the pat was unwanted, but it had been a while since anyone had patted my knee.

Ben's gaze went to mine. I smiled and mouthed, "Sorry."

I turned to Max to find him looking at me. I could tell that something was on his mind, but it didn't look like he was ready to spill it. Probably about Daman and me. He liked Ben, but D-Rod was tough to beat.

"What's the homework situation?" I stood, gathered the empty paper plates, and threw them in the trash can under the sink.

"One sheet of math." Max stood also, grabbed the trash I'd missed, and took it to the trash can. "I'll go get started."

Max headed toward his room.

He was such a good kid.

I gathered up all of the empty food containers and tossed them. As for the ones with food still in them, I closed them up and stored them in the refrigerator.

"Feel free to take these home, I'll just put them in the refrigerator for now." I didn't want to seem like I was keeping all of his leftovers. There were still seven containers of things that I couldn't identify.

"I don't do leftovers. Keep them." Ben reached out and took my hand. He pulled me close to him. Since he was still sitting and I was standing, this put him at eye level with my breasts. To his credit, he only glanced at them before looking up at my face.

"I know I probably shouldn't tell you this, but I've spent a fair amount of time daydreaming about spending more time with you on your sofa." He kissed the back of my hand. "Just the two of us."

I plastered on a wide fake grin. It was nice to be wanted, but I had a lot on my mind. Maybe he was just the thing to take my mind off of my troubles. I'd found that sometimes when I put the problem I was trying to puzzle out on the back burner of my mind, the answer would come to me.

Maybe that's what men did with problems they needed to solve, too? They back-burnered them—only I was pretty sure they forgot to turn the burner off and their ideas caught fire and burned up some brain cells.

Bitch alert, was I being overly bitchy?

"I think that can be arranged." Okay, so I felt a little guilty about the dating-two-guys thing, but I was doing this for me and all of womankind who'd ever been two-timed by an asshole. Only in this scenario, I was the asshole.

I could live with that.

Ben scooted his chair back, stood, and stretched. His white knit polo shirt pulled free of his jeans and a three-inch swath of washboard abs peeked out. Nice... really nice.

He caught me looking and stretched even further so more of his shirt rode up. "See anything you like?"

"Maybe." My gaze lingered on the peaks and valleys of his abs and then finally made it all the way to his face. He must work out a lot... a whole lot.

He slid an arm around my shoulders and we headed to the sofa. He stopped short and I ran into him.

"I can't believe I didn't notice that before." He pointed in the general direction of my TV.

"What?" I scanned the area for something out of the ordinary, but all I saw was my old TV. Was there a hidden camera or something that he'd noticed? I stepped out of his arm and walked in the direction he'd pointed to see if I could find it.

Ben tugged my arm playfully and pulled me back against him. "I was talking about your TV. I haven't seen a tube TV since I was a kid."

"I'm into antiques." And by antiques, I mean hand-me-downs. I'd had to sell our good flat-screen TV to cover my first and last months' rent here.

"It has to be desirable to be an antique. That's junk." He squinted to get a better look. "Wow, it still has buttons on the front you use to turn it on and off."

"I've got news for you. Those buttons also change the channels. This was my parents' old TV, and the remote has long since been lost." I had nothing to be embarrassed about. This is what I can afford. "Know the best thing about renting from your aunt? She loves her some TV. So we get cable and all of the movie channels."

He probably got all of the movie channels too, only he had to pay for them. So there. My TV may be crappy, but free movie channels are awesome.

"She likes you." He sat on the sofa and pulled me down next to him. "She called me the other day to tell me to marry you so we could give her some cute grandnieces and nephews."

That was awkward. This was like our second or maybe third date. "What did you tell her?"

"I told her that I've begged for your hand in marriage, but that you're not ready to commit to a family as crazy as mine. My aunt agreed to try and be less crazy, but I don't see that happening." He slid his arm around me. "You always smell coconut-y." He sniffed my hair. "Is that shampoo or something?"

"No, it's Burt's Bees Coconut Foot Creme." Another luxury that I couldn't afford, but some things made life worth living, and not having dried-out, cracked feet was one of those things.

"I could always tell when you'd been in to visit David because his office smelled like coconuts." He kissed the palm of my hand.

Just hearing my ex's name smothered any good mood that I'd been trying to convince myself I felt. Should I ask him about David? It was probably the wrong moment, and Daman had said that I shouldn't trust anyone.

"Once, I smelled my way through the perfumes at Macy's trying to find the one that smelled like you." He kissed the inside of my wrist. "Okay, more than once. I like it." He kissed my forearm.

So he hadn't been lying when he told me he'd had a thing for me for a while. That was sweet. Ben made me feel safe. I liked it.

"Turn around and let me rub your shoulders. You seem tense." His voice was mellow and soothing.

I turned my back to him.

His hands slid up my arms to my shoulders, and he kneaded lightly. "Tough day?"

I forced myself to relax. "Yes, this hot cop almost gave me a ticket. Luckily I talked him into bringing me dinner instead."

"You think I'm hot." There was a smile in his voice.

This was nice.

"Of course I do. You have a fantastic butt." I only lied when I needed to, or to get out of a ticket, or if I needed to cut in line at the grocery store, or pretty much whenever I had something to gain by it. Now, I felt like telling the truth, or at least some of it.

"So you've been looking at my butt." He sounded pleased. His hands moved to my neck. It was wonderful.

"You have a very nice body, and I think you're well aware of that." I closed my eyes and willed myself to relax. Ben was bending over backward to be nice. I liked it, but something was off. It felt like he was trying too hard.

Was this about him being jealous of Daman? Had he somehow found out about the kiss we'd shared an hour ago?

"Mom, I'm ready for you to check it." Max walked in holding his math homework.

I sat up straight and Ben dropped his hands. Why did I feel like I'd been busted by my parents for making out on the couch? At least we hadn't had to straighten any clothes.

"Let me see." I took the paper and scanned it. It looked good, except for one problem. "Take another look at number four. I think your answer is a bit too high."

Max took the paper and his gaze zeroed in on number four. "Oh, it's sixteen. I got it."

He set the paper on the sofa back, erased, and wrote the correct answer. He tossed the paper on the sofa. "I'm going to get ready for bed."

"Homework in your backpack, please, so we don't have to look for it in the morning." I picked up the paper and handed it to him.

He sighed like I'd just asked him to vacuum the entire house, but took it and lumbered down the hall to the bathroom.

"You're a great mom. Ever thought about having more children?" Ben slid his hands back to my shoulders.

That was a little too much. Yes, I'd like to have another child, but it seemed a little soon for that conversation.

His front left jeans pocket vibrated, and I'm not going to lie, I was a tiny bit excited. A man with a vibrating penis could take over the world.

I turned around to check it out. Unfortunately, it was his phone.

He worked it out of his jeans and glanced down at the screen. "Sorry, I need to take this. It's work."

I stood. "I'll just go check on Max."

Giving him some privacy seemed like a great idea. I walked to the hallway and knocked on Max's open door. I peeked inside. He must be in the bathroom. I remembered that I'd left my work tote bag with the murder board and all of Molly's medical records on the kitchen counter. Best not to leave it lying around even if the bag was zipped. I walked back down the hallway and was about to step into the living room when Ben's whispered voice caught my attention. With the peculiarity of the house's architecture, sound from one particular spot right by the front door was crystal clear in this one square foot of tile. I'd used it more than once to spy on Max.

"I told you, I'm making progress. She trusts me. Just give me time." He shoved a hand into his front pocket and leaned against the front door.

Was he talking about me?

"I'll find out what she knows, but I'm telling you now, she's not involved. Just because she and Molly were friends doesn't mean that Molly told her anything."

My heart dropped to my knees. That bastard, I knew he was too good to be true.

Son of a bitch. Ben had been playing me. Did I have stupid tattooed across my forehead? He'd seemed so sincere, if a little pushy. And I'd fallen for it.

"I can't right now. I'm in the middle of something." Ben waited for whoever to stop talking. "Okay, fine. I'll be right there."

He ended the call and slid the phone in his back pocket.

I stepped into the living room and smiled brightly. "Is everything okay?"

He plastered on that aw-shucks-ma'am smile and shook his head. "I hate to cut our evening short, but something just came up at work. Rain check?"

Rain check on what, the fake romancing of me or the planting of more bugs in my house? Now I knew for sure who was bugging my house, but I still didn't know why.

"Sure." I walked to him. "No problem. I'm used to police emergencies."

I made my way to the door and opened it for him. "Call me sometime."

Or never; that was fine too. Now I questioned everything he'd ever told me.

"Dinner tomorrow?" He leaned down and kissed me on the cheek.

"Absolutely." Not. I'd find some way out of it.

He walked out the door and to his fancy silver truck. I waved like a lovesick teen, closed the door, and leaned against it. I walked over to my kitchen table and ran my hand under the table where he'd been sitting. I'd gotten all of two inches when my fingers encountered a small square of plastic. I bent over and looked at it.

It was a bright, shiny new listening device.

I hated when I was right.

CHAPTER 22

The next afternoon, I left work early, claiming I was still nauseated from the fake stomach flu I'd been ailing from. I picked up Max from school and met Haley and her girls at the Lakeside Park. Unfortunately, Monica refused to get the fake flu and leave her one-day conference, so she couldn't join us.

I glanced up at our kids climbing on a giant spiderweb of ropes. They were having a wonderful time and not paying attention to us.

I pulled the lipstick jammer out of my pocket and turned the bottom. "This is a signal jammer so that in the event someone is listening to us, they won't hear a thing."

"Wow, where'd you get it?" Haley picked it up and examined it.

"Daman, but I don't want to talk about it." Only I really did. I hated that I couldn't tell her about Daman or his suspicions about David. Not that I thought Haley would tell anyone, but Daman had asked me to keep quiet.

"Ben is the one who bugged my house, but he isn't working alone. I don't think he killed Molly, but I think he knows why she was murdered. I overheard him talking to someone on the phone last night about how I wasn't going to be a problem and how he was making headway with me." It still pissed me the hell off.

Haley's mouth dropped open. "What?"

I nodded. "Yep, I fell for the old romance the information out of her."

I am such a sap. I'd never really thought of myself as particularly sappy, but obviously my capacity for sap was growing.

"He seems so nice and genuine." Haley always wanted to believe the best about people. I'm pretty sure she'd have tried to find the good side of Osama bin Laden.

"I didn't see it coming, either." I hunched my shoulders. "It sucks because I like him."

I liked Daman, too, which might or might not suck depending on if he was also romancing info out of me. This dating-two-guys thing was tough, especially when I didn't know whether they were dating me because of my sparkling personality or because they wanted to monitor my activity.

"What a jerk." She put the lipstick down. "Do you think he bugged my and Monica's houses?"

I shook my head. "Clearly he works for someone else. He had the opportunity to bug my house and maybe Monica's when she wasn't home, but yours is a problem. Someone is there all the time." I sucked on my bottom lip. "Can you make a list of all the people who've been in your home since the night of Molly's viewing? It's probably a little bit further than we need to go back, but it's better to be safe than sorry."

"Good idea." Haley's gaze stayed on the kids, making sure they were okay. "I'll start as soon as I get home. I'll need to ask Pierre and Anise."

Pierre was her personal chef. He was French and snotty and hated Americans, but he could do amazing things with vegetables that actually made them taste good. I asked him how once, but because he's French and snotty, he yelled at me for a long time. I left the kitchen when he picked up a knife and started waving it around to drive home whatever point he was trying to make in French. Evidently, vegetables were a touchy subject with him.

I unzipped my tote bag and pulled out the stack of medical records. "Let's go through these again. I'm out of leads. I don't think we'll ever find out where all of that money came from, or the gold."

I sucked in my bottom lip again. I should tell her about the new info I'd found out about Molly. I'd just leave out where I'd gotten it.

"I've found out something new about Molly. I can't tell you how I found it out, but she was into something illegal... possibly money whitening or turning black money, which is dirty, into white money, which is clean. Apparently Lakeside has a seedy criminal underworld thing going on. Money laundering for terrorists or something." It still sounded so impossible.

Haley crossed her ankles and leaned back. "My gut reaction is, huh? But now that I think about it, there are lots of things about Lakeside that don't make sense. We have more banks in this town than the entire countries of Switzerland and the Cayman Islands combined. I know for a fact that they do the bulk of their deposits in cash. Where else do you see people take Whole Foods sacks full of cash into a bank for deposit?"

"I've never really noticed. Then again, my paycheck is direct deposit so I never go to my bank." It's not like I have extra cash lying around that I throw into a Whole Foods bag and carry into the bank. Hell, I can't afford to shop at Whole Foods.

"Banks are supposed to report any deposits of ten thousand dollars or more by filling out a suspicious funds report, but I've never seen one being filled out, even when I deposited twenty thousand in cash." Haley was so blasé. Like depositing twenty grand in cash was something she did every day.

It was on the tip of my tongue to ask her why she was carrying around twenty grand. Daman had told me to trust no one.

"It was the weekly deposit from one of my parents' Chik-fil-As. It had been a particularly good week, and they didn't want all of that cash in the safe," she explained.

I hated that even for a second I'd doubted her.

"Since I have no idea where to look to find out what Molly was into, let's go through these again." I handed her half of the stack of medical files. "I hope we missed something, because I've got nowhere else to look."

"Okay." She slid her pile in front of her and thumbed through a quarter inch of the stack, picked it up, and turned it facedown beside her.

"What are those?" There was no way she'd read through them that quickly.

"Files from her pediatrician. We decided they were no use." Haley leaned down, picked up a rock, and placed it on top of the stack she'd just turned facedown, to keep the pages from blowing away.

"That's right." I moved the rock and grabbed the pile. "I guess I'll check them just in case."

I skimmed the first page and the second and so on. Nothing but routine childhood illnesses. About three quarters of the way through, things got interesting. I thumbed to the next page and the next. I went back and reread the dates, counting. "Can you think of a reason why Molly met with Dr. Turley every Friday for the last two years? Always the last appointment and there are no treatment notes, just an entry of the date."

Slowly Haley lowered the handful of papers she'd been reading. "No."

"It doesn't make any sense. Dr. Turley is a pediatrician, so seeing her is out of his scope of practice. If he billed it, her insurance company would deny it. So she paid cash for her visits?" Not that any of this mattered, but my work brain had kicked in. I knew the scope-of-practice thing all too well. Before Lakeside Regional, I'd worked for a doctor who liked to throw in the occasional pelvic exam for his cute female clients; only he was an orthopedic surgeon. Trust me, when your orthopedic surgeon offers free pelvic exams with every knee surgery—say no and find a new doctor.

"We now know that she had plenty of cash." Haley set the papers down and put the rock on top of them. "Why every week? Clearly Molly had other doctors, so if she had some sort of medical problem, which isn't in these records, she would have gone to another doctor. In some cases, I know that adults with special needs will often stay with their pediatrician because they feel comfortable, but Molly didn't have special needs. Or did she?" A slow smile curled on her lips. "Last appointment of the day?"

"Yes." Something else was going on, something that didn't have anything to do with medicine.

"They were having an affair." Haley's shoulders shook with laughter. "She told us that she was seeing a doctor. We all assumed it was Dr. Dick, but it was Dr. Turley."

I wrinkled my nose. "Ewww. He's like seventy and married and he was her pediatrician."

I tried not to picture the two of them going at it, but the image kept popping into my head. I couldn't help the gag building in my throat. Dr. Turley had always reminded me of a crazy-eyed Santa Claus. He was fat, overly jolly, smelled like peppermint, and one of his eyes wandered. I never knew which eye I was supposed to look at.

"It's the only thing that makes sense." Haley looked a little dazed, like she was trying to wrap her head around it, too. "Think he was the father of her baby?"

"Makes sense if they really were having an affair." Had he killed her because she'd told him about the baby?

"He's a pillar of this community, I guess an illegitimate child wouldn't be a good thing?" I couldn't even convince myself of that. In this day and age, illegitimacy wasn't a big deal.

"Maybe." Haley wasn't buying it either. "Okay, I can almost see the affair—almost—and the baby could happen, but I don't see him killing her... now wait a minute." She pointed to me. "Have you met Puddy Turley, his wife?"

"Puddy?" God, I hoped that was a nickname.

"It's short for Prudence. Anyway, she makes Edna Miars look like Miss Congeniality. When Lisa Beth, Dr. Turley and Puddy's daughter, was a junior in high school, Lisa Beth was the second alternate on the varsity cheerleading squad. Two cheerleaders both had bizarre accidents and couldn't finish out the season. One fell out of the second-story window of her house, breaking her leg, and the other was the victim of a hit-and-run car accident and broke her pelvis. And that's not all. Once, when Puddy tried to join the garden club but didn't have enough votes from the membership committee, the whole committee mysteriously came down with food poisoning. You don't cross Puddy. My money's on her for the murder." Haley crossed her arms.

"Wow. I bet she's fun at parties." If I hadn't been sure before, I was now 100 percent convinced that the people of Lakeside were batshit crazy. "So, where do we go from here?"

"Hold on..." Haley threw up a hand. "There's something else about Dr. Turley. Something Daniel told me years ago. What was it?" She looked down like she was sifting through memories trying to find the right one. She snapped her fingers and looked up. "Oh, I know, he told me that Dr. Turley is usually the person who signs the death certificates for any deaths in the area that aren't suspicious. The ones that aren't natural causes or overdoses go to the Travis County medical examiner. Since Molly's death was ruled an overdose, Dr. Turley was probably the one who signed her death certificate."

"If his wife murdered Molly, he could have covered it up as a heroin overdose." So Molly's death might not have anything to do with the money whitening at all. It was a simple case of jealousy. "But if he was having an affair with Molly, presumably he loved her, so why would he help his wife kill his girlfriend? Why not just leave his wife to be with Molly?"

"Puddy has all of the money. He probably makes low six figures as a pediatrician, but she's worth millions. If he leaves her, he gets nothing; but if he's stuck it out this long, trust me, he'd wait for the payday." Haley nodded.

If Puddy was as crazy as she sounded, the money wasn't worth it, but I was in the minority because here in Lakeside, money meant everything.

Haley shook her head. "Hold on a second." She pulled her cell out of her coat pocket. "A couple of weeks ago, Humberto sent me a text. He was redoing all of Puddy's front flowerbeds while she was on a month-long European vacation. He started the day after she left, which was almost three weeks ago. Unless she hired someone to kill Molly, she didn't do it. Knowing Puddy, she'd want to do the killing herself."

There was no denying that Haley had Lakeside wired.

"She left the week before Molly was murdered? Don't you think that's a little suspicious? The wife is out of town when the mistress is murdered? Does Puddy usually go out of town for a month at a time?" I felt like we were on to something. I wasn't sure what, but Dr. Turley was involved.

"No. This was a birthday present from her husband for her seventieth birthday." Haley tucked a loose lock of hair behind her ear. "Humberto said that she was shocked, but pleased."

"So we're back to Dr. Turley killing her. Maybe Molly threatened to tell Puddy about the affair or the baby, and Dr. Turley sent his wife away so that he could do his murdering in private?" It still felt like we were missing something. The death certificate thing was interesting, and

Dr. Turley was involved in some way. "I think we need more information on Dr. Turley."

I wasn't sure how we were going to get it, but everything pointed to him.

"What kind of information?" Haley drummed her fingers on the plastic-coated metal picnic table.

"We need his schedule. I'd love to see if he sees a new patient on Fridays now. Also, if he was having an affair with Molly, did they meet anywhere else? I guess they could have met at Molly's house." I thought about it for a second. "Molly said something once about spending the weekend at her boyfriend's ranch a couple of months ago. Do the Turleys have a ranch?"

"Not that I know of, but I can ask Humberto." She pulled her iPhone out and began typing.

I was a little jealous of her ability to thumb type so quickly. My thumbs weren't that nimble. Starting tomorrow, I was going to do thumb exercises so I could up my texting abilities.

I glanced up to find a young mother walking toward us, holding the hand of a four- or five-year-old. Did I mention that this is the only place at the park to sit and watch your kids? The last thing we needed was an audience.

I turned back to Haley and said loudly, "Did you know that it only takes eleven pounds of force to strangle a human? It's getting rid of the body that makes murder so hard to get away with. I vote for chopping the body up into manageable-sized pieces and then running it through a wood chipper."

"Then what do you do with the pounds and pounds of shreddings? It's not like you can bag them up and set them out on garbage day." Haley had a point. Since the mom and her child were behind Haley, I was pretty sure she didn't even know that we had eavesdroppers.

Without turning my head, I cut my gaze to the woman and her child. Her eyes were the size of Oreos, and she was backing away. Mission accomplished. The way to clear out a park is to start talking about murder in very graphic terms... works every time.

Haley's phone beeped. She picked it up. "Humberto says that Dr. Turley had him install a sprinkler system for a friend on some acreage on the east side of Austin. It's in this old neighborhood surrounded by businesses. The friend was putting in some kind of orchard."

Haley started thumb typing again. "I just asked him if it was Dr. Turley who paid for the sprinkler system."

I nodded. "If Turley paid, then possibly the acreage belongs to him. Why tell Humberto that it was for a friend?"

Haley shrugged. "No idea. Maybe Puddy doesn't know about it?"

Her phone beeped again. She read the words on the screen. "Turley paid."

"Sounds like we might have found the ranch. Does he remember the address?" We were on to something.

She thumb typed and then her phone beeped again. "No."

"I have an idea." Damn, I was good. "Don't your girls each have an iPhone?"

I gestured toward the girls climbing on the ropes.

"Yes." Haley's brows scrunched together. "Why?"

"Ever lost one?" I can't believe that I was asking the queen of organized if she'd ever lost anything.

"Yes and we used the Find My iPhone app." Slowly she nodded. "I get it. Slip one of their phones into his car and we can track where he goes. But what if he finds the phone and links it to my daughters?" When Haley was scared, her voice turned high and squeaky. Right now, I was pretty sure she could communicate with dolphins.

"Good point. We can't use any of our phones because they could be bugged." We needed a phone that wasn't linked to us, still had service, and that we could track. "I know. I'll borrow Astrid's phone. Dulce regularly hides it just to mess with Astrid. I'll ask her to get it for me and we can slip it into Dr. Turley's car."

I'm so devious that sometimes I amaze myself.

CHAPTER 23

Two nights later, we left the kids at my house with Monica's mother and followed the Find My iPhone app to a house on the east side of Austin. This was our first stakeout.

We really needed T-shirts to commemorate the occasion, but as I sat behind the wheel, I was willing to admit that it was a little too late. Better planning next time.

We were parked across the street and down the block from the house where the Find My iPhone app led us. This was a very bad neighborhood. Back in its heyday, circa 1950, the rambling ranch houses were probably cutting-edge. Now they were surrounded by seven-foot-tall chain-link fences with razor wire on top. The one we were parked in front of sold discount tire rims and offered an oil change for ten dollars if you brought your own oil and didn't mind all of the scattered junkyard car parts everywhere.

"I can't believe the phone thing worked." Monica leaned in between the front seats of the black Toyota Corolla I'd borrowed from Dulce's nephew's neighbor. Or it might have been Dulce's neighbor's nephew. All I know is that when staking out a possible murderer, don't use your own car.

"Why does this car smell like bean nachos?" Haley sniffed. "And dirty feet. It smells like bean nachos and dirty feet."

"No idea, but it's one of the most popular cars on the road. We're blending in." I pulled the black knit cap over my ears. Blending in meant no heat, and it was like forty-two degrees outside. In Central Texas that's polar-ice-cap cold. I fully expected to see polar bears frolicking on the street in front of us. Sadly, dark street was the only thing frolicking in front of me. To make matters worse, I couldn't feel my pinky toes and I was pretty sure it was hypothermia. Or it might have been the black high-heel boots I was wearing. They were a half size too small, but they'd been on sale and they were so cute.

"On TV, stakeouts aren't this boring." Monica propped an elbow on the passenger's seat back. "Anyone want to sing 'Ninety-Nine Bottles of Beer on the Wall' again?"

We'd already sung it twice and eaten a bag of potato chips. Haley had brought a cooler full of drinks that were in the trunk, but we'd all agreed that peeing outside was a man's job, and the gas station down the street looked like a crack house, so using their restroom was out of the question.

"We could play I Spy." Monica sounded as bored as I felt. "I'll go first. I spy something that smells like bean nachos and dirty feet."

"I don't know. That's a tough one." I laughed. "How about this car?"

"Nope. It's me. I've been sitting in this thing for so long the smell is sticking to my hair and clothes." She reached back, twisted her long, dark hair into a bun, and shoved something through it to hold it on top of her head. "Think the scary gas station has some of those Christmas tree car deodorants we can hang from the rearview mirror?"

"Just hold your horses. I've got a surprise coming for us." Haley breathed into her black-leather-clad hands.

We'd all three worn black, of course. It was the color of choice on stakeouts according to Hollywood, and since we were making this shit up as we went along, Hollywood was all we had to go on.

"I hope it's a car deodorant delivery person." You know, like Domino's, only they deliver a clean smell to cars across the nation. Now there's an entrepreneurial idea ready to pop.

"Maybe we can set the upholstery on fire? I think it might be an improvement." Monica touched the faded purple fabric.

There was a knock on Haley's passenger's-side window, and my heart just about jumped out of my chest. Haley rolled the handle, and the window slowly descended. "Kim-Li, thank God you made it."

Who the hell was Kim-Li?

"Yes, Ms. Haley, when you say emergency, I leave right then." Kim-Li was a tiny Asian lady carrying a huge square suitcase of some sort.

"Ladies, this is Kim-Li Ho, my manicurist. I figured that we were going to be here a while, so I booked us all manicures." Haley pointed to the backseat. "Hop in."

Haley rolled up the window. "Monica, can you open the door for her?"

"I'm not so sure this is a good idea." Stakeouts were serious business, and I was pretty sure that James Bond and Veronica Mars wouldn't get manicures while watching for the bad guy.

Monica opened the door, but the overhead light didn't come on. Thank God she'd had the presence of mind to flick it to the off position before opening the door. "How can she work if we keep the light off?"

Kim-Li slid in beside Monica.

"No worries, Kim-Li work in low light all time. My eye good." She slammed the door.

I hoped that she had more than one eye.

"Works for me." Monica pulled off her gloves. "My toes could use some pedicure love too."

"Kim-Li only do hand, no feet only hand." Kim-Li was firm. "You want feet you call somebody else."

"Okay." Monica sounded a little disappointed.

Haley leaned over the front seat. "George is the best pedicurist in the state. People come from all over the world just for a pedicure. He's a legend."

"You've had a pedicure by George?" Monica was awed. "I hear they last for six weeks—no chipping."

"Yes, check it out." Haley unzipped her black boot, took it off, peeled off her sock, and stuck her leg over the seat. "This is four weeks old."

"Wow." Kim-Li and Monica said at once.

"He do good work." Kim-Li drew out the last word as she nodded.

"Is it true that George is a little difficult? I've heard he takes diva to a whole new level." Monica still sounded impressed that Haley was on George's client list.

Haley pulled her leg back into the front seat, slid on her sock, and put on her boot. "The pedicure takes about two hours and there's no talking. George doesn't like distractions. If you talk, you're out. Don't even think about chewing gum. The last person who smacked her gum during her pedicure was never heard from again. And don't go expecting a foot massage. George doesn't do frills. He spends the whole two hours on your feet, but when you leave, your heels are supple and soft. He's a miracle worker."

"Sounds complicated." I wasn't that good at following the rules, so George would probably disappear me in less than five minutes, and I bet he was really expensive. Since I can barely afford fish sticks and toilet paper, pedicures are right up there with thoroughbred horses and private jets on my list of things I'll never have. Don't get me wrong, I'm okay with it... mostly. I am willing to admit that in sandal season I do have the pedicure blues.

Kim-Li took Monica's hand. "You cuticle terrible."

She clicked the locks on her case. The top folded out, revealing three large compartments. One side of the top was used as a table. It even had a cup holder. Kim-Li balanced the contraption on her lap. She poured something into a red plastic cup and set it into the cup holder. "You stick hand in cup and soak."

She shoved Monica's ungloved hand into the cup.

"You pick color." Kim-Li waved her hand like a game show hostess, revealing the nail polish colors in the middle bottom compartment.

She looked up at me. "You choose too. Ms. Haley only want pale pink. I try new color and she say, 'No, no, Kim-Li, only pale pink.' She boring."

I looked at Haley. "Are you sure we should be doing this?"

"Kim-Li is very discreet. She won't tell, will you, Kim-Li?" She turned around in her seat to watch the manicurist.

"No, no. Kim-Li know all Lakeside secret but never tell nobody. Kim-Li keep quiet." She nodded. "Ms. Haley nice lady and good tipper. Kim-Li lock mouth and throw away."

She made the lock mouth motion and then threw away the key. She pulled out a towel, plucked Monica's hand out of the cup, and dried it off.

"You cuticle so bad it make Kim-Li sad, but Kim-Li fix." The manicurist nodded to herself.

An hour and a half later, Kim-Li stuffed the money Haley handed her into her bra, packed up her kit, opened the door, and stepped out.

"Bye, Ms. Haley. I see you next week. If other nice lady need Kim-Li, ask Ms. Haley for card. Bye-bye." She walked down the street like she did car manicures in the 'hood every single day.

"Hands down, that was the best manicure I've ever had." Monica studied her pink glittery nails. "Kim-Li has got some serious hand massaging skills."

"I know. My hands are as soft as a baby's bottom." I couldn't get over it. Kim-Li really could see in the dark. My nails were painted a glittery purple and looked fantastic.

"I told you." Haley waved her arms to dry her nails. "I'm going to book her for all of our stakeouts."

"You're a planner. That's why we love you." Monica patted her shoulder.

Headlights cut through the blackness at the house where we'd followed the Find My iPhone app. I leaned forward and squinted. Dr. Turley got out of the car, walked to the gate, unlocked it, went back to the car, and drove through. He stopped, got out, and relocked the gate.

"Duck down," I whispered. Not sure why I whispered since he was a block away, but we all hunched down. As he drove by, headlights illuminated our car and then they were gone. The car didn't stop, so that was good. "Let's wait a good ten minutes before we go over there, in case he forgot something."

"Are we staying hunched down for the whole ten minutes?" Haley blew on her fingernails. "Just checkin' because I think I smudged a nail."

"Yeah, I vote we stay hunched," Monica said from the backseat. "There's a surprising amount of legroom back here. And now that the car smells like nail polish instead of bean nachos, it ain't half bad."

Clearly, Monica was high on nail polish fumes. This car was a piece. Still, it was better than Bessie. Sorry, Bessie.

I stared at my wristwatch. Ten minutes dragged on... and on... and on. "Okay, ten minutes—"

A car's headlights sliced through the inky black of the starless night. "Stay down."

I eased up far enough to peek over the dash. The car didn't stop at Turley's, it drove right past and kept on going.

"I think it's all good." I sat up and stretched. My back was killing me. Hunching over was painful. It looked so easy on TV.

Haley's head popped up. "You're sure?"

"Yes, the coast is clear." I looked around. "We're the only ones here."

"Okay, let's go see what we can find." Monica sat up and opened her door.

"Okay." Haley opened her door, stepped out, stretched her back, and then grabbed her Louis Vuitton cross-body purse. It was about the size of an envelope. She looped it over her head so that it rested on her left shoulder.

"Really? You need your purse?" It seemed as ridiculous as the Queen of England carrying a purse. Seriously, did the Queen of England need to carry identification? A thought hit me. "Is there a gun in that purse?"

Haley grinned. "Maybe. You can't be too careful."

She unzipped the purse and pulled out a tiny pink-handled gun. "It's my derringer. Only two forty-five-caliber shots. You have to pull the hammer back and let go." She pulled the hammer back, showing me, and then released it. She slipped it back in her purse and zipped up.

I rolled my eyes and followed them out. I wasn't sure having a gun with me made me feel safer. It just seemed like a bad idea. I have a temper, so giving me a means to hurt people I think I want to hurt at the time can't be good. Haley's not as quick to get angry. Maybe that's the key. Anger management. But I kind of liked my anger just the way it was. It helped me think up new and inventive ways to torment Salina Atan, and it never let me back down from people who'd stolen my parking place. Occasionally it does get me into trouble, but in all fairness, I get myself into way more trouble than my anger does. Yes, I was in a good place with my anger.

We all closed our doors as quietly as we could. We jaywalked across the street and walked down the sidewalk. I hadn't really figured this part out yet. To be honest, I was amazed that we'd gotten this far.

"Anyone know how to break and enter?" I worked my car keys out of my front right jeans pocket. Tonight, I'd brought my keychain flashlight because I couldn't find my big flashlight. I figured I'd wait to turn it on because in this neighborhood, we'd stick out like Hell's Angels at a Scentsy party.

"No, I thought you did." Monica looked at me. We felt lost, and then ...

"I've got it covered." Haley pulled a metal key out of her back pocket. "I looked up lockpicking on the Internet and learned how to make a bump key. I hope this works." Haley held up the key. "The YouTube video said that this type of key is the most common residential model."

"Did you use your computer?" Monica eyed her suspiciously.

"No, I used my next door neighbor's when I went over to visit her last night. I was careful." Haley was the slightest bit defensive.

"Just worried about you." Monica put her arm around Haley. "If you got killed, I'd lose all chance of getting another Kim-Li hand massage."

"You just love me for my manicurist." Haley elbowed Monica.

"She does up your value, there's no denying that." Monica shrugged. "Kim-Li is brilliant."

We walked to the locked gate.

"I don't think my bump key will work on this." Haley held it next to the padlock. "It's only for house locks. It's too big for this."

Well, crap. Here we were and we couldn't get in the gate, much less the house. James Bond wouldn't have this problem. He'd just hit that lock with the laser in his watch and call it a day. I glanced at my watch. It barely told time correctly, and lock-melting lasers were more expensive then the $19.99 I'd paid for it at Target. I should have sprung for the forty-dollar one. I bet it had a laser.

"Any suggestions?" I looked up at the fence. "I think we can climb it, but the razor wire part is a problem."

Monica eyed Haley's Sherpa-lined coat. "I have an idea."

Haley pulled the coat tighter closed. "Why are you staring at my coat?"

"It's really thick. Take it off and we can throw it over the razor wire and then climb over it. If we slip, we'll land on the coat." Monica looked at me as she shrugged out of her coat. "We'll stack all of our coats so it's really thick."

"It will get demolished. I like this coat." Haley took a step back. "Can't we come back tomorrow with some bolt cutters?"

"Seize the day, chicka." Monica held her hand out for Haley's coat.

I unzipped mine and took it off.

"Oh, all right." Haley huffed as she removed her purse, slid off her jacket, lobbed her purse back over her shoulder, and handed Monica her coat. "First it was my favorite scarf at the viewing and now my favorite coat. Next it will be one of my kids."

"Your sacrifice is noted." Monica handed me the coats. "I'll climb the fence. Hand me the coats when I get closer to the top."

Since this was the only plan we had, we went with it. Monica scaled the fence like a pro, threw the coats over the razor wire, eased one leg over and then the other one, and hopped down. If I didn't know better, I'd say that she'd done this before.

Haley was next. She climbed the fence, tossed one leg over and then the other, and hopped down. I stuck my foot into a chain link at about knee level. My foot slipped out. I tried it again and my foot slipped out.

"What's taking you so long?" Monica heaved a sigh.

"Not my fault. Y'all made this look so easy." I finally got up the fence, hooked one leg over, and the heel of the other foot caught in the chain link. I hovered a mere inch above the razor wire. I'm not a man so there was no chance of my manly bits being mangled by razor wire, but still, I didn't want to land on it.

"Crap. You're stuck." Monica was so helpful.

"Really, I hadn't figured that out all on my own." Sarcasm is my go-to emotion during times of crisis or boredom or pretty much all of the time.

"Don't get your panties in a wad." Monica climbed a few rungs up and worked on my heel. "I can't believe you wore high heels to a stakeout."

"They were the only black boots I had. Hello, my only other boots are pink and don't match this." Sometimes Monica was so dense.

My heel came loose and I went ass over teakettle, landing with a splat on my back in the dirt. "I think I broke my ass."

I looked up at the black night sky and tried to remember why we were here. Oh yes, Molly Miars had been murdered.

"Don't move her in case her neck is broken." Haley stood over me. "Is your neck broken?" she stage-whispered.

"I broke my ass, not my ears." I sat up. "I'm sitting up, so I think my neck is fine." I rolled to my knees. My butt really did hurt, but I didn't think anything else was damaged. Slowly, I stood. "Let's get this over with."

"I vote we don't break in through the front door. Going around back gives us more cover." Monica pointed to another gate that led to the backyard.

"Works for me." Haley held up her right index finger. "I broke a nail. Can you believe it? Kim-Li's going to be so mad."

"If that's the worst thing that happens to us all night, we might get out of here alive." Monica was so levelheaded. Maybe she was a spy instead of an insurance claims adjuster. I'd never actually been to her office, so ...

"Are you a spy?" Sometimes words just fall out of my mouth. I don't know why.

"Nope. Just grew up in a rough neighborhood. Maybe I've done this before." Monica waited for me to catch up.

I flicked on the flashlight and handed it to her. "Here, you might need this."

She turned it off. "Better if we don't draw more attention to ourselves."

"Good point." She was so smart.

I was happy for her to take point.

Monica held the backyard gate open for Haley, who in turn held it open for me.

Monica aimed my flashlight at a tree. She moved the flashlight around to reveal an orchard of five-foot-high trees. All were covered in individual clear plastic pup-tent greenhouse things.

Apparently, flashlights were okay in the backyard.

"Is this the tree you saw in Molly's yard?" Haley pointed to the closest tree.

"Yes, but these have those red fuzzy pod things. But yeah, I'm sure that it's the same tree. Looks like a cross between marijuana and a chrysanthemum." Why in hell would Dr. Turley have the same tree in his yard as Molly had in hers? Was he the one who dug it up?

"This is a castor oil plant. I know because there's one on the Lakeside walking trail. Riley brought one of these pods to me and asked what it was. I looked it up. Incidentally, that tree was donated by Dr. Turley." Haley stepped closer to the tree. "It's used to make castor oil, but the seeds..." She pointed to the pods. "…can be dried and made into ricin."

I work for a hospital that has a disaster plan for everything. I know exactly what ricin is.

If ricin is ingested, it causes severe diarrhea and vomiting, but if it's inhaled, it causes respiratory failure.

"I don't think Molly was killed because she was pregnant or whitening money, I think she was killed over this." I pointed to the trees. "I think Molly was making ricin in her garage."

CHAPTER 24

"That's ridiculous." Haley shoved the bump key into the back-door lock. She jiggled it around and turned the doorknob. The door swung open. "Um, I don't think that key actually worked. I think the door was unlocked."

Well, that was disappointing. Here I'd been waiting my whole life to see a bump key in action.

Monica walked in, sweeping the flashlight around the room. I stepped in next to her.

"This is just like the lab I saw in Molly's garage." The floor was white tile, the walls were painted white, and a massive chemistry setup dominated three long tables. There were lots of beakers, Bunsen burners, and other chemistry stuff I semi-recognized from high school chemistry.

Haley stepped around us and picked up a giant Ziploc bag full of beans. "Are these the beans you saw at Molly's house?"

She held them close to the light for me to see.

"Yes." I had a bad feeling that Molly was into something much worse than money whitening.

"They aren't lima beans, they're castor oil beans." Haley set the bag down.

"Okay, for the sake of argument, let's say that Molly was making ricin in her garage... why?" Monica shined the flashlight on the wall by the back door until she found the light switch. She flipped it on and the overhead fluorescent light hummed to life, pouring light down on the white room.

"Are you sure that's a good idea?" Haley looked over her shoulder at Monica.

"Think about it, which looks more suspicious, a flashlight bouncing around or the lights on? With the lights on, it just looks like Turley's home." Monica turned off the flashlight and handed it back to me.

I nodded. "She has a point."

Haley's eyebrows arched. "Makes sense."

"Wait a minute." Haley unzipped her purse and pulled out three tiny gold Godiva chocolate boxes and handed one to me and then to Monica. "Time to celebrate. I got us these in case we actually were successful in breaking in. There's one cherry cordial and one dark chocolate ganache heart for each of us."

I slipped the heart into my mouth. Heaven. And then the cherry cordial. It was even better. "Do you always have chocolate in your purse?"

Haley nodded. "Pretty much."

"How did we not know this about you until now?" I enjoyed the lingering cherry taste in my mouth.

"Don't know. Chocolate is important. Without it, life doesn't make sense." Haley popped her own cherry cordial in.

"That should be on a T-shirt. 'Without chocolate, life doesn't make sense.' I'd buy one." Or better yet, the T-shirt should be made out of Godiva chocolate, so I could eat my way out of it.

"Me too." Haley unzipped her purse and pulled out some individually wrapped Handi Wipes.

"What all do you have in that purse?" I really needed to know where she got these purses that looked so small on the outside, but you could actually park a Volkswagen bus in them.

She dug around in her tiny purse. "Um, my gun, a couple credit cards, some cash, lip gloss, Handi Wipes, emergency tampon, and my car keys. We just ate all the chocolate."

"You said you always have chocolate in your purse, but is it Godiva?" Monica popped in her cherry cordial.

"If you're going to eat chocolate, it should be the best." There was a big, fat duh in her voice.

"If you're ever involved in a run-by purse snatching by someone who looks like me, it's not me. Just saying." I'm a criminal mastermind. She totally won't suspect me at all.

"So Molly was making ricin in her garage." Monica pointed to the chemistry set. She was so useful in getting us back on topic. "What does that have to do with all of the money and gold that we found?"

"And the cell phone with the names," Haley added.

"Molly made ricin for money." Where had she learned to make it? Was there a book called *How to Make Ricin for Fun and Profit*? I seriously hoped not.

"I guess that works." Haley let out a long, slow sigh. "I can't believe we're having this conversation about Molly."

"I know." Never in a million years would I have imagined that she could be tangled up in something illegal.

"I guess selling ricin could be profitable. I don't know." Monica leaned down to get a better look at a huge beaker and the hoses running to and from it. "What if Molly wasn't selling the ricin, but she was using it?"

"I don't understand." Haley looked like she just couldn't get her head wrapped around the idea that Molly was using the deadly product she was making.

"Okay, stick with me here, it's just an idea, but what if Molly was using the ricin to kill people. Every single one of the people on the cell phone list died of respiratory failure—"

"If inhaled, ricin causes respiratory failure," I added. This was so surreal. Here we were standing in a house we'd broken into, and we were actually discussing the possibility that Molly was a killer.

"Right. All of those people died of respiratory failure. What if that was Molly's murder list? Molly was crazy for making lists. One time I saw her make a list of the lists she needed to make. Let's say that was her murder list, why kill those people? Why is Mustang on the list?" Monica was trying to put the puzzle together. Her eyes got big. "It's a hit list. Molly killed all of those people for money."

"Bravo," a deep male voice said from behind us.

I turned around to find Dr. Turley leaning against the open door, holding a gun pointed directly at me.

Oh, crap.

"I'd applaud, but a one-handed clap sounds funny." Dr. Turley smiled and his wandering eye looked off to the left.

I was probably supposed to look at the one that was trained on me. Note to self, right eye is the good eye. Watch that one.

He'd lost weight—a lot of weight.

"You've lost weight." I figured that it couldn't hurt to compliment the guy. He had lost a considerable amount of weight, and he was holding a gun on us.

"Thanks." With his free hand, he patted his stomach. "I'm Paleo."

I glanced at Haley for translation.

"The Paleo Diet is where you eat like a caveman. Lots of meat, no refined foods, no processed carbs, and lots of salad." Haley shot me a weird look like we had more pressing matters than the Paleo Diet.

"We were just leaving." Monica grabbed my hand and Haley's and tugged us closer to the door.

"You're not going anywhere." He shrugged one shoulder. "I can't let you leave. Before, you were just a pain in the ass, now you know too much."

"How can we know too much? We don't know anything. As far as we're concerned Molly died of a heroin overdose." I sounded halfway convincing... I think.

Haley, Monica, and I moved as one large group toward the door.

Turley cocked the gun. "I can shoot you all for breaking and entering. As long as I say the magic words, 'I was in fear for my life,' I fall under Texas's Castle Law. I believe Mrs. Hansen has a concealed handgun permit. Am I right?"

We stopped.

"Yes." Haley's voice was high and squeaky.

In the movies, this is the point where the SWAT guys come crashing through the windows and take down the bad guy. I glanced at the window to my right and waited and waited. Maybe the SWAT guys were out to dinner and would be back any minute.

"How did you find this place? It isn't under my name, I was very careful." Turley moved inside the door, reached behind him, closed the door, and locked it.

"Dumb luck." I really couldn't think of anything else. Apparently my keen lying skills had run for the hills. It was probably the fear. If I didn't die tonight, I was totally going to work on my lying skills.

"Somehow, I don't believe you." Turley cocked his head to the right, and his left eye wandered to the ceiling. Oh, crap, I was supposed to watch the right one.

"I've never met three bigger pains in my ass. I liked things better when ladies stayed home and had babies. Women's lib has ruined the world. Things were so much easier before y'all decided to take jobs away from men." Turley was taking that Paleo Diet to a whole new level. He was actually turning back the clock and becoming a caveman. All he needed were some knuckles to drag on the floor and a cave to sleep in and he'd be all set.

This is the point where I should have busted out my ninja moves and kicked his ass, but sadly, I have no ninja moves. The only thing I could think of was talking him to death. Many people had pointed out that talking someone to death was my superpower.

"Okay, so we figured out that Molly was a contract killer. Did you kill her?" I was still holding out hope for the SWAT guys. Plus, this was always the part in *Castle* where the murderer confessed to everything.

"What? You haven't figured out the rest? Cervantes credits you with more brains." Turley rolled his shoulders like his neck muscles were tight. If he was any indication, being a murderer was stressful.

Cervantes? Hadn't Daman mentioned him?

"No, we only just now put together the whole contract killer thing." I leaned forward slightly, in the universal "please elaborate" gesture.

Turley studied me and then shook his head. "Damn, you really don't know. Molly was hired to kill you. When she refused, I had to take her out."

All eyes went to me.

"Who hired her to kill me? And why?" True, Salina Atan hated me, but I was pretty sure she couldn't afford to hire someone to kill me. Unless she'd recently come into an inheritance or she'd hit it big in the lottery. In either case, I would have expected her to quit her job. Then again, maybe she'd stayed at the job to throw me off. Salina was sneaky, there was no denying that.

"Cervantes." His brow scrunched up like he couldn't believe I was that stupid. Well, the joke was on him. I *was* that stupid and more, because I still had no idea what was going on.

"Molly wouldn't kill Mustang so you took her out. That's what you said," Monica jumped in. "What happened to her body? Only her head made it to the funeral home, how did that happen?"

"That was Chief Stanford. He's such an idiot." Turley shook his head like there was nothing he could do about

Stanford's stupidity. "What can you do? He's an idiot, but he does what he's told."

"Huh? I don't understand where Stanford fits into things." Maybe talking people to death really was my superpower. Being a badass ninja would be a better superpower.

"Molly was my apprentice."

"Wait, like the Donald Trump show?" I'd never actually seen it, but I was pretty sure that it didn't involve killing people.

"No, apprentice as in contract killer in training. I taught Molly how to make ricin and the best ways to use it." His tone suggested that I was mentally challenged and that his patience was wearing thin.

"Molly was a contract killer... she was the Kindergarten Killer? Wow, I know it's wrong, but it kind of sounds cool." A few other things finally fell into place for me. "So this is how she could afford Lakeside Living."

"Said she'd rather kill people for a living than have her mother move in with her. It turns out that she had a talent for it." There was no mistaking the pride in his voice. He really felt like Molly's mentor.

Having met Edna Miars, I'm not sure I could fault Molly for choosing contract killing over living with her mother.

"It was unfortunate that I received orders to kill her. She was my finest creation." His voice turned sad. As crazy, wandering-eye killers went, he was pretty creepy.

"When I slipped some ricin in her dinner, she didn't notice until it was too late. She struggled and damn my tender heart, I didn't like watching her suffer. She was just like a daughter to me. So I administered a lethal dose of heroin through eyedrops I keep for emergencies." Turley actually sounded upset... in that creepy, emotionless way.

He always had killer eyedrops on hand? It was good to be prepared, I guess.

"That was very kind of you." Monica's tone was flat.

"I'm not heartless." He waved it off.

Obviously, sarcasm was lost on Turley. I wondered if all contract killers missed the nuances of sarcasm. Maybe it was something genetic, like the gene that caused some people to hate cilantro. Perhaps contract killers are missing the sarcasm gene.

"What about the bodiless head?" Monica prompted. She was a stickler for staying on topic.

"I called Chief Stanford over to clean up the mess. I explained that I'd just found her and that she'd ingested ricin. I gave him the time of death, told him we would call it a heroin overdose, and then I left. Puddy had dinner waiting, and she gets so mad when I'm late for dinner." He sighed long and hard.

It was all so normal, just a day in the life ...

"In hindsight, I should have just told Stanford that she overdosed. The idiot got ricin confused with something contagious like Ebola and dismembered the body before burying it." He shook his head. "I have no idea why he thought dismemberment was necessary. The man has lost his car twice in the Target parking lot and reported it missing both times."

See, I wasn't joking about that. It really happened... twice.

"After he buried her, he called me in a panic because he thought he might be exposed. It was just easier to tell him that I'd mixed up the cause of death, and that she'd actually died of a heroin overdose." He shrugged again. "Like I said, he's an idiot. Not once did he question how I knew it was a heroin overdose."

"And the head. How did that make it to the funeral home?" Haley kept her eyes on Turley, but I noticed that her hand was moving slowly to her purse. I hoped she was going for her gun, because I didn't think Turley was going to let us go.

"Actually, that's the normal part of this whole thing. Edna Miars threw a fit to have an open casket, so Stanford dug up Molly's head." Turley made it all sound so normal.

"Wow, he really is an idiot." I nodded in agreement. Agree with the man trying to kill you, that was my plan. Well, that and talking him to death. "So, um..."

I had nothing. We'd set out to find out who killed Molly, and here he was about to kill us. Oh, wait, "Why kill me?"

"No idea." He shrugged. "Cervantes wants you dead."

"I don't know anyone named Cervantes." How could I have pissed off someone that I didn't know?

"What about the baby?" Monica watched Turley very carefully.

"What baby?" His brushy, gray eyebrows shot up.

"Molly was pregnant." Haley's hand slowly unzipped her purse.

Dr. Turley blinked twice. "Molly was pregnant?"

"A little over two months." My eyes stayed on Turley.

"Oh, my. I told her not to mix business with pleasure, but she slept with Cervantes anyway. She was in love. Useless emotion. Cervantes ordered the death of his own child. I have to tell you, I did not see that coming." Turley didn't sound appalled or even upset, just matter-of-fact.

"He's a monster." Monica's tone implied that Turley was right up there with Cervantes.

Turley shrugged one shoulder. "It's the business, it dehumanizes people. What can you do?"

With the gun in his right hand, he wrapped his left hand around his right and shifted, aiming at me. "Don't worry. I was a pretty good shot back in Vietnam. I hit half of the people I was aiming for, so this might not hurt much." He hunched his shoulders. "Provided I get you in the heart. If I clip the stomach or kidneys, all bets are off."

So I had a fifty-fifty shot at dying in terrible pain. I didn't like those odds. I stepped to the left. A moving target was harder to hit... right?

"So, how long have you been in the contract killer game? Is it good money?" My talk-him-to-death superpower had been restored. "I see that you have an opening. I'd like to apply."

I moved over even farther.

"What?" He tracked me with his gun. "Stand still. I might miss if you don't stand still."

Which was the point. I zigzagged right and then left.

"Damn it, hold still." He dropped his left hand and glanced down. "Hold on, let me get my glasses."

As he felt around in his left breast pocket for a pair of glasses, Haley yelled, "Dive!"

She shoved her hand in her purse and shot off two rounds. She didn't even bother taking the gun out of her purse, she just shot clean through it.

Turley got one round off. My left shoulder burned like it was on fire.

Dead center of Turley's chest, twin bullet holes bloomed with blood. Turley staggered back against the door and collapsed.

He mouthed, "You shot me." His eyes turned vacant and his head lolled to the right. He still held the gun.

I turned back to Haley. Her blue eyes were wide and her hand was still holding the gun inside of her purse. "Daman always told me to carry a revolver in case I ever needed to shoot someone but didn't have time pull out my gun or flip off the safety."

Monica laid her hand on Haley's forearm and lowered it. "I'd say that was some great advice."

"I'm calling 9-1-1." I tried to lift my left arm and pain rocked down it. I looked down. Blood was oozing down my arm and dripping onto the floor. I'd been shot and I couldn't call 9-1-1 because I'd left my phone in the car. I just stared at the blood flowing down my arm. I couldn't make sense of it all. My legs felt heavy and pulled me down to the floor.

"Mustang's been shot." Monica sounded so far away.

"She's going into shock." Haley was at my side. "Call 9-1-1."

"All our phones are in the car," I managed before my knees buckled.

"Not all of them." Monica slid a phone out of her back pocket. "I've got Molly's."

The irony was fantastic.

The world around me faded into darkness.

CHAPTER 25

I woke with the feeling that I was flying through the air. I opened my eyes to find myself on a stretcher, being lifted out of an ambulance and into the emergency bay of Brackenridge Hospital. I could see the sign, a little blurry, as they set my gurney gently down on the concrete. I guess it was the closest hospital. I was strangely relieved that they hadn't taken me all the way back to Lakeside Regional, because a bullet hole would have been hard to explain when I'd just gone home early with the fake stomach flu. Come to think of it, I was still going to have to explain a bullet hole. Damn it. Maybe no one would notice.

I looked around. Haley was on my right, holding my hand, and a really cute paramedic smiled down at me. "Ms. Ridges, you're going to be okay. You were shot in the shoulder, but we stopped the bleeding."

"I got shot... in the shoulder?" I tried to sit up so I could look at my shoulder, but the straps across my chest, waist, and knees prevented any movement. It was weird, my shoulders didn't hurt, in fact I felt really mellow... like I'd had three or four margaritas. "Are you sure?"

"I'm pretty sure." The paramedic winked at me. "You enjoying that morphine?"

"I have morphine?" I looked around trying to figure out where I'd gotten morphine. "Are you sure?"

"Yes, ma'am." He leaned down. "I'm the one who gave it to you."

He pointed to an IV bag.

There was a hose running from that bag to my arm. "I have an IV? When did that happen?"

All sorts of strange things were happening to me. I really needed to get on top of this situation. If I could just figure out why my body was floating in the air, I could get a handle on things.

"I bet she's a fun drunk." The paramedic looked up at Haley.

"You have no idea." Haley patted my hand.

"Haley, I got shot in the shoulder. Did you hear?" I watched her face as she nodded slowly... like super-slow-mo slowly. In fact, the entire world seemed to be in super-slow-mo.

"Wait a minute... you were there. You shot Dr. Turley. Is he still dead?" I couldn't quite remember if it was a dream or real. I think Channing Tatum had been there dressed as Elvis, but I couldn't remember why.

"Yes." Her hand shook a little bit in mine.

"Don't worry. He was bad—Turley, not Channing Tatum—it's okay to shoot bad people because they deserve it." My eyes were very heavy.

Sometime later, I peeled my eyelids open to find that I was lying in a bed in a room I didn't recognize. There was an IV taped to the back of my right hand and some clear liquid was dripping into my vein. I tried to sit up, and pain rocketed through my left shoulder. Oh yeah, I'd been shot.

"Try not to move your shoulder, doctor's orders." Monica grabbed the remote control by my hand and clicked the up arrow. Slowly, the head of the bed tilted up.

"Max?" I choked out. My throat was so dry. It felt like I'd swallowed a prickly pear cactus and washed it down with the Sahara Desert.

"Haley is with him. She has all of the kids at her house for a big sleepover. He's fine. We decided that one of us needed to be with the kids and the other would stay here. I figured that her being around the kids would take her mind off of Turley." Monica wrapped the cord of the remote around the rail close to my right arm. "If nothing major happens, like you rip your stitches or contract some hideous infection, you'll get to go home in a few hours. They did surgery on your shoulder to remove the bullet and patched up the hole. Your orthopedic surgeon should be by in an hour or so."

"It's not Dr. Chambers, is it? He likes to give free pelvic exams." He was the last person I'd want looking at my shoulder or my cervix.

"No, it's Dr. Wong." Monica scooted her chair closer so she wouldn't have to lean. "We explained everything to the Austin Police Department and they aren't filing charges. It was clear that our lives were in danger, and they found all of the ricin that Turley had been making."

"How's Haley?" She was the one who'd take the brunt of the blame. And she'd killed a man. Yes, he was a bad guy, but still ...

"She's doing okay. A bit shaken up and worried about you, but she's going to be okay. Being around the kiddos will take her mind off of things." Monica laid her hand over mine. "We did it. We found out who killed Molly."

We sure did. The case was closed on Miss Molly Miars.

"Unfortunately, we uncovered something much worse." It just hit me. "Where's your phone?"

This whole bugging thing was getting on my nerves.

"I took the battery out of your phone and mine. Also, I swept our phones and purses in case they were bugged. Nothing. This room is clean." Monica pulled the lipstick jammer out of her pocket. "I found this in your pocket. I left it on."

I'd turned it on at the beginning of our stakeout and had forgotten to turn it off. Oh well, the bad guys probably already knew that Turley was dead.

There was a knock on my door.

I looked at Monica. She slid the jammer under the blanket by my right hand.

"Maybe it's the doctor." She yelled, "Come in."

A giant bouquet of flowers walked into the room with a man behind it. He put the flowers on the tall rolling table next to my bed. It was Ben.

Of all the nerve. We'd found out who killed Molly, so I didn't have to be nice to him anymore.

"I just heard and I was frantic." To his credit, he looked frantic. His hair looked like he'd finger-combed it a thousand times and his shirt was untucked, but he'd had time to buy a giant flower arrangement.

"Get out," I hissed. I'd had enough manhandling for one day. "You bugged my house. Get out."

His eyes turned enormous. "I don't know—"

"Really, lying. That's your play here?" Monica glared at him.

"I know it was you. You used me and you bugged my house." If I hadn't been shot in the shoulder and could lift the flowers that he'd brought, I'd have thrown them at him. "Get out."

His face turned the color of oatmeal. I hate oatmeal.

"Get out!" Now I was using my loud voice.

"It's not what you think." He backed up a foot. "I was trying to protect you—"

"I don't know about you, Monica, but my bullshit meter is going off." I pointed to the door. "I don't want to ever see you again. And all the bugs in my house and Monica's and Haley's had better be gone by the time I get home."

Screw the stitches. I reached over with my right hand and grabbed the rim of the vase one-handed. "I trusted you, I let you in my house, I let you play with my son. Get out."

I hurled the vase all of four inches, where it caught on the edge of the table and crashed onto the floor. Water, glass, and flowers went everywhere. I'm pretty sure some water splashed on his boots. Not quite the destruction I was aiming for, but I'd take what I could get. My left arm burned and I doubled over in pain.

"Get out." It was weak at best.

"Let me explain." His voice shook with controlled rage.

"There is nothing to explain." I needed him out of my room and out of my life. "Get the bugs out of my house... now."

Monica stood. "Don't make me call the cop that just left and have you dragged out of here."

"Don't threaten me." He shoved his index finger in Monica's direction.

She picked up the phone. "I don't threaten. You forget, we're the heroines who just uncovered a hoard of ricin and a contract killer. APD loves us."

Ben turned back to me. "Let me explain."

"Are you the one who put the contract out on me? Or was it Cervantes?" I'd just remembered that my name had been on Molly's hit list and that I was the reason she was dead. I didn't feel bad for her anymore.

"Contract? There's a contract out on you?" All his swagger broke and he looked honestly rattled. "I'll take care of it. I'll make it safe for you."

He turned to go, and as he reached the door, he looked back at me. "One day, you're going to let me explain, and then you'll know the truth."

He opened the door, walked through, and it swung closed behind him.

"Don't forget to remove the bugs from my house," I yelled after him.

"What an asshole." Monica walked over to the door and cracked it. "I guess we should keep the door open so maintenance can clean up this mess."

I hit the nurse call button.

"Yes," said the voice over the intercom in the hospital bed remote.

"We had a little mishap with some flowers, can you please send maintenance to help us clean it up?" I said.

"Of course." The intercom voice hung up.

"I'm proud of you for throwing the vase. It didn't go far but your point was made. It was very dramatic." Monica knelt down and picked up the larger broken pieces of glass and the flowers and tossed them in the garbage can.

"I try." I sat back. My shoulder was on fire.

"How are your stitches?" Monica continued to throw things away.

I glanced down at my left shoulder. "It hurts, but it's not bleeding. I think I'm okay."

The fact that Ben had the nerve to show up here was amazing. I felt like an idiot because I couldn't stop liking him even after knowing what he'd done.

"Why are the cute ones always bad for us?" Monica stood, grabbed a towel from the sink that was outside of the bathroom, and knelt down again.

"I have no idea." I lay back. "He seemed like he was really into me."

"That's because he is. Trust me, he wasn't just using you, but it doesn't matter now. He's a liar." Monica mopped the floor.

She was right. It wouldn't matter if Ben declared his undying love for me, I would never believe him. Call me a cynic, but I didn't believe in undying love.

All I wanted to do was get home to my son.

My life wasn't going too great. I'd been shot, there was a hit out on me, and my ex-husband might or might not have been dead. But my house would no longer be bugged... that was something.

The door burst open, bounced off the wall, and nailed Daman right in the nose.

"Damn." He rubbed his nose and kicked the door out of his way. He looked terrible. His clothes were wrinkled, his hair was a mess, and his eyes had dark circles the size of half dollars. He practically ran over to my bed. "I got here as fast as I could."

"I can see that." It struck me that he hadn't stopped off for flowers, he'd just come. Somehow, that was more important than flowers.

"I was so worried. When I got the call that you'd been shot, I walked out of my meeting, drove to the airport, and hopped on my plane." His eyes scanned my body to make sure that I was in one piece. He zeroed in on my shoulder. "The doctor told me that he removed the bullet without any complications and that you shouldn't move your arm for a while."

"When did you talk to my doctor?" I hadn't talked to my doctor. Clearly my doctor had never heard of HIPAA. I most certainly had not given him permission to disclose anything to anyone.

"He called me as soon as you were out of surgery." He pulled the chair right out from under Monica as she was about to sit down. He looked over at her like he'd just noticed she was there. "Hey, Monica."

"Seriously? Am I invisible?" She stomped to the door. "I'm going to the cafeteria. Anyone want anything? And by anyone, I'm talking only to Mustang, as I don't care if you starve to death."

"I'm good." I grinned at her.

She rolled her eyes as she huffed out the door.

"The doctor said that you're going to be okay, but I wanted to make sure for myself." His eyes were beginning to look less frantic as he scooted the chair next to my bed and took my right hand. "I've spoken to Max four times and he's fine."

"How did you track him down at Haley's house?" It meant a lot that he'd thought of Max. I glanced outside. I had no idea what time it was. The sun was low on the horizon.

"As soon as I'd heard you were shot, I called Haley. She told me everything." He placed his other hand on top of my hand. "How could you go after Turley? You could have died."

"We didn't go after him so much as follow him and get caught breaking into his house." I was willing to admit that possibly we should have planned things a little better... Next time.

"Have you lost your mind?" His hand tightened on mine. "He was a killer. You can't do things like that."

I wanted to believe there was more between us than just a promise he'd made to my ex-husband, but right now, my man-reading abilities weren't in top form.

"I think you and Max should move in with me. You can pick any of the twenty-two guest bedrooms in my house." He was completely serious.

I stared at him for a moment, waiting for the punch line, but his black coffee eyes didn't crinkle in the corners and his dimples hadn't made an appearance.

"That's not going to happen. Believe it or not, I can take care of myself." I glanced at the IV sticking out of my hand. Okay, so that wasn't my finest argument. "Wait, you have twenty-two guest rooms? I don't even know twenty-two people I'd want to spend the night at my house. Come to think of it, I don't know four people I'd want to spend the night at my house."

He worked his phone out of his pocket. "Let me make a call and I'll have all of your things moved over within the hour."

"Hold on. I'm not moving in with you." This was ridiculous. "I can't move in with you. I have a life."

It wasn't the greatest life, but it was mine.

He nodded. "Okay, then it's settled, I'm moving in with you."

Seriously, it was like talking to a fence post.

"No, when I leave here I'm going to my house, and when you leave here you're going to your house. We are not moving in together. My house and your house... two separate houses." I was dying to use my hands for some serious hand-talking, but my shoulder hurt and he had my other hand in lockdown.

"I can't protect you if I'm not near you." His tone suggested that I was two years old and he was explaining that the oven is hot and I shouldn't touch it.

Were we back to the protecting thing? I thought we'd already covered that. "Really, I can take care of myself. I'm not in any danger now. All of the contract killers are dead, so there's no one left to take me out."

His mouth dropped open. "There's a hit out on you?"

Oh, crap. I was losing ground—well, I really hadn't had that much to begin with, so it wasn't like I'd lost much. "Maybe."

"Ay dios mío, cariño." He sat back but kept hold of my hand. "How do you get yourself into so much trouble?"

I tried to shrug and pain shot down my arm. Not being able to shrug was seriously going to suck. How was I supposed to get my point across without a shoulder shrug?

"I don't even know Cervantes, much less know why he wanted Molly to kill me. According to the email, he ordered my hit on October 1. Nothing happened in or around then that I can remember. I don't know Cervantes." I enunciated the last sentence in case he suddenly couldn't understand English.

"What email?" His tone was level.

Double crap.

"Nothing. Did I say email? I meant... um..." I had nothing. Must have been all of the pain medication.

"What email?" Slowly, one eyebrow arched.

How come everyone else could do that but me? Was there some surgery I could have that would allow me to do the one-eyebrow-up thing?

He stared at me for a good minute.

"Okay, we found an old cell phone in the..." He didn't know about the safety deposit boxes. "Um... same place we found the diamonds. Molly used it to get instructions from Cervantes or whoever she worked for."

Daman closed his eyes like he was praying for patience, and then he opened them. "Where is this phone?"

"In the cafeteria in Monica's back pocket." Now that I thought about it, we probably should have hidden it with the money and gold, but it was too late now. "When she comes back, you can have it."

It's not like we needed it anymore.

"Did it ever occur to you to hand the phone over to me when I told you about who I really am?" he whispered.

"We're good. This room is bug free." And come to think of it, so would be my house when I got home. That was going to be wonderful.

Daman shook his head. "Bugs are only one type of listening device. There are many others."

"I have the signal jammer on." I conveniently left out the part where it had been on the whole time, but he didn't need to know that I'd turned it on before the manicures. I certainly couldn't have turned it on immediately after. I looked down at my purple sparkly nails. Kim-Li really was amazing. I'd been shot and no chipping. "Speaking of your diamonds... do you want them back?"

He stared at me like he hadn't heard me. "I'm sorry. I thought you were going to put them back where you found them."

"Well, you know... there's a tiny problem with that." I held my right index finger close to my right thumb, indicating how itty-bitty this problem was. "You see the thing holding the phone and diamonds accidentally..." on purpose, "got run over by Haley's Rover. Since the thing holding everything was destroyed and we found it outside, we couldn't put everything back."

I smiled brightly in the hopes that my radiant smile would distract him.

He looked at me the way Ricky Ricardo looked at Lucy when she went on a game show to win a thousand dollars because she'd blown all of the grocery money on new furniture.

"Did you find anything else with the diamonds and the phone?" He looked like he really didn't want to know.

"Nope." I continued the radiant smile in case he finally noticed its radiance.

"I don't believe you." He scrubbed his face like he wasn't sure what to do with me, so scrubbing his face was better than strangling me. "Since you won't move in with me and you don't want me to move in with you, I'm installing a security system in your house."

He glanced at his watch. "In fact, they should be finished with it right now."

"You played me... again." I would have crossed my arms in indignation except for that whole bullet hole thing. "I can't believe it."

He grinned and the dimples finally came out. "Can't play a player."

"You think you're so cute, don't you." I had to bite my bottom lip to keep from smiling. He was cute, damn it.

"There's one more tiny little thing." This time he held his index finger close to his thumb, showing me how itty-bitty of a thing it really was. "Your van is gone."

I sat up. "I beg your pardon."

"Your old, ugly, brown van had a small accident." The itty-bitty thing was starting to get on my nerves. "Unfortunately, it was parked at a jobsite downtown—"

"How did it get downtown?" I couldn't imagine anyone stealing my van.

"I had it towed down there," he said. "And the strangest thing happened, a large metal beam fell on it."

"What?" I leaned forward and white-hot pain shot down my arm.

"Your van is significantly smaller." He was very satisfied with himself.

"How much smaller?" This was bad. Please let Bessie be okay. She's a piece of shit, but she's my piece of shit.

He shook his head, completely unapologetic. "Ever seen what happens when you step on a loaf of bread?"

"Bessie?" I squeaked out as I put my right hand over my heart. "Bessie's dead?"

What was I supposed to do now? I couldn't afford another car. Hell, I couldn't afford to have what was left of Bessie towed away.

"Who's Bessie?" Daman looked confused.

"My van." I felt like I was going into shock again. Where was that cute paramedic when I needed him? Maybe he could scrounge up some more morphine. "Why did you have it towed downtown?"

"So a large metal beam could fall on it. Cariño, you're better off. That van was a death trap." He patted my knee.

"But she was *my* death trap." Lord knows I couldn't afford another one. Maybe Dulce's nephew's neighbor would sell me his stinky bean-nacho Corolla for a good price. Or maybe that discount rim place we'd parked in front of for the stakeout could fix me up with a car. I didn't care if it was stolen as long as it looked legit. I was too broke to be judgmental.

"My insurance company assures me that it's cheaper if I just write you a check." He patted my knee again.

"What does your insurance company have to do with anything?" I wasn't following him. If I was going to buy a stolen car, could I tell them what kind of car I wanted? Really, I was paying for it. Shouldn't I get to choose?

"I own the building where this terrible accident happened." He touched his breast pocket looking for something, and when he didn't find it, he felt around his trouser pockets. He pulled out a set of keys... well, key fobs. "I saved us both some time and took the liberty of picking out something for you."

He handed them to me.

"I don't understand." I looked down at them. "Why is there a Porsche logo on these?"

"Because you now own a Porsche Cayenne. After Bessie's terrible demise, I thought you should have something sportier and nicer, not to mention safer." It was his turn at the blinding smile.

I just stared at him and tried to figure out if that was a good thing or a bad thing. I didn't like charity, but he had killed Bessie, so maybe it was okay... plus, it was a freaking Porsche.

Goodbye Bessie... hello Portia de Glossy. I was going to have to park way at the back of the Target parking lot so no one would ding my door during the stampede to the Black Friday sales. That jogged my memory.

"Did you know that the world's going to end on Christmas Day?" I hated to be the bearer of bad news, but he needed fair warning.

"No, I hadn't heard that. Personally, I think the world should end on Black Friday." Gently, he brought my hand to his mouth and kissed the back.

"That's what I said."

There were still so many unanswered questions. Who was Cervantes and why did he want me dead? What had happened to my ex-husband? And then there was all of that gold and money Haley, Monica, and I had stashed at TFBH. But we'd found Molly's killer, and that was enough for today. The rest could wait for tomorrow.

About the Author

Katie Graykowski is an award-winning author who likes sassy heroines, Mexican food, movies where lots of stuff gets blown up, and glitter nail polish. She lives on a hilltop outside of Austin, Texas where her home office has an excellent view of the Texas Hill Country. When she's not writing, she's scuba diving. Drop by her website www.katiegraykowski.com or send her an email at katiegraykowski@me.com.

Other books by Katie Graykowski

The Marilyns Series
Place Your Bets
Getting Lucky

The Lone Stars Series
Perfect Summer
Saving Grace
Changing Lanes

CPSIA information can be obtained
at www.ICGtesting.com
Printed in the USA
LVOW08s1502280217
525683LV00008B/690/P